SCANDAL IN THE SECRET CITY

SCANDAL IN THE SECRET CITY

A Libby Clark Mystery

Diane Fanning

This first world edition published 2014
in Great Britain and the USA by
SEVERN HOUSE PUBLISHERS LTD of
19 Cedar Road, Sutton, Surrey, England, SM2 5DA.

Trade paperback edition published
in Great Britain and the USA 2015 by
SEVERN HOUSE PUBLISHERS LTD

British Library Cataloguing in Publication Data

Fanning, Diane author.
  Scandal in the secret city.
  1. Women scientists–Fiction. 2. Oak Ridge (Tenn.)–
  Fiction. 3. Murder–Investigation–Fiction. 4. Detective
  and mystery stories.
  I. Title
  813.6-dc23

ISBN-13: 978-07278-8404-6 (cased)
ISBN-13: 978-1-84751-527-8 (trade paper)

Typeset by Palimpsest Book Production Ltd.,
Falkirk, Stirlingshire, Scotland.

FOREWORD

The story in this book is a work of fiction. The characters, with the exception of cameo appearances by historical figures, are fictitious as well. The Secret City, however, did exist. It was created out of forest and farmland by the federal government in the early 1940s as part of the war effort. It was not on any map.

As the United States entered World War Two, military and industry began a partnership to end that war by developing a weapon more fearsome than any ever seen before. They established one of their top secret development facilities on 52,000 acres of Tennessee land in the foothills of the Great Smoky Mountains.

In a far shorter time than anyone would have thought possible, they built a secret fenced-in city of 70,000 residents dedicated to ending the war. Corporations recruited chemists and engineers from all over the country along with a huge cadre of high school-educated women to work as Calutron girls.

The scientists knew they were working with Uranium, but only the top management among them knew the final goal of the facility. The Calutron girls knew even less. They were trained to monitor and adjust calibrations of the control panels but had no idea what their adjustments affected.

Originally, it was identified as the Kingston Demolition Range, in the announcement of its existence that Congressman Al Gore sent to his constituents. It was then called the Clinton Engineer Works. We know it today as Oak Ridge, Tennessee.

In this high-security environment, people with disparate geographical locations, education, upbringing and social standing were tossed together in close proximity, breaking down the barriers that kept them apart in the real world.

It was a happenstance of dormitory room assignments that brought together country girls Ruth and Irene Nance and the more urbane and highly educated chemist Libby Clark. What happened in the Secret City intertwined their lives and transformed all three women.

CHRISTMAS 1943

'It was the best of times, it was the worst of times, it was the age of wisdom, it was the age of foolishness, it was the epoch of belief, it was the epoch of incredulity, it was the season of Light, it was the season of Darkness, it was the spring of hope, it was the winter of despair.'

Charles Dickens, *A Tale of Two Cities*

PROLOGUE

I spent a solitary day this Christmas. It was an unsettling experience but I made the most of my time alone, taking a walk, reading my new book, relaxing to Christmas carols on the radio. Just before ten that night, I snuggled in an armchair by the cozy warmth of the coal stove, reading one more chapter before going to bed. Sudden, loud pounding on my front door made me lurch to my feet. I winced as the book hit the floor with a thump but didn't pause to pick it up on my way to the door. Only bad news comes late at night. I flung open the door with dread.

'Merry Christmas!' two voices shouted.

'Ruthie!' I couldn't believe my old roommate was standing on my doorstep. 'I didn't think you were coming back until Sunday.'

'Changed our minds,' Ruth said. 'Hey, you haven't met my sister. This here is Irene. Irene, Libby. Irene doesn't work in our building, she's got a job up at the guest house.'

The two young women slipped off their shoes and stepped inside. Irene reached her hand forward and said, 'What do you know, what'd you say?'

I couldn't help grinning at the latest slang and replied with some of my own, 'Doing swell.'

Ruth continued, 'Yep, Irene meets a lot of important people working up at that place.'

Irene shrugged. 'Who knows? Those cats act like they're important and they're treated like they're important, but I don't know who they are really. There was this funny-looking, little fella with a big gap between his front teeth here last month. He spoke with an Eye-talian accent – couldn't quite figure that one out – I thought we were at war with Italy. But anyway, he said his name was Mr Farmer. An Eye-talian named Farmer? I just said, "swell".'

'The all-purpose answer,' I laughed. I wondered if Mr Farmer was actually the brilliant physicist Enrico Fermi – the description did fit the photographs I'd seen of him. And he certainly would be important enough to have a code name.

'Sure is cold out there tonight,' Ruth said. 'But we brought something back from home that'll warm us up.'

Both girls reached up under their skirts and pulled out a bottle of Jack Daniels. 'Good old Tennessee sipping whiskey,' Ruth said, 'made right in our hometown.'

'How did you get it through the gate?' I asked.

Ruth snickered, 'We stuck it in our underpants and slipped it up under our waistbands to hold it in place. They might be particular about security, but there are still places they wouldn't dare search.'

'Or at least, they'd better not try,' Irene added. 'We were raised on this stuff – put it in our bottles from the time we were babes. It's a sin it's illegal in this part of Tennessee – downright un-American.'

'Oh, stop it, Irene. You'll have Libby thinking we're a bunch of backwood moonshiner trash.'

'Well, Grandpa, did . . .'

'Irene!' Ruth scolded.

Irene laughed. 'Ah, Libby knows I'm just joshing. Still, this stuff is Killer Diller. Have you ever had any, Libby?'

'No, I can't say that I have.'

'You're in for a treat, honey. It's pretty loco, but we live in a dry county, too, and yet we make barrels of hooch,' Irene said.

'Not any more,' Ruth added. 'They're still distillin' alcohol but instead of using it to make this fine whiskey, it's all going to fuel for torpedoes. It's a good cause but it sure is a high price to pay.'

'How did you manage to get these bottles, then?'

Irene and Ruth exchanged a grin. 'Uncle Reuben!' they said in unison.

'He was a taster before the war,' Ruth said.

'And he was a smart one,' Irene added. 'He saw the war coming long time afore it got here. He spent a couple of years buying a bottle a week to tuck away in his cellar.'

'Now,' Ruth said, 'he's got cases of this mighty fine stuff. He's not too willin' to part with it but he said since we were doing work to end the war, least he could do was give us each a bottle for Christmas.'

'God bless Uncle Reuben,' Irene said, hoisting her bottle in the air. 'Well, gotta run. My fella's waiting.' Irene stuck her bottle back under her skirt and was gone.

Ruth slipped out of her coat and said, 'Got any glasses?'

I went into the kitchen and pulled two juice glasses out of a cabinet. Ruth filled them both with whiskey. 'Now, sip it slow,' she warned.

I brought the glass to my lips, hesitating for a moment before taking a tiny sip. My tongue went numb and burning heat sped down my throat and into my stomach. I felt my eyes pop and my jaw drop. 'Oh my!'

'Good, isn't it?' Ruth said while laughing at what must have been a comical expression on my face. 'Packs a lot more kick than that puny 3.2 Barbarossa beer.'

I nodded and dared to take a second sip; this swallow was different. I felt a warm, soothing smoothness as the liquid trickled down. I felt as if I were glowing from the inside out. I led Ruth back into the living room where we both sat on the floor in front of the coal stove.

'That Irene is somethin' else, Libby. Just as I think she's a pig-headed, selfish little thing, she does or says somethin' sweet. Like on the ride back on the train, she said that we oughta give you one of these bottles and split the other one and I said that was a good idea. So I'll leave this one here when I go,' Ruth said.

'No, don't do that,' I objected. 'Take it back to the dormitory and give some other girls a treat. It wouldn't be a good idea for me to sit around here drinking alone.' I hadn't been raised in a teetotaling household but I'd heard plenty of stories from Prohibition of friends and neighbors whose lives were destroyed by excessive consumption of bathtub gin and corn whiskey distilled in someone's barn. I just didn't feel comfortable with anything stronger than sherry around the house.

'Are you sure?' Ruth asked.

'Absolutely. Now, tell me about your Christmas.'

'We had so much fun! Christmas morning, we opened presents and the best part of that was watchin' our little brother. Nothing like a kid to make Christmas special.'

As I listened, my mind drifted off like wisps of smoke in a breeze to those long ago Christmases when Dad was still alive.

The bittersweet memories stirred up comingled feelings of happiness and sadness that left a dull ache in my chest. I shook it off and turned my full attention back to Ruth. 'Sounds like you were having a great time. Why did you come back early?'

'Oh, it was Irene's idea. She's really been worryin' me. She's been edgy all weekend like somethin's bothering her. On the ride up, I thought maybe she was afraid I'd tell Ma she's seein' a married man. So I told her I wouldn't say a word. She just snapped at me saying she didn't care what I said to Ma. Then, she started on me about returnin' earlier than we planned. She didn't let up the whole time we were there.'

'Did she say why?' I asked.

'She said she missed her boyfriend, but I think there's somethin' more to it. She was so touchy and when she didn't think anyone was lookin', she had this awful expression on her face like she was standin' in front of a firing squad. Even Ma noticed. Asked her what was wrong.'

'What did she say to your mother?'

'She didn't really answer. She just got on Ma's case for agreein' with me about the two of us being roommates. She reminded Ma that she wasn't a kid no more and that I wasn't her mother and she was real tired of my bossiness. But I can't boss that girl around. She don't do nothin' I say anymore. Hey, forget about my sister. She said she wouldn't stay out late tonight so I'll see her soon enough in the dormitory.'

We chatted and sipped for a couple of hours, slipping back into the easy exchange we had developed when we lived jammed together in a room built for one occupant. It was pleasant to set aside the turmoil of the world around us and be nothing more than two women who enjoyed each other's company. The commonalities of our childhoods had drawn us together while work, our relative positions in the workplace and even the war itself faded into the background.

Around one in the morning, Ruth pushed herself to her feet and said, 'I'd better get up and get going while I can still walk.'

'You want me to walk you to your dorm?' I offered.

'If you do that, Libby, who's gonna walk you home?'

Why didn't I think of that? I shook my head, stirring up a wave of dizziness that made me realize how tipsy I felt. I had to focus hard to untangle my thinking and respond. 'I'll watch you go down the street. And you come back soon. We can listen to some radio shows.'

'Do you like *Fibber McGee and Molly* and *The Shadow*?' Ruth asked.

'They're two of my favorites – it's a lot more fun when you have someone to laugh with or get scared with.'

'I'll be back for sure and we'll listen together.'

'I wonder if we'll ever have television in our homes?' I mused, not realizing I'd spoken out loud until Ruth responded.

'Television? You mean moving pictures in our house? You've got to be kidding.'

'I saw one at the Chicago World's Fair a few years ago. I thought we'd have them by now.'

'Maybe after the war, then. A lot's gonna change after the war,' Ruth said.

The falling temperatures after nightfall made the steps treacherous. We helped each other down to the boardwalk. 'You could stay here, Ruthie.'

'Nah, if I don't get back to the room, Irene will be worried. I'll be all right. You be careful going back up those stairs.'

I watched Ruth's back as it grew smaller and then disappeared at a bend in the road. I went back up the steps with exaggerated care. I thought about banking the fire or cleaning up the kitchen but it just seemed too much. I dropped face forward on the bed believing I'd rest for just a minute and then get up and take care of everything.

Next thing I knew, early morning light was streaking into the bedroom under the curtains. I was clutching myself from the cold and my head was pounding so hard, I could hear it. It took me a moment to realize that the noise was coming from the front door, not a hangover. I rolled over and sat up. The alarm clock read 7:30. Although I was usually up by that time, on this morning, it seemed far too early. Served me right for enjoying a little too much whiskey the night before.

Before I could throw my legs out of bed, I heard the front door bang open. 'Libby, Libby, Libby!'

Ruthie? What would she want at this time of morning? 'Is something wrong?' I asked as I slid my reluctant feet onto the floor and forced my unwilling legs to carry me into the living room.

'Irene never came home last night.'

'Are you sure? Maybe she came in and left early.'

'She would've left a note – well, maybe she wouldn't, but she sure would have made a mess. I'm cleaning up after her all the time. She never makes her bed and it was as neat as it was when I made it before we went home for Christmas. I'm scared, Libby. I know Irene can be a little wild. And sometimes she stays out too late. But she always comes back to the room . . .'

'Could she just have spent the night in someone else's room?'

'I checked with all her friends. None of them saw her last night. And she wouldn't be working, she wasn't due in again until Monday.'

'Do you know where she went last night when she left here?'

'She said she was meeting her boyfriend.'

'Where?'

'Towncenter.'

'But all the shops were closed yesterday, all day long. Why would she meet him there?'

'She said they always met there. I don't know. I'm worried she might've fallen down and broke somethin' or stepped in a big mud hole somewhere, sprained her ankle, broke her arm, and can't pull herself out. And it's so cold this morning the way the wind is blowin'.'

'Let's go find her.'

I quickly got myself ready and then off we went. I was startled by the dramatic difference in the noise level outside. Yesterday, a blanket of quiet peace had spread over the community. Today, life had returned to normal as if Christmas had never happened. Even though it was Saturday, I could hear bulldozers roaring at the construction sites and see legions of workers streaming to the bus stops.

At Towncenter, none of the stores had opened for business yet but lights shone in the back of the A&P as workers got ready for a new shopping day. Ruth and I looked around the front of the shops, peering in the windows and then circled around behind them, lifting up trash can lids and searching behind piles of cardboard boxes. No sign of Irene anywhere.

'Let's go up to the high school,' I suggested.

'You think Irene went up there?'

'I don't know. Maybe her and her boyfriend wanted to take in the view.'

'Maybe they went up for the view. Or maybe they went up there to make-out – I hear it's a pretty popular place at night. Probably oughta check the picnic grounds behind the Chapel on the Hill – that's another spot.'

Well, that was a surprise. The high school and the picnic grounds as trysting spots? News to me. 'How do you know that, Ruthie?'

'Never you mind,' Ruth said with a laugh.

We walked around the semi-circular driveway in front of the school and looked out over the Towncenter, the administration building and the dormitories. I wasn't sure why I stared down at the scene below for so long and I doubted that Ruth had any idea of what answers she expected to find down there, either. After a few minutes of watching the bustle of a town awakening for the day, we turned back toward the school and trudged around the perimeter of the building, then over to the athletic field.

When I spotted the shoed feet twisted at an unnatural angle under the wooden seats of the bleachers, I turned to Ruth. She did not seem aware of them yet. When I saw no signs of life – no rising and falling of breath, no twitch in any of the limbs, something that felt solid lodged in my throat, making it difficult to breathe. I wanted to run toward the stands but didn't want to excite Ruth, so I didn't alter my pace as we drew closer to the ominous sight.

When Ruth gasped and broke into a run, I rushed after her. 'Wait, Ruthie, wait.'

But Ruth would not stop. I could tell her gaze was riveted on those shoes and heard her whisper her sister's name. A flash of memory sparked and I recognized the coat and hat as the ones Irene was wearing the night before. Ruth crawled under the end of the bleachers on her hands and knees and threw herself on top of her sister's body. 'Irene, Irene, Irene,' she wailed.

I kneeled on the seat right above them. I saw a scarf tied tight around Irene's neck and turned my head away from the bulging eyes dotted with pinpricks of hemorrhage. Acid rolled up from my stomach, dissolving the lump in my throat. I swallowed again and again to keep the tears from flowing. This was a crime scene and it had to be preserved. I forced a calm I didn't feel into my words. 'Ruthie, Ruthie. Come out. We have to get help.'

'No, no, no. She's just sick. Everything will be okay.'

I wanted to crawl into that seductive cocoon of denial with her but knew I didn't dare. I slipped under the bleachers to Ruth's side, wrapping an arm around her shoulders. 'C'mon, we can't do anything here. Let's go get security and let them take care of her.'

Ruth pushed me away. 'No. No, you go. I'll stay here.'

I lifted my head and looked around the field, fearing that someone lurked on its edges, frightened that it would not be safe to leave Ruth here alone. 'Ruthie, we need to get help. You can't stay here. Whoever did this to Irene might still be nearby.'

'Watchin' us?' Ruth's brow furrowed as she stared at me.

'Maybe. Let's go. Being here is making me very nervous.'

Ruth looked down and stretched her hands toward the scarf. I grasped them firmly in mine. Ruth struggled to pull away. 'Look at me, Ruthie. Look at me.'

Ruth turned her head away from her sister and faced me.

'Don't touch that. It's evidence.'

'How can I leave that around her throat?' Ruth moaned.

'You have to. The investigators will need to see that. It might help them find who did this. Let's go.'

Ruth sighed and made no further move to loosen the scarf but she didn't budge an inch either. 'I have to stay here, Libby. This is my sister. I can't leave her here all alone – in the cold. I can't. Go, get help. I'll stay with Irene.'

'Are you sure?'

'Yes. She's my little sister. I'm supposed to take care of her. I promised Ma. Just hurry, Libby. Hurry!'

I ran down the hill on the boardwalk, past the Towncenter, to the police station in the administrative building. I was panting by the time I reached the officer at the front desk. 'Please help me! My friend's sister is dead. We found her body under the bleachers. In the athletic field. At the high school.'

'Okay. Slow down. Catch your breath. Now, you found a body?'

'Yes. It's Irene Nance. Someone killed her.'

'You saw a body?'

'Yes. We need help. Please send help,' I turned away from the counter and took a step towards the door.

'Miss. Hold it right there. I've got to get more information from you.'

'I can't leave my friend out there alone,' I objected.

'I thought you said she was with her sister.'

Idiot! I came back to the desk and slapped my hands on the wood. 'You're not listening to me. My friend is with her sister's body.'

The officer pulled out a sheet of paper. 'Okay. Your name please.'

'I've got to go back out there.'

'Miss. I have to fill out this report if you want help.'

Exasperating! 'Libby, uh, Elizabeth Clark.'

'Your address?'

'384 East Drive.'

'Where do you work?'

'Y-12. Beta lab.'

'Secretary?'

'No. I'm a chemist.'

The officer raised an eyebrow. 'Wait right here.'

'I've got to get back to my friend.'

'I'll be right back, Miss,' he said, nodding over my head at someone or something.

I turned around and saw an officer stand in front of the door, his legs spread wide, his hands behind his back. He stared up at the ceiling but I suspected he would not miss a move I made. I paced the width of the room until the first officer returned.

'Follow me, Miss,' he ordered and led me back to an office where the door was marked Captain Wilson. 'Elizabeth Clark, sir.'

'Have a seat, Miss Clark,' Wilson said.

'Thank you but I really need to get back to my friend.'

'We have people on the way, Miss Clark. You'll just be a distraction. We need you to wait here. Can I get you a cup of coffee or glass of water?'

I grew more restless with every passing moment. It seemed as if it was taking him far too long for the simple task. I stood back up and resumed my pacing, wondering if I ought to try to leave. Would the officer really physically stop me? It was hard to believe but, still, I hesitated, afraid of the man's reaction. Right now, Ruth needed a friend, not some nameless police officers. I cooled my simmering impatience by turning my thoughts to recollections of Ruth and the unlikely sequence of events that conspired to make us fast friends.

APRIL 1943

'Old fashioned ways which no longer apply to changed conditions are the snare in which the feet of women have always become readily entangled.'

Suffragist Jane Addams

ONE

I tried to concentrate on where I was going and the reason for the trip, but everything around me conspired to catapult me into the dramatic moment that placed me on this particular train at this unique moment in time. The clack of the wheels, the hum of the rails, the ebb and flow of the sound of rushing air as the train passed trees, buildings and fields rang in my ears, growing louder and louder with every passing mile, until it transformed into the buzzing of planes, the roar of flames and the shattering cacophony of exploding munitions. When murmurs of voices passed down the corridor and drifted into my compartment, I heard the faraway echoes of shouted orders and agonized screams. Breathing in the air, I inhaled the scent of the worn leather upholstery, the musky odors of previous passengers, even a trace of the sweet aroma of fruit eaten by an earlier traveler. The jumbled fragrance was overcome by the noxious scent of a fire that incinerated fuel, rubber and human flesh.

The walls of the compartment pressed against me, creating the same feeling of isolation from the real world I found inside a movie theater. As I gazed out of the window, it mutated into a projection screen. The view, clips from newsreels and my fevered imaginings of Sam's death merged. Echoing in the distance, like the voice of God, I could hear the opening words of Franklin D. Roosevelt's announcement to Congress and the citizens of the United States: 'Yesterday, December 7, 1941, a date which will live in infamy, the United States of America was suddenly and deliberately attacked by naval and air forces of the Empire of Japan.'

My fevered filmstrip rolled. Airplanes rose on the horizon, darkening the skies like a swarm of termites, casting long shadows on the ground and water below as they zeroed in on the harbor, summoning up dread. I'd fallen into this waking nightmare so many times and yet I still hoped that the ending would change, that the planes would turn around and head back to the land of the rising sun. Instead, as always, they grew nearer, taking on a sinister cartoon cast with fang-festooned grins painted on their nose cones and evil, distorted faces that leered from the cockpits. As one aircraft lost altitude, I saw Sam standing on a pier, his head thrown back, a look of puzzlement on his face as he squinted up into the heavens.

I sucked in a deep breath and tried to dislodge the vision from my mind. I knew where it was going. I knew what would happen next. Still, I held my breath, holding on to the fervent wish that somehow, this time, the outcome would be different. But it pushed on following a relentless and irrevocable path. The lowering plane zeroed in on Sam. Its belly opened and disgorged a bomb. I watched as it plummeted down, it's high-pitched whine foreshadowing the obliteration to come. When the smoke cleared, every trace of the spot where Sam had stood was gone along with the life of my childhood playmate and beloved cousin.

I shook my head to chase away the morbid thoughts that had no factual basis. I am a scientist. I know better than to succumb to raw emotion to reach conclusions. I did not know exactly what killed Sam – no one did. I knew he died on that day of infamy but nothing more. I forced away the haunting image of smoke and flames rising in the sky and sought grounding in the here and now by focusing on the mundane and material.

I straightened my posture and raised up to make sure the skirt of my tan gabardine suit was not bunched beneath my legs. I sat back down and made a ritual of planting my open-toed brown pumps firmly on the floor. I pressed on the front of the skirt, smoothing the twin pleats. Then I shrugged my shoulders to adjust the fall of the jacket. But my hat? I touched the slouched beret. It was undeniably stylish but might be a bit too informal to wear with a suit? Aunt Dorothy insisted it was a perfect combination. Was she right? I folded my hands in my lap to keep them still. This trip was so important. I couldn't allow some little, superficial thing get in the way of my goal.

The last sixteen months had been so frustrating. I had been more than a semester away from my baccalaureate in Chemistry and Physics when the attack happened at Pearl Harbor and hadn't even started working on my master's degree in Analytical Chemistry. Still, after all my endless efforts, no opportunity had been offered to allow me to use my education and expertise to do my part for freedom and for my country.

Instead, I'd watched male colleagues, both undergraduates and graduate students, putting their education on hold to leave the school for important jobs. I was happy for them but angered at the companies that chose one of them over me when I was just as qualified – in some cases, more qualified – for the required work.

I often did not get an interview simply because I was a woman. Many acted as if I were committing a violation of the laws of God and nature when I expressed a desire to work in Chemistry or Physics. More than once, in social situations and interviews, someone asked, 'Did you choose that field to improve your chances of finding a husband?' One prospective employer even said, 'With a position this vital, we cannot afford to hire someone who will, in a year or less, quit the job to get married or have a baby.'

The only thing further from my mind than getting married was raising children. Sure, I liked men and dated a lot in high school and college but I had a rule and, for the most part, I kept it: no more than two dates with any man. Anything more could lead to something serious – the kind of relationship that posed a threat to my professional aspirations. All the young men I'd dated regarded my career goals as a lark that kept my mind occupied until I settled down in acceptance of my lot as a woman.

Aunt Dorothy only intensified my ire by regarding my failure to secure a meaningful position as good news. She wouldn't stop insisting that no woman had a chance without an advanced degree and I needed to accomplish that before I even thought about employment. I argued that I could continue my education after the war. She called that notion intellectual dishonesty. I loved that woman, but sometimes her belief that, war or no war, my schooling should be my chief priority was maddening.

I had to admit, with more than a little admiration, that she reached that conclusion the hard way, through her struggle down a path that blazed a trail for women like me to follow. Against all odds in that earlier time, she left rural Virginia for a successful undergraduate stint at Smith College and then earned an ScD from Cambridge. Right now she was the department head of the School of Social Work at Bryn Mawr, where I'd earned my baccalaureate degree.

Our heated discussions about my future, though, rarely lasted long. We were too obsessed with following the news as it ping-ponged between the Pacific and Europe and Africa. Good news, bad news, it was an endless stream where hope was our only antidote to pain. Because of the conflict, we had to reorganize our lives to accommodate government-sanctioned deprivations. The February after Pearl Harbor, shoe rationing began.

Three months later, prices were frozen on many everyday commodities like sugar and coffee. We received our ration books and tokens – without them, we could not buy gasoline, silk, nylons and a lot of other things, no matter how much money we had. By year's end, gasoline rationing was the law of the land but by that time, the situation was looking very encouraging for the Allies.

The best news from the two war fronts often left me feeling empty and excluded. The tide turned in the Pacific with the first victory against Japan that began their long retreat; allied troops scored victories in battles in northern Africa; and the Russians had halted the advance of the Germans. But the Germans launched the A4-rocket, the first man-made object reaching space. Our government was determined to top that accomplishment. Here I was, unutilized in that effort, even though I had the kind of skill sets and education they needed. Some days I worried the war would end without anyone giving me an opportunity to make a contribution. As soon as that thought crossed my mind, I was ashamed of my selfishness – but that didn't stop the worry from returning.

It was the reason I was on this Detroit-bound train in April 1943, on my way to the American Chemical Society meeting. A lot of corporate recruiters were booked for the event and interviews were guaranteed. Word was that the demand for chemists was at an all time high, the number of applicants was short of the growing need and many positions went unfilled for months. Surely they could no longer overlook me simply because I wasn't a man.

I'd actually lined up fourteen interviews before boarding the train – more than I'd managed to secure in the whole previous year. I'd done it without making any attempt to conceal my gender as many other women had advised. 'Use your initials or a nickname in place of your given name,' they urged. But I'd seen that ruse fail for others. Those girls might have secured more interviews but they sabotaged their chances in the end.

I walked into my first interview with high hopes that were quickly dashed. We'd barely gotten past the pleasantries when the representative from Union Carbide asked, 'When are you planning to have children?' It all went downhill from there. Next up was Heinz. A jolly interviewer offered me a job almost right away. He wanted to hire me to study the vitamin C in tomatoes. He was nice enough but his statement that 'it would almost be like being in the kitchen' made me clench my jaw tight to keep my abusive thoughts to myself. And, frankly, there was nothing about that job that was vital to the effort to win the war no matter how hard he tried to expand the definition of that phrase.

By the time I walked into the interview with a man from Eastman Kodak, I was on the verge of giving up. When I asked what the job entailed, he said, 'Do you know anything about Eastman Kodak?'

'I've used your cameras and was pleased with them.'

'Good,' he said and leaned back in his chair smiling.

Really? Was that it? I pushed on. 'What kind of work would you want me to do?'

'It's war work. We are hiring a number of technical people for vital war work.'

'What kind of technical people?'

'We're hiring chemists.'

'I have a baccalaureate from Bryn Mawr with a double major in Chemistry and Physics. Next month, I will receive a Masters degree in Analytic Chemistry from the University of Pennsylvania.' Is he hearing me? Is he really listening to me? Or had he already looked at my skirt and scratched me off his list.

He leaned forward slowly and steepled his fingers and said, 'Good. Good. You're definitely the kind of technical person we are looking to hire as chemists for this work and your additional background in Physics is an added bonus.'

'What kind of war work?' I asked. His answers were vague and evasive – why? I wanted more details about the scope of the position but if I pushed too hard would I offend him and ruin my chances of receiving an important job offer?

He smiled, brushed a lock of hair off his forehead and leaned back in his chair. 'I can't tell you. It's a secret.'

A secret? Now, that sounded like war work. 'Where would I work – at your headquarters in Rochester?'

'Oh, no.'

'Then where would it be?'

'Sorry. Can't tell you. It's a secret.'

A secret location? That does sound promising. 'But it is vital work that could help win the war?' I asked.

'Most certainly. I can assure you it's good.'

I wanted to know more. 'What is the goal of the work?'

'I can't tell you. It's secret.'

'How long will the job last?'

'Until the war is over.'

'Are you offering me a job?'

'I can't tell you. It's secret,' he said, setting his mouth in a grim line.

I was dumbfounded. That was the most ridiculous thing that I'd heard all day.

His eyes twinkled as his face broke into a broad grin. 'That was a little joke,' he laughed. 'Of course, I am. Your country needs you, Miss Clark. Will you answer the call?'

I nodded my head faster than I could think. 'Yes, yes, I will,' I said, surprised at the recklessness of my spontaneity. What had I just agreed to do?

'Good. You will be hearing from us shortly about the transportation arrangements for your trip to Rochester for your orientation with the company.'

My head was spinning, looping like a roller coaster, staggering under the burden of unanswered questions. I felt numb. I had one more appointment scheduled but it wasn't for an hour. I hunted down the recruiter from Ames and cancelled our session telling him I'd accepted another offer, but didn't really believe the words even as I said them.

I had a job. I had achieved my goal. On the train ride home, doubts rose to the surface. Had I been right to trust that evasive Eastman Kodak man? The work had to be important if it was top secret, didn't it? Maybe I shouldn't have cancelled that last interview. I hoped I hadn't made a naive mistake.

What kind of work could be that secretive? Spy work and weapons development? Was there any reason someone would want a chemist for espionage? I couldn't think of any. So it had to be weapons development. But what kind of weapons? I recoiled from thoughts of the lethal poisonous gases used during the last war and the terrible toll on those who survived exposure to mustard gas. I recalled a farmer who returned home seeming like the living dead, suffering as he coughed his way to an early grave. The Geneva Protocol banning these weapons had been signed by most countries more than a decade earlier – but not by my country. We were one of a handful of nations keeping that option open. What if they wanted me to work on that? I would have to walk away. I could not bear having poison gas on my conscience. Some means were not justified, no matter the end.

TWO

B ack at home, I attacked my dissertation in a frenzy, hoping to complete it before I had to report to Rochester. On the day I received the first piece of Eastman Kodak mail, I finished writing and hand-delivered the paper to my professor. That first piece of mail was followed by a flurry of correspondence. Within a week, I knew I had to report on May 26 and received the train tickets to get there. I'd miss walking across the stage to accept my postgraduate degree, but I had secured it before I boarded the train and headed north.

I arrived late that evening and reported to the personnel office at nine the next morning. At the reception desk, I waited until a woman about my age, with freckles sprinkled across her cheekbones and tightly curled bangs of brilliant red hair on her forehead, came out to the lobby to greet me. 'Hello, Miss Clark. I'm Miss Farnham. But you can call me, Betty. Come have a seat at my desk.'

In her office, I sat down in a straight back, wooden chair, and realized right away that it had been built for utility not comfort. Betty slipped around the desk extension that held a black typewriter and ran her hands under the back of her gray rayon jacket dress as she slid into a swivel chair. 'First we have paperwork,'

she said with a smile, pulling out one sheet of paper after another
from a file drawer in her desk.

She rolled the first page into the typewriter. For an interminable
hour, she asked questions, I answered and she typed. Finally,
Betty jerked a sheet out of the roller and announced, 'That's it.
Last one. I have cousins in Pennsylvania. You don't sound like
you're from Philadelphia.'

'I didn't move there until I was twelve years old,' I explained.

'Where did you live?'

'Virginia – out in the country.'

'Oh, Virginia is such a pretty state. Not that I've been there.
But I have seen pictures. I imagine it's even prettier than that.
Why did you leave?'

I didn't want to talk about the death of my father. I didn't
even want to think about the sequence of events that brought me
north to live with Aunt Dorothy. Instead of being totally honest,
I said, 'Yes, it was a lovely place to live but I got a better education after I moved.'

Betty cocked her head to the side as if she was about to ask
more questions. I quickly changed the subject. 'What's next?'

'We need to review the employee handbook,' she said, pulling
a large binder out of her drawer. She opened it to the title page
and read: 'Eastman Kodak Employee Procedures and Policies,
Revised March, 1943.' She looked up and smiled, then turned
the page.

'Introduction,' she read and placed her finger on the first line
moving it under the words as she continued, 'Welcome to the
Eastman Kodak Corporation. Employees wear their Eastman
Kodak badges with pride. The name Eastman Kodak has long
stood for leadership in photography. Now with freedom at stake,
the men and women of Eastman Kodak are pioneering in new
fields, helping free tomorrow's world. Your hands are needed to
help us win the war.' Betty continued on through three pages in
a monotonous reading voice that threatened to put me to sleep.

When she paused to clear her throat, I said, 'I'd be glad to
read through this on my own. It would be a lot easier on you
and quicker, too.'

Betty closed her eyes and exhaled forcefully. Placing one palm
on top of the open book and putting her other hand on top of
that, she stared at me with exasperation and irritation sparkling

from her eyes. 'Miss Clark, I must ask for your patience. We are trained in proper procedure and that requires that we go through this handbook together, page by page. When a war is at stake, we must always follow procedure. And, you need to give me your utmost attention.'

I'd certainly said the wrong thing – so much for efficiency. 'Sorry for interrupting, Miss Farnham.'

Betty smiled. 'Betty is perfectly fine.' She cleared her throat again and returned to the reading, her finger moving smoothly from one word to the next.

I jiggled a foot, crossed and uncrossed my legs, shifted from one side to another in my struggle to remain alert through the endless list of details about vacations, pay periods, rules and regulations. Then I thought it was about to get interesting when Betty read the title page for the section on laboratory protocols. My optimism fizzled fast when instead of specifics, all she read were vague and generalized rules with no real substance.

When Betty shut the cover on the book and said, 'Now, let's go to the cafeteria and have some lunch,' I felt as if I'd been rescued from a deadly fate. Walking down the corridor to the cafeteria, she explained, 'You can bring in a lunch if you like, but the food provided here is inexpensive and rather good. Today, however, you are our guest. I'll be charging our meals to the department.'

We entered a long room, filled with rectangular tables with seating for four or six. The noise of dozens of simultaneous conversations bubbled around us. The aroma of meatloaf and macaroni and cheese made me aware of how hungry I was. I handed my plate across the counter and asked for a serving of both along with some green beans. Then I picked up a cup of coffee with chicory and a small bowl of tapioca pudding for desert.

I followed Betty to an empty table near the back of the room. After spending hours playing the role of rigid bureaucrat, Betty now chatted to me like a long-lost friend who needed to be caught up on the latest news. I heard about her grandmother's health, her dreams of marriage and child-rearing and her worries about her boyfriend on the frontline. She was so earnest, I didn't dare laugh at the latter remark but knew that although everyone said their boyfriend was on the front, more often than not, they were in some boring place like Hoboken doing nothing more life-threatening than counting socks.

Betty took me on a tour of headquarters after our meal. I peered in rooms filled with desks and bent-over heads hard at work before we reached a laboratory with rows of black tables. It appeared to be as up-to-date a facility as I'd ever seen. Each station marked by a fume hood, with sparkling glassware and pristine equipment distributed at every work area. Not a stray paper anywhere. Not a fingerprint on any surface. It didn't seem as if the room had ever been used. I turned to Betty and asked, 'What's done in this laboratory?'

'Nothing yet,' she said. 'It was all built for you.'

'Me?'

'Well, the whole group of you who are coming in for training. We're hiring hundreds of new employees.'

The room was large but nowhere near big enough to accommodate that many people. 'Hundreds?'

'Oh,' Betty chuckled. 'Not all of them will come to the corporate office for training. You're in the first group, though, there's about fifty of you. A lot of the new employees will be trained on site.'

'What are we going to do here?'

'You'll be going through training.'

'Training for what?'

'I'm no scientist,' Betty said with a laugh. 'I wouldn't understand it if they did tell me.'

'You said that some people would be trained on site?'

'Yes.'

'Where is that?'

'You don't know?'

'No,' I admitted, hoping I'd finally get an answer – but no luck.

'That's peculiar. They didn't tell me but I thought they'd tell you. I would think your mother would want to know where you're going.'

My mother – another thing I didn't want to discuss with a stranger. 'Well, I sure can't tell her since I don't know.'

'I guess they'll tell you when you need to know. They say that to me a lot when I ask questions. I have the feeling, though, that I'll never have a need to know much of anything. Ah, wartime . . . Well, that's it for today, Miss Clark. Tomorrow morning at nine, you will be expected in room 238 for your orientation. Make

sure you're not late. They said they'll be locking the d
keep the rest of us from interrupting. That's what they
have a feeling they just don't think we need to know what's
going on under our noses.'

THREE

R oom 238 looked like an ordinary classroom and it was
packed full. I kept looking through the group for another
woman but it seemed as if I were the only one there. Dr
J.G. McNally walked to the front and began the real first explanation I'd heard about the work ahead of us. 'Gentlemen, Lady,'
he said smiling at me, 'Welcome to Eastman Kodak. We're pleased
to have you as members of our staff. We're engaged in a very
important project, war work. And it will involve you. You are
chemists, and we need to have you work on the chemistry end
of the project.

'As chemists, you need to know that you will be working
with Uranium.' He paused and watched for the reaction of the
group. Some squirmed, nervous about the prospect; others
appeared rather excited by it. I was pleased for two reasons.
First of all, any talk of a radioactive element evoked visions of
Madame Curie dancing through my head. Secondly, I feared
he might have said Chlorine or Phosgene, chemicals being used
in the ongoing experiments to create airborne substances that
would eat away at the protective masks worn by the enemy and
defeat that line of defense against poisonous gases. Uranium
also meant I wouldn't be involved in any lethal gas experiments.
Uranium required such a high temperature to vaporize there
was no way it could be implemented as deadly airborne fumes
on the battlefield.

'That is the last time you will ever hear me use that word.
And you will not use that word. Not here. Not anywhere. Not
ever. When you need to call it anything, you will call it Tube
Alloy. You will be prosecuted and persecuted if the proper word
ever crosses your lips. If you say it, even among yourselves,
you're subject to immediate arrest and very likely a jail sentence.

'Tube alloy. That is its code name. And your hexavalent compounds will be called tubelineal oxide. Your tetravalent compounds will be tubinous suflate or tubinous tetrafloride or so on. You'll get used to it. We're going to use code names because we don't want anybody to find out what's going on. You will be trying to develop methods for separating the tube alloy from solutions that hold iron, copper, nickel, cobalt, molybdenum or whatever.'

After this speech, I then spent two months in the Rochester laboratory becoming familiar with the equipment, using extraction and refinement processes on 'tube alloy', separating it from other substances on the basis of their differences in weight. I couldn't stop wondering what the expected end result was. Before I'd finished at the University of Pennsylvania, I'd heard rumors of fission experiments being conducted at a secluded facility at the University of Chicago. Was I being trained to work there? Would I be developing a new bomb? I didn't dare ask.

Most of my free time, I had only myself for company. The strong emphasis on secrecy built a communications barrier, making all of us chemists avoid any of the employees outside of the circle of those who needed to know. After hours, we were encouraged not to discuss our work and were too nervous to talk to each other about the possible projects that lay ahead. The men seemed to find non-work oriented camaraderie outside of the laboratory but being the only female meant I didn't have a roommate as all the others did. Conversations seem to center around whatever it was that men talked about and tended to stutter and stall whenever I entered a room.

On the bright side, I was performing well during training. More often than not, one of the scientist/trainers would stop by and ask questions about my methodology and results, but after the first ten days not one of them uttered a word of criticism or corrected any of my procedures, as I'd overheard them doing to many others working nearby.

It was an exciting opportunity for learning because although I'd studied uranium as a rare earth in college, the chemistry of it was unknown. There were no textbooks on it, all that I'd ever read was one little paperbound pamphlet which had only a single page on the chemistry of uranium. We were all becoming experts on the subject – how it worked, how to test it, measure it, weigh it and purify it. I felt like a pioneer on the edge of a limitless frontier.

Two or three recruits seemed to disappear overnight. At first, I thought they were sent to the site to work and grew impatient about when my turn would come. But then I talked to the chemist at the station next to me, he said that his roommate was sent home after Dr McNally deemed him inappropriate for the work ahead.

'What does that mean?' I asked.

'I don't think they gave him a reason,' he said with a shrug.

That's why I got so nervous when I was told to report to Dr McNally's office. Had I failed to measure up? I couldn't think of any area where I'd fallen short in my performance or in my adherence to security, but I imagined none of the others who were sent home had seen it coming, either. My knees were shaking when I poked my head through the doorway. 'Dr McNally, sir?'

He looked up and smiled. 'Come in, Miss Clark, come in.'

He wouldn't be smiling if he were sending me home, would he? Or was he that glad to be getting rid of me?

'Miss Clark, all reports have indicated that your work in the laboratory has been impeccable. You have been chosen as one of the first to go out in the field.'

For a moment I couldn't speak. Did I hear him correctly? 'You think I'm ready to go out in the field?'

'You shouldn't be so surprised, Miss Clark. You must have noticed that you are no longer as closely supervised as the others.'

I did hear him right the first time. 'Thank you, sir. Where will I be going, sir?'

'I'm not at liberty to provide you with that information. Go home and pack for a long stay away. The ticket for your destination will be handed to you at the train station in Philadelphia.'

'When do I need to go to the station?'

'You have no need to know that at this time. You will be informed when the time comes. Be ready to leave at a moment's notice.' McNally looked back down at the paperwork on his desk.

It seemed as if I'd been dismissed but I wasn't sure of what to do next. And I couldn't manage to find the words to ask.

After a moment of silence, McNally looked up with a surprised expression on his face. 'Yes, Miss Clark?'

'I–i–is that all? Sir?'

'Oh, yes. Sorry. Just stop at my secretary's desk on the way out. She'll give you your tickets home.'

On the train ride back to Aunt Dorothy's place, I was baffled. I did get a lot of answers in Rochester, but every one of them seemed to have raised three or four more questions to take their place. Where was I going? Would it be Chicago? Or further west? And when would I have to go? And what did they mean by a moment's notice? Could I be sitting down to breakfast one morning and have to drop my toast and run? What if Aunt Dorothy were teaching class at the time? Would I be able to say goodbye? I had to admit all the unknowns made it all feel like a cinematic adventure that was thrilling but also very frightening.

What would I do with myself while I waited in a timeless purgatory for the directions to move to some uncertain location? How could I focus on anything at all? But I clung to the one certainty I now possessed: it was only a matter of time before I'd be contributing to the war effort – doing something positive to destroy the enemy who caused Sam's death.

AUGUST 1943

'Once basic knowledge is acquired, any attempt at preventing its fruition would be as futile as hoping to stop the earth from revolving around the sun.'

Enrico Fermi

FOUR

My scheduled departure wasn't quite as abrupt as I feared it would be. I had forty-eight hours from the time notice arrived until I was due at the train station. Aunt Dorothy acted quite stoic about it – exhibiting the stiff upper lip she'd claimed to have acquired as a student at Cambridge – but I saw tears welling up in her eyes before she quickly turned away. Our housekeeper and cook, Mrs Schmidt, was far more maudlin in her farewell. She couldn't stop sniffling, hiccupping and apologizing for her German ancestry as I walked out the front door. At the train station, I quickly located a man in an army uniform holding a sign with my name on it. He handed me an envelope and said, 'When you reach your destination, you'll find someone waiting for you there.'

He spun around so crisply, I felt like I should salute. Instead, I tore open the envelope. Chicago! Since leaving Rochester, I'd been devouring scientific journals looking for more information about the research on uranium. I'd learned that the physicist Enrico Fermi was hard at work on his theories about fusion in that city and had also read vague discussions about the fission experiments that were thought to be ongoing at the Metalurgical Laboratory at the University of Chicago. Fermi's work was top secret. Is that where I would work? With Enrico Fermi? I grabbed the wall as a spell of light-headedness came over me. Would he share his secrets with me? Could I possibly provide a tiny, fresh insight that would lead to a breakthrough? As I rode the rails, I roamed through a daydream terrain, my excitement building with every clack of the train.

Disembarking, I could hardly contain my anticipation at the thought of heading for the laboratory. But, instead of a uniformed officer offering to collect my bags and giving me a ride to my new workplace, he handed me another envelope. He, too, said that when I reached my destination someone would be waiting for me.

I looked at the ticket. Knoxville? Tennessee? That made no sense. How could anything important be happening in Knoxville? How could I possibly do significant work with uranium – no,

that word is not allowed – tube alloy. How could I expect to
make a valuable contribution if they were shipping me to the
middle of nowhere? But, maybe – maybe – it was just another
stop on my route to someplace else. If it was my final destination, was I being banished for the duration of the war? Was it
my punishment for being a woman?

It was nearing midnight as the train pulled into the station. This
time the man holding a sign with my name on it was wearing a
suit. And he wasn't holding an envelope. I tried not to let my
shoulders slump and telegraph my disappointment that this back-
woods place was the end of the line. All the uranium talk must
have just been a ploy to keep me interested and excited about the
work ahead. After the devastation of the depression, I should have
known better than to trust any corporation. Eastman Kodak had
a good reputation, but it seemed now that it was only a charade.

'Miss Clark? Miss Elizabeth Clark?' the man in the suit asked.

'Yes, I'm Miss Clark,' I said as I reached out to shake his
hand.

'Charlie Morton. I'm head of Analytical Chemistry here at
Clinton Engineer Works. You'll be helping me set up our lab.
But not until tomorrow. Because of the late hour, you'll get to
experience the best Knoxville has to offer: the Andrew Johnson
Hotel. After breakfast, we'll head out to the facility.'

Morton claimed my bags and we drove off to the hotel on
Gay Street, the tallest building in town. 'The local radio station
is up on the seventeenth floor,' he said. 'Not my kind of music
– it's all hillbilly music to me but they call it country. I was
raised in the countryside but that was Massachusetts. No one
there sang like they do here.

'The area feels very primitive,' Morton continued. 'A lot of
the scientists call this place Dogpatch, but it's the home of the
Tennessee Valley Authority and gateway to the Great Smoky
Mountains National Park. It really does have a lot to offer. But
don't count on anything but formal southern hospitality from the
natives here – you won't be making any friends. There's a bit of
bitterness about the land the government took from farmers to
build our little experiment in the sticks.'

By the time I'd climbed into bed, my future seemed a bit
brighter than it had when I arrived at the Knoxville station. It
certainly sounded as if there might be potential to do something

significant, no matter how unlikely the location. The next morning, I was too excited to eat. I just moved my food around the plate with my fork as I drank coffee from a thick, white mug.

We set out for Clinton Engineer Works and in a few miles, the paved city streets gave way to a dirt and gravel road running through rolling, lush, green and cow-filled countryside that reminded me of the hills of Virginia. Despite their primitive composition the roads were smooth and free of ruts. Things changed when we crossed a bridge. It was jarring to travel through all that natural beauty only to confront long barbed-wire-topped fences which ran for as far as I could see. Even more intimidating were the ponderous tanks squatting like all-powerful trolls, their turrets pointed straight at the entrance – straight at us. And not just tanks, I also spotted a machine gun barrel poking out of a pillbox-shaped shack.

A uniformed man emerged from that little building with a pistol prominently displayed on his hip. Charlie showed his identification badge to the soldier and the gate opened. Once inside, the smooth dirt and gravel road we'd travelled up to that point turned bumpy with a sparser smattering of stones and a plentiful supply of potholes.

We passed naked dirt fields littered with upturned stumps not yet cleared away. The earthy aroma of moist earth filled the air, resurrecting memories of long ago spring planting times. Then we went by a collection of wooden buildings, some still under construction, others shining like newborns – all of them emitting the scent of fresh sawn timber and sawdust.

A billboard sprouted up on the side of the road. On it, a man looked back over his shoulder. The message beside him read: 'Who me? Yes you . . . keep mum about this job.' Further along, another one displayed an eye with a swastika embedded in its pupil and read, 'The enemy is looking . . . for information. Guard your talk.' The mandate for secrecy was even more strident here than it had been in Rochester. But instead of the hushed quiet of whispered confidences, energetic bustle was everywhere. Heavy machinery moved dirt and dumped debris with no attempt to muffle the sound. Soldiers zoomed by in jeeps. People coming and going, working and doing – the hyperactivity of a city rising from bare soil like a bumper crop. The air jangled with the electricity of unceasing motion, tingling my nerve endings. A feeling of eager anticipation overcame me with the realization that I had entered a whole new world with a universe of promises and possibilities waiting to be discovered.

Charlie pointed to the left at an odd looking building with two smaller segments followed by a large one, and said, 'That's Y-12. That's where we'll be working.'

The structure seemed to stretch into forever. The thrill of working there nearly made me speechless but somehow I stammered out, 'How long is Y-12?'

'Oh, about four hundred feet. The second section is where our lab is housed.'

A little further down the road he turned into the drive of a large, boxy, utilitarian, and boring piece of architecture. 'This is your dormitory. I'll help you take your bags inside and then they'll take it from there. They are expecting you. As soon as you get your badge, are assigned a room and get unpacked, go down to the bus station right over there,' he pointed to a sign less than a block away. 'Get on a bus marked Y-12 and come find me in the middle section.'

Inside the building, the smells of new construction were even stronger than outside: the slightly chemical scent of fresh-laid linoleum and the nose-wrinkling odor of freshly applied paint swirled through the air. The sun streaked through windows dancing on a fine haze of sawdust.

In my assigned room, all the furniture was brand new and made of wood – even the door knobs were wooden. They said I would have a roommate, in a matter of days or weeks. But as I surveyed that small space, I knew I'd be comfortable here alone, but it was going to feel cramped when someone else joined me. I wanted to rush to the lab but I dutifully unpacked my bags into the dresser and closet.

It was easy to find my way to Y-12 but when I stepped off the bottom step of the bus, my foot did not hit solid ground. Instead, it plunged into a pit of mud. I struggled to pull it out of the muck. When I did, though, my pretty, strappy shoe did not come out with it. I looked down in despair – one foot was a block of mud, the other still looked as cute as ever in its darling shoe. I couldn't possibly go to work like that. What would Charlie Morton think? How would I ever recover my shoe? And where could I clean off my foot?

I started at the sound of a male voice. 'Give up, sweetheart.'

I looked up at a soldier. 'You'll never find it,' he added. 'You might as well ditch the other one and don't plan on wearing anything but tie-on shoes and make sure those laces are cinched up tight.'

Was he crazy? He looked perfectly normal.

He laughed and said, 'Hey, don't worry about it. It's not an unusual sight here. You going into Y-12?'

I nodded, stunned that he found my predicament amusing.

'No one will be surprised to see you walk in missing a shoe – or even barefoot. Happens here all the time. They'll just want you to wipe off your muddy foot before you go inside.'

What kind of place was this? No one surprised by someone coming to work in bare feet? This really was a hillbilly town. Even at the farm in Virginia, I was expected to exhibit more decorum unless I was mucking the stables or shoveling the chicken coop.

Not knowing what else to do, I limped into the laboratory area feeling mortified – one shoe off, one shoe on. How was I going to explain this to Charlie Morton? To my surprise, he looked down at my feet and grinned. 'I see you've gotten your official welcome to Clinton Engineer Works. Everybody loses shoes in the mud. We're building changing houses attached to the buildings with lockers and sinks for cleaning up, but they're not finished yet. And soon the boardwalks will connect just about every place here so you'll be able to walk on them instead of slogging in the mud. In the meantime, did you pack a pair of galoshes?'

Was he really undisturbed by my dishevelment? Or was he just humoring me? 'No. I didn't. I didn't know where I was going until I got here,' I said.

'Right. Well, you can't buy any now with the rubber shortage going on – and it probably won't ease up till the war is over. Do you have a pair at home that somebody could ship down to you?'

'Yes, I do.'

'Write a letter back home tonight and get them to do that. Just remember, all your mail goes through censors so don't say anything about this place or where it is located. You can mention the abundance of mud – but no other details. You'll have your official orientation tomorrow and they'll fill you in on all the rules. A lot of what you hear won't be applicable to you because you have clearance for more information. Still, it will be useful.'

'If I can't tell my Aunt Dorothy where I am, how can she ship anything to me?'

'Everything goes to a drop box. I'll jot the address down for you so you have it. Now, let's give you a tour and you can get a general idea of what is going on here. In your position, you will know more than most of the other chemists. Remember not to volunteer information to anyone – or answer any questions. If they don't know, they probably don't need to know.

'As you see, our laboratory is in the beta chemistry building, the second section of this structure.' A sparkling room of long black tables and fume hoods looked capable of housing dozens of scientists. 'You and I will have to figure out what we will need and order the supplies and instrumentation so it's all ready by the time the others arrive.'

I struggled to forget about the condition of my feet and focus on what Charlie was saying but every uneven step refreshed my memory of my encounter with the mud.

'Follow me to the first section,' he said walking up the corridor. 'This is the alpha chemistry building, for bulk treatment. They'll be purifying the tube alloy and turning it into tube alloy tetrachloride.'

The long lab counters were all framed but only one section of stations was completed with fume hoods in place.

'They'll be stocking their own lab when they arrive so we don't have to worry about them. Our lab will be testing their results, looking for ways to improve methodology and tracking the efficiency of the process. Are you wearing a watch?'

'Yes,' I said, holding up my wrist.

'Take it off and leave it in here,' he said as he unbuckled his watch band and laid it on the small counter.

How odd? Shoes are optional and watches forbidden? I complied and I also discarded my only shoe since the sound of my uneven walk was nerve-wracking. My thoughts must have been clearly etched on my face because when Charlie looked at me, he laughed again.

'You'll see why in a minute,' he said. 'We'll also handle any problems connected to chemistry in the third section where the Calutron is housed.'

'Calutron?'

'You've heard of the cyclotron out at the University of California, haven't you?'

'Of course.'

'This machine is a variation on that – the name is a combination of cyclotron and California.' He shrugged. 'Don't ask me why. You will have clearance for all three sections of Y-12, unlike most of the others. People in the alpha lab go in and out of their entrance and never see the rest of the building. Your badge is color-coded for your clearance. You probably noticed the guard at the door glance at it before you came inside. If it hadn't been the right colors, he would have stopped you and refused your admittance. Now, here is the Calutron,' he said, flinging his arm wide.

It was monstrous. Charlie explained that the oval-shaped hunk of metal was a 77-foot wide, 8-foot tall, 122-foot long, oval-shaped piece of machinery. It looked a lot like a racetrack, but instead of horses' pounding hooves, it was raw ore that sped around the curved field.

Charlie continued, 'This is where the electromagnetic isotope separation of the tube alloy takes place. The raw material is heated up and vaporized; the vapor rises, passes through an ionizing process and gets an electrical charge. Then it goes through a slit in the vacuum and the magnetic field makes it arc as it curves sending the heavier material in a bigger radius and into one receiver and the lighter material into another.'

While Charlie spoke, I translated the code in my head. The heavier material is Uranium 238. It is separated from the light Uranium 235, the product they needed.

'This single unit has gaps for ninety-six tanks, which sounds mind-boggling. But if you just think of it as a massive mass spectrometer, it makes a lot of sense,' he continued. 'Both it and the Calutron achieve acceleration using electrical fields, both use magnetic forces to separate isotopic ion species, both operate in a vacuum and both have ion sources and collectors. The main distinction between the two is that we use the spectrometer for detection and analysis. We use the Calutron for production.'

'So, technically, we could do the work of the Calutron with our spectrometer in the lab?'

'Yes,' Charlie answered. 'But the quantities produced would be exceedingly small and reaching our production goals would be impossible.'

'What's the ratio of the heavier and lighter materials in the original?'

'For every one thousand pounds of the original ore that we send through the process, we should get seven pounds of the needed lighter substance. The separation is based on a simple principle and what it does is vital and priceless for the war effort. But even if this piece of machinery was useless, it would have an incredibly high value – far more than the engineers envisioned in the original design. The specifications called for electromagnets wrapped in copper coil. When that requisition was submitted, it was rejected in record time. All the copper available was tied up in the production of munitions for the military.

'It was difficult for the engineers to get the army brass to understand that they couldn't just cobble together the electromagnets with anything that might be on hand. Eventually, the officers accepted that the laws of physics trumped military desires every time. So, General Groves got Roosevelt to raid the US Treasury and deliver 14,700 tons of silver coin to melt down and use it to wrap the coils.'

'Nearly 300,000 pounds? That's one seriously expensive piece of equipment.'

'It certainly is. The vacuum pumps are downstairs but not much to look at. Let's go upstairs where we have the monitors and controls,' he said. I followed him into an area filled with a series of panels covered with levers, dials and meters. 'The Calutron is a very temperamental piece of equipment requiring constant supervision. At the moment, we've got PhDs running this equipment – just like they do in California with the cyclotron. That's going to change. For one, the PhDs are always slowing down the works trying to figure out the why of everything. For another, there is simply not a large pool of available doctorates to man these controls once we go into full production.

'When this gets rolling, women with high-school educations but no real background in science will sit in these stools, monitoring the meters around the clock They will know the parameters of acceptability, however, they will not know they are monitoring the balance between the electrical and the magnetic forces. They will know which levers to switch or dials to turn with each variance in the readings but will have no idea of how their actions are impacting the equation. They will simply know that they have done the right thing when the meter readings have stabilized. We will not explain anything to them other than to say that they're making a catalyst that will be vital to the war effort. You must always remember not to provide those employees with any additional information, no matter how innocent a question might sound. The less they know, the safer we all are – the whole country is.

'Follow me this way,' Charlie said, 'we're going across the catwalk. Can you feel the magnetic field pulling on the nails in your shoes?'

Abashed, I looked down at my feet and felt the warmth of a blush rising into my cheeks. 'Well . . .'

'Oh, right. Forgot you learned about the mud today,' he said with a chuckle. 'Anyway, it feels as if you have glue on the soles of your feet. And that is why I had you remove your watch. The magnetic field will yank the steel parts inside out of their positions and smash the inner workings to bits.'

The next morning, I arrived at the main building, joining a gaggle of other employees, mostly women, for orientation. 'Most of you here will be Calutron Girls,' the man intoned from the front of the room. 'Today is the last day you will wear hair pins. The machines you will be operating will pull them right out of your hair and stick them like glue to the nearest metal surface. It could be a little painful. So leave them in your rooms. If you want to keep your long hair, a snood or head scarf will be required on the floor.

'You are the first of many coming here to help win the war. Everything is more primitive than it will be in the near future. Roane-Anderson, that's the company who administers our little community, announced that the first drug store is opening later this week and the first grocery store days after that. By mid-month, we'll have a post office. By the end of the month, we hope to open the movie theaters. And we have much more planned in the fall – bowling alleys, a bank, a newspaper and you'll be happy to hear, ladies, in a little more than a month, our first beauty salon will open. So if you're ready for a shorter cut, we'll have beauticians trained in the latest styles ready to make you beautiful.

'You are our pioneers. We will train you and you will help train others. We cannot tell you what you are going to do, but we can tell you how to do it and we can only tell you that if our enemies achieve what we are attempting before we do, God help us!

'Always remember this: what you do here, what you see here,

what you hear here, when you leave here, let it stay here. The enemy is looking for information – guard your tongue. Don't be fooled by tricky characters. Your country is depending on you.'

After my stint in Rochester, I wasn't at all surprised by this high security talk, but looking around the room, I saw an ocean of gaping mouths and eyes as wide as Thanksgiving pies. By the time the session was over, though, every one of them stood a little taller and looked a little prouder. Obviously the atmosphere of secrecy was enough to convince them all that what they were doing was vital to the war effort – what they accomplished would bring their brothers, fathers and friends home from the front.

FIVE

I worked long hours at Charlie Morton's side, selecting the equipment and supplies needed for our laboratory. At last, we were ready to analyze samples provided from test runs of the Calutron as the engineers worked out the glitches. It didn't seem like there was much to do and yet it swallowed up ten, twelve, sometimes fourteen hours a day, six days of every week. The overwhelming sense of urgency at Y-12 was so keen; at times, I thought I could smell it in the air the moment I stepped inside the building to start a new day.

We broke for hurried meals in the cafeteria. Charlie Morton kept up an encouraging spiel throughout our meals, constantly offering me assurances that as soon as the process was up and operating smoothly, we would have time to relax. As occupied as I was with work, I hadn't noticed the swelling population of women pouring into the Calutron area, replacing scientists at the controls until there was hardly a PhD on the floor.

I had, however, noticed that every time I went back to the dorm to sleep, there were newcomers. It seemed as if legions of additional women were roaming the halls every evening – not that I had any time to socialize with them.

I met Ruth in mid-August. Returning to my room, I discovered the amount of furniture in my space had doubled in my absence and a woman I'd never seen before stood between the beds. She was rail thin with tawny brown hair. She turned toward me and said, 'Hi there. You must be my roommate. I'm Ruth Nance from Lynchburg, Tennessee. Pleased to make your acquaintance.'

'Hi Ruth. I'm Elizabeth Clark.'

'My good friends call me Ruthie. Considering we'll be living in this little room as close as a large flock of fat hens in a small chicken coop, you might as well start out calling me that, too.'

'Ruthie, it is. My given name is Elizabeth, but Libby is actually what friends call me.'

'Good. Now Libby, I hope you're fixin' to tell me a bit about yourself 'cause no one else in the building seems to know a thing about you.'

'You talked to other people about me?'

'I've been here for hours with no sign of hide nor hair of you. So I've been asking questions but not getting many answers. All I learned is that you're never here. Where y'all from?'

'I was born on a farm in Virginia but then later went to Philadelphia to live with my aunt after my father died,' I said, surprised when that little bit of information popped out of my mouth. What was it about this woman that had already broken past my normal reticence to discuss anything personal?

'You poor thing. An orphan? Or is your mamma still alive?'

'Yes, she is. She . . .'

'My pa died, too. Ma's never been the same. Life's been hard on her these last ten years. That's why I came here, so I could make enough money to send some home to help her out. How old were you when your pa died?'

'Ten,' I said. 'What about you?'

'I was twelve. Did you have any sisters or brothers?'

'I had a younger brother but he died in the same fire that killed my dad. Now, I have a half-brother.'

'Your pa and your brother at the same time? That's awful. But my ma never remarried. And I was the oldest when Pa died but Ma was carrying a new baby that was born three months after he was gone. I also have a sister Irene – she's two years younger than me and a brother Hank, two years younger than her. Little Frankie – he's ten years old now – he was a big surprise to all of us. And soon, he'll be the only one at home. Hank's about to turn eighteen and as soon as he does, he's signing up. All he can think about is fighting in the war. And Irene works here, too.

'After Pa died, Ma pretty much had her hands full with the baby coming along and all her grieving. I pretty much had to take charge with Irene – that girl was running wild. Even at ten years old, she was too pretty for her own good. She's a good girl but there have always been a lot of boys – and men – ready to take advantage of her. And she was an easy mark. She never met a person she didn't like. And ever since she started school, all she could talk about was movin' out of the sticks. I figured any fella promisin' to make that dream come true, could get her to do most anything.

'So I kept a close eye on her, but like I said, she really is a good girl. She listened to me real good back home. But here, it's gettin' harder every day. Wish my two big brothers were still around.'

Did I hear her wrong? 'Older brothers? I thought you said you were the oldest when your father died?'

'Well I was then, but my parents had two sons who died when they were babies.'

'How horrible!'

'It was for Ma and Pa but I never knew them. I hadn't been born yet when they caught that influenza after the Great War.'

'That was an awful time. My parents lost a baby then, too.'

'Guess we're lucky we weren't around yet – might not be here to talk about it if we were.'

I reached out and squeezed Ruth's hand. She threw an arm around me, enveloping me in a tight hug. When we broke away, Ruth wiped a tear from one eye and said, 'Well, where do ya work here?'

'In Y-12 . . .'

'Really, well I be. I'd figured ya weren't one of us Calutron girls on accounta nobody on any shift can ever remember seeing you at work. I guess I was wrong.'

'No. Not at all. I'm not a Calutron girl. I—'

'Are you a secretary?'

'No, I—'

'A cafeteria worker?'

'No, I—'

'Post Office?'

'No, I—'

'Well, what do you do, Libby Clark?'

'I've been hired as a chemist.'

'A chemist?'

'Yes, you know, a scientist.'

'I know what a chemist is, Libby. What I don't know is: how did you manage that?'

'I went to college—'

'Really. I know that it's possible. But personally I never did know of any woman who did that. Were there a lot of women there?'

'I went to Bryn Mawr, a college just for women.'

'You're kidding me. They have colleges just for women? My word, I never heard of such a thing. And you got a degree there?'

'Yes, I—'

'In chemistry?'

'Yes, and in physics.'

'So you're a smart one.'

'Well, I do have some education—'

'Don't be modest, Libby. You're smart. And, you,' she said, poking my chest with her index finger, 'you are the future for women. Makes me proud to know you. Maybe I'll get a little smarter, rooming with you.'

'I wouldn't—'

'Could happen. You might teach me how to use what brain I do have – that'd make me smarter.'

'I guess that's—'

'Did you know that Tennessee is the state that gave women the right to vote?'

'Tennessee?'

'Yessiree. Right here in Tennessee. We are the state that put the amendment over the top and made it law.'

'That's right. My Aunt Dorothy told me about that once.'

'Well. Before everybody starts going to bed, it's time you met some of your neighbors.'

'But, I—'

'Never you mind. We're all girls here. You don't have to comb your hair or fix your lipstick or put on a fresh dress. It's just come as you are,' Ruth said, sliding her arm through mine. 'Let's go.'

Out in the hallway, Ruth announced in a big, booming voice, 'Look y'all, my roommate came home at last.'

Immediately, Ruth was surrounded by a swarm of women. She seemed to know everyone's name and each one of them

treated her like a long-lost friend even though they'd met her for
the first time that day. Initially, they were treating me the same
way. I had no illusions that I'd suddenly become that captivating.
I knew it was because of Ruth, not on my own merits. The truth
of that conclusion became obvious once my new roommate told
the others I was a scientist. They all seemed to shrink back like
one amorphous mass at the sound of the word. One even snapped,
'Well, I guess you're smarter than the rest of us. I hope you don't
rub our noses in that every day.'

Before I could respond, Ruth jumped to my defense. 'Libby
ain't no snobby Yankee. She was raised on a farm in Virginia.
She can milk cows and slop hogs. She's one of us.'

'She's a scientist, Ruth. Don't kid yourself. She's only with
us because she has no choice.'

'And there's something not natural about a career woman,'
another woman chimed in.

'Yeah,' said another. 'All of us are just doing our part for the
war. When the men come back home, all we want to do is get
married and have babies. What about her?'

'Land's sakes! Libby is a woman, too,' Ruth said. 'She can't
wait to get married and have babies.'

I started to object to that statement but felt a sharp pinch on
my upper arm as Ruth hustled me into the stairwell. 'Now, what
were you going to say?' she asked.

'I doubt if I'll ever get married or have babies, Ruthie.'

'You're just saying that 'cause you haven't met the right fella
yet.'

'No, Ruthie, I—'

'Never you mind, Libby, I won't say that again. It doesn't
matter. C'mon, I've got more girls you need to meet.'

On each floor, the same scene repeated itself. Ruth, already
beloved and me quickly scorned. I was surprised that none of
the negative reactions of the other girls seemed to affect Ruth's
attitude at all. She continued to treat me like a prized trophy,
presenting me to one and all with pride. When we got back to
the room, Ruth said, 'See, I am the only girl with a scientist for
a roommate. Ha! None of them can top that.'

'But, Ruthie, they don't like me,' I objected.

'Pshaw, they're just all green with envy.'

Over the following weeks, Ruth's loyalty and commitment to

our friendship never wavered, no matter what anyone said. Her constant refrain became an admonishment that we needed to spend time having fun together. She kept saying, 'Girl, you need to stop workin' so darned hard. I finally gave in to her urging and the two of us went to see the first movie airing in the new theatre. It was a British film, Noel Coward's *In Which We Serve*, a dramatic recounting of the Battle of Crete in 1941, aboard the ship of the HMS *Torrin*.

By mid-September, our dormitory was overflowing. Many girls had three to a room. We breathed a sigh of relief after each new group of arrivals settled in and we realized they wouldn't have to cram one more person in our space.

In October, an influx of additional Eastman Kodak scientists flooded into the laboratories. I searched the incoming in vain for just one more female face. Not a single woman in the whole lot.

My male colleagues were friendly enough for the most part and I recognized more than a few faces were familiar from Rochester, but a lot of those men grew suspicious when they learned that I had arrived two months ahead of the rest of them. Once again, there were frequent instances when conversations halted when I walked into a room and I overheard many snide remarks when I walked away. Four years at a women's college had its downside: it didn't prepare me for the real world where the backward attitudes of men were in plentiful supply.

The male scientists had no ulterior motives to be friendly to me, either. There were plenty of women around; they outnumbered the men with ease. Those young chemists, no matter how low they were on the totem pole, had no problem getting dates with Calutron girls, secretaries and other gals working here. I treated them all like peers but they could count on being admired and placed on a pedestal by the others. All I had to offer was a definite step backward in status. I accepted that many of them would be threatened by an equal, but I certainly didn't like it.

Still, I was excited when the Shangri La Club of Bachelors announced their first soiree – a Sadie Hawkins dance, where girls asked the guys to dance – on October 30. I was pretty sure I wouldn't be the first name listed on anyone's dance card. But I also knew I'd be a star on the dance floor if I could get the music away from the slow dances and into some jitterbug. So I taught a willing Ruth the basics and she was a natural. By the time the dance rolled around, she was eager to try out her newfound skills. I packed up my records and dance shoes and we slogged in our galoshes over to the cafeteria. I expected to see the dining tables moved out of the way but didn't think I'd see any other changes. I was wrong – streamers and bunting were everywhere, brightening up the boring place considerably.

We abandoned our boots at the doorway, slipping into our party shoes. We stood on the sidelines for a while, observing other dancers. Then Ruth took the records up to the turntable where a surprised scientist from New York was delighted to learn that a Tennessee girl actually had a clue about the latest dance moves. He quickly put one on, grabbed Ruth's hand and headed to the dance floor.

I wrapped my fingers around the nearest male hand I saw and took my place beside them. At first no one was paying much attention. I knew how to remedy that. I dropped into a split and a beat later was back on my feet. I heard a smattering of nearby applause and, in a short time, every imported Yankee male who knew the Lindy Hop or any one of its variations was standing in line for a turn to dance with me or Ruth. We wore them out one by one. I went to bed exhausted and exhilarated.

The next Monday morning in the lab, I saw the effect of that night out on the men in the lab; they were much friendlier. You wouldn't believe the number of invitations I got for the next dance. But I wouldn't commit to anyone. I told them all that I'd be there and be sure to save him a dance but was not about to spend a whole evening with one partner; variety was much more fun. It also minimized the possibility of anyone thinking that I had romance on my mind. Jitterbug was a true gender equalizer and a great way to blow off steam, make friends and get exercise. It's hard to get serious about anything when you're not standing still.

DECEMBER 26, 1943

'Try as much as possible to be wholly alive, with all your might, and when you laugh, laugh like hell, and when you get angry, get good and angry.

Try to be alive. You will be dead soon enough.'

William Saroyan

SIX

Wilson's return jerked me from my pleasant memories and dropped me into the decidedly unpleasant present. He handed me a steaming, white coffee mug and offered a cigarette. I declined the latter and he lit one for himself, inhaling deeply and blowing smoke off to the side. 'Are you sure you saw a body?'

My jaw dropped at his stupid question. 'What do you mean by that? What could I possibly have seen that I thought was a body and wasn't?'

'Your eyes can play tricks on you, Miss Clark.'

'Sir, I crawled under the bleachers until I was right beside her – closer than you and I are now.'

'Could she have been asleep?'

'Sir, I touched her body. It was cold. It was stiff. She was unresponsive. There was a scarf wrapped tight – too tight – around her neck.'

'A deep sleep, perhaps. Maybe she'd been drinking too much.'

'Her eyes were wide open, sir.' I didn't like the direction of this conversation one little bit.

There was a light tap on the door and Wilson rose, excusing himself again. Things were not going as they should. They'd had plenty of time to get to the bleachers and verify what I'd seen. What was the purpose of this line of inquiry? Was Wilson trying to confuse me for some reason? Did he think I had something to do with Irene's death? Unless I was a suspect, his questions were a serious waste of time. It had to be a temporary tactic until Wilson received confirmation about the body. I just had to be patient enough to let them do their job and become satisfied that I had no role in Irene's murder.

Wilson returned to the room and his seat behind his desk. Folding his hands on the surface, he asked, 'Had you two been drinking?'

'Not today,' I snapped, my irritation rising despite my best intentions.

'Well, what about Miss Nance – Miss Ruth Nance.'

'We both had a little to drink last night – a Christmas celebration.'

'We didn't find any spirits in your home—'

'You went into my home?' I bit my tongue to prevent my surrender to the sudden urge to emulate Aunt Dorothy's house-keeper and spout a string of German invectives.

'Miss Clark, you came in here on a serious matter. We had to take it seriously. We did find an open bottle of Jack Daniels in Miss Nance's dormitory room. As you know, we are located in dry counties. We have to respect the local laws. All alcoholic beverages are illegal here.'

Agitated, I rose from the chair and leaned across the desk. 'What are you doing searching Ruth's room? Why are you not out at the bleachers taking care of Irene?'

'Please be seated, Miss Clark, and try to remain calm. We've been to the bleachers.'

'OK. Then why all of these nonsensical questions? You saw Irene's body. You know we didn't imagine it. Why are you trying to make me think otherwise? Do you think I killed her?'

'Miss Clark, we have been out to the bleachers. There is no body there.'

'What?' The ground no longer felt solid beneath my feet.

'There is no body under the bleachers.'

'What?' I could not have heard him correctly.

'There is no body anywhere near the high school.'

I swallowed hard and took in several deep breaths, fighting to maintain my composure. 'Captain, I did not imagine Irene's body. It was there.'

'Miss Clark, for now, we are going to assume that you two were mistaken.'

'We were not mistaken.'

'If you were not mistaken, then you were playing a prank – a serious one that could result in charges being brought against both of you for filing a false report.'

'But that—'

'That is the way it is. There is no body at the high school. You cannot prove that there ever was a body at the high school.'

I bit my lower lip as I stared at him, looking for signs of deception in his eyes. His pupils did not shift, he did not blink.

His expression was clear of malice. I didn't know what to think. Something was happening here that made no sense at all.

'Is this situation clear to you, now, Miss Clark?'

It wasn't at all clear. But I said, 'Yes, sir,' hoping I'd figure it all out with a little more time.

A man's voice boomed behind me, 'I'll take it from here, Captain.'

I turned around. An attractive man who appeared to be in his early forties stood just inside the doorway. His hair was almost military short but not quite. His blue eyes were intense and humorless. He wore a navy blue suit, white shirt and a striped navy blue and white tie.

After the captain left the room, the man said, 'Miss Clark, I trust I do not need to remind you of your oath of secrecy.'

'I do not see the connection between the death of Irene Nance and any of the work we are doing here; therefore, I do not understand why you would need to remind me. I don't believe we've been introduced, sir.'

His lips twitched as if he wanted to smile but could not remember how to make his mouth form the right shape. 'Everything that happens inside these gates needs to stay inside these gates, Miss Clark.'

'Yes. And all indications are that Irene Nance was killed inside these gates and I have come to the appropriate authority, inside these gates, to report that fact. Again, I do not understand your concern and I do not know who you are.'

'You do not need to know who I am. And you don't need to understand what happened this morning. All you need to know is that there is no body – not in the bleachers, not at the high school, not anywhere inside of our secured area.'

He reminded me of a schoolyard bully who understood nothing but a show of force; however, I knew I could not overpower him. Maybe if I softened my stance, I'd get further. 'Sir, even if I accept what you are saying as fact, that still does not explain where Ruth's sister has gone. If Irene is not dead, then she is a missing person.'

'Possibly. But until Monday when she is due to report to work, we have no reason to believe that there is a problem at all. It's a holiday weekend. She could be simply out and about enjoying the festivities.'

'Sir, Ruth is very concerned about her sister.'

'I'll leave word with the guards at the gate. They'll let Miss Nance know if her sister is seen entering or leaving.'

The remnants of my patience were as ragged as a hobo's shoes. Before I said anything I'd regret, I needed to get out of here. 'So that's it?' I asked.

'Until Monday morning, yes it is.'

I took a few steps towards the door, then stopped and turned around. 'Where is Ruth? Did you leave her at the athletic field?'

'No, of course not. She has had a shock, one of her own imagining, but a shock nonetheless. We wouldn't just leave her there.'

'Is she back at the dorm?'

'No, Miss Clark. We took her to the hospital.'

'Hospital? What did you do to her?'

'She was hysterical, Miss Clark. The doctor administered a sedative to calm her down. We wanted to keep an eye on her for a couple of days.'

'I'll bet you did,' I said, walking away as quickly as I could. I was frightened but I could not give a name to my fear. It was more a primitive, visceral response to unanswered questions lurking in some impenetrable fog of the unknown than it was a reaction to a real, tactile threat. I followed the boardwalks to the hospital.

A military guard stood beside Ruth's room. When I approached, he stepped sideways in front of it and came to attention. 'Sorry, miss, doctor's orders. No one to disturb the patient while she's sleeping. Doc gave her some medicine and said she'd probably sleep until the next morning. Meanwhile, no visitors.'

I wanted to force my way past him but that was another battle I couldn't win, so I left and walked back to the athletic field at the high school. I needed to find something to confirm that what I saw was true. There had to be some small scrap of evidence that Irene had been there or some subtle indication of what happened to her body.

I walked up to the spot where Irene had lain lifeless such a short time ago, close enough to peer at the flattened grass. A lot of it looked trampled. Someone – a lot of them – had been out here. It must have been the people charged with taking her body away, but who and where was her body now?

I circled the bleachers making a progressively wider arc with each orbit. I spotted discarded cigarette butts, broken pencils and small scraps of paper. Then I saw an odd shape nestled in the blades of grass. I squatted down beside it. It looked like a woman's lapel pin with a broken clasp. I picked it up and turned it over in my palm: a little, pale blue, ceramic fawn with white spots and pink Lucite ears.

It looked familiar. Was this the pin Irene been wearing when she came by the house on Christmas night? I closed my eyes and tried to remember. There had been of a spot of color on Irene's lapel – was it this? Maybe. I just wasn't sure.

I slipped it into a pocket, planning to show it to Ruth. I completed a few more circuits of the field and, finding nothing else, returned home.

I had seen Irene's body. I hadn't imagined the scarf cinched too tight around her neck. Irene was dead; there was no possibility that she simply got up and walked away. What happened to Irene on that football field? And what happened to Ruth while I was at the police station?

I lay awake in bed in my little bungalow that night, thinking I'd never get to sleep. To push my thoughts of the current ugly predicament out of my mind, I forced myself to recall the surprising turn of events that had brought me here into my new home.

THANKSGIVING 1943

'Let me be something every minute of every hour of my life. And when I sleep, let me dream all the time so that not one bit of living is lost.'

Betty Smith
Author of the 1943 best-seller
A Tree Grows in Brooklyn

SEVEN

My current housing situation was a direct result of the problems in Y-12. Nothing was going as smoothly as the planners had expected. The first fourteen-ton race-track magnets wrapped with silver windings tested at the end of October were leaking electricity and shorting out the coils. The engineers first suspected moisture. I was dubious about that because the heat of operation should have evaporated it all away. They brought everything to a halt to manually dry off the magnets. When they were certain all of them were completely dry, they started the system up again but it still shorted out. I kept turning the problem over in my mind, trying to figure out the reason and find a solution.

It would help if I could ask the right questions but I wasn't sure what they were. I ran a sample of product from the alpha lab through the spectrometer recording the distances different substances traveled from the filter. The contaminants I found were not found in the ore and I doubted if the chemists added it during processing. I took the discovery to my supervisor. 'Charlie, I've found copper and plain old dirt in the sample from alpha. I suspect it came from the processing in the Calutron but I can't be sure without taking samples directly from there and running tests.'

'What samples will you want to test?'

'I'd start with the ore, run it through an acid bath and see what shows up there. Then, I'd want to test the end product before it goes to alpha. And finally, I'd just like to look around and see what other substances are introduced during the procedure that could be sources of contamination and test those as well.'

'Do you think you'll find anything to explain why the line is shorting out?'

'I don't think the spectrometer analysis will answer that question but who knows what else I'll find. There could be some misapplied physics the engineers aren't recognizing within the mechanical design. I could check that out as well.'

'You won't be able to do that while it's in operation and I doubt if I can get them to shut down the line for one of my people to crawl around on their equipment. How would you feel about coming up here on Thanksgiving – they'll be shutting the line down for the holiday. But I wouldn't be able to help you with it. I'm taking my family over to Virginia to visit my wife's relatives.'

Would I have to give up a homemade Thanksgiving meal to find the answers? My stomach churned in rebellion over that possibility. Maybe I could do both. 'I'm supposed to have dinner with the Bishops but I can come up here early and see what I can find. I might get lucky. Meanwhile, I'll run what samples I can before then.'

'See what you can do, Libby, but don't ruin your holiday plans.'

'I guess that means you don't think I have much chance of success.'

Charlie sighed. 'It's not that I don't think you can find an answer, Libby. I'm just not sure there is an answer.'

Now, that was a challenge. Intriguing enough to miss out on Thanksgiving dinner? Maybe. I could only hope that it would not come to that. The invitation to spend the holiday with the Bishops came after I met Dr Bishop's daughter. By the time the last month ended, Eastman Kodak had 4,800 employees on the site – and they were only just one of a number of employers on site. They'd all hired a lot of women but none of them were working as professionals in the labs in Y-12. Somehow, they all seemed to know I was a scientist and nearly every day, one of them sidled up to me with a question about what we were doing and where was it leading. And I wouldn't – couldn't – answer even the most innocuous questions. That certainly didn't make me popular with the women in the building.

Dr Marc Bishop's daughter, Ann, was an exception, probably because of the way we met. She was secretary to the managers of the Y-12 facility. Both of us thought we were the only person using the women's restroom in our section until I walked in one day and heard her crying in a stall. At first, I wondered how a Calutron girl had got past security to find this lavatory. The anguish in the unseen woman's voice, however, pushed that concern out of my mind.

'Hello,' I said, raising my voice to be heard over her wailing. 'Can I help you?'

'I'm way past help.'

'What happened?' I shouted through the door.

'He's dead.'

'Your boyfriend? Your husband?'

'Noooo. I knew him all my life.'

'Your father?'

'Noooo. My favorite cousin. He was like a brother to me.'

'Did he die in combat?'

All I got in response to that question was a deep moan.

'If you come out,' I urged, 'it would be easier to talk. I lost a close cousin at Pearl Harbor.'

Sniffles followed by the loud honk of a blowing nose leaked out of the cubicle, followed by the sound of rushing water when the toilet flushed. Then the door creaked open.

To my surprise, instead of the neck to ankle overalls that the Calutron girls wore, she was dressed in a brown-and-white checked dirndl skirt and a tucked front white blouse with a lace collar. 'Where did you come from?' I asked.

'In there,' she sniffed and pointed back to the stall.

'No, I mean, do you work here? And where do you work?'

'Oh. I'm a secretary for a bunch of scientists,' she said and paused to blow her nose again into a piece of toilet tissue. 'My dad got me the job. I'm Ann Bishop. He's Dr Bishop. Do you know him?'

'Yes, I do. I work for Dr Bishop, indirectly anyway. My supervisor works under him. I'm Libby Clark. How long have you been here?'

'About a month. Are you new?' Ann asked. 'What do you do?'

'I've been here about a month, too. I'm a chemist.'

'A chemist? But you're a woman.'

'Yes, I am, that's why I'm using the ladies' room.'

'I didn't know there were any lady scientists here. That's really swell.'

'I didn't know there were any women in Y-12 except for the Calutron girls.'

'I think I'd go loco working over there. All that time sitting and staring at dials with a bunch of girls. No thank you.' Without warning, she burst into tears again.

I put my arm around her. 'There, there, I know how much it hurts. It gets better with time. It still makes me sad and sometimes makes me angry that my cousin died so far from home but it doesn't hurt quite so much now. How did your cousin die?'

'His plane crashed in the Mediterranean somewhere,' she said with a sniff.

'Was he a pilot?'

'No, he was a gunner. They said he went down firing,' she choked on her words and sobbed. 'Like that did him a lot of good. And they won't even tell us how it happened or who shot him down or anything.'

I patted gently on her shoulder. 'I know, I know. My cousin died in Pearl Harbor but I don't know how. And was he on a pier? On a ship? Walking down the road? I have no idea.'

I suppose it was our shared loss that broke down the barriers and formed a bond that strengthened as we went to lunch together a few times each week. Ann didn't particularly understand me but was clearly fascinated by my different outlook. One day at lunch she said, 'I never considered doing anything but finding a husband, getting married and having babies. Whatever made you even imagine doing something else?'

'I guess I was pushed in that direction by the circumstances following my father's death, Ann. But I am happy I was. I wouldn't mind having a male companion, but men . . . They all want to shove you in a mold of their own design. It might be nice to be married to someone who treated me as an equal, who saw value in my work as much as in their own – one who didn't feel a need to prove their manhood through procreation. It seems as if all my life, the world has been in turmoil. Why would I want to bring a child into this mess? Why wouldn't I want to have control of my own life, since there is no way I can control the world and its chaos?'

'We're women. That's just what we do,' Ann said.

'This woman will not.'

'Amazing. My mom needs to meet you – she doesn't seem to believe there are other options.' From that idea, a Thanksgiving dinner invitation followed the next day.

EIGHT

Before leaving work on the Wednesday before Thanksgiving, I went up to the Calutron to look it over while it was in operation and to plan my course of action for the next morning. As I walked around the circumference, observing the moving parts, I heard a belligerent voice that seemed to be directed at me.

'Hey, what're you doing up here, miss? You're no Calutron girl.'

I turned around and faced a middle-aged, balding man with a bulbous nose and downturned mouth. I read his badge and said, 'I'm authorized to be here, Mr DeVries.' Then, I turned away from him and back to the Calutron.

'Don't turn your back on me, missy. Let me see the clearance code on your badge or I'll call security.'

I really wanted to ignore him and his rude request but thought better of it. If he did call security it might cause a lengthy delay in my work.

He looked hard and long at my identification as if he were interpreting a coded message and said, 'OK. OK. You have a right to be here but that doesn't mean you have a right to monkey with the equipment. Hey, wait a minute – Elizabeth Clark? Aren't you that girl scientist rooming with the Nance girl from over in Lynchburg?'

'You know Ruth?'

'Nah, never met her. But I know her sister Irene.'

'How nice for you,' I said. 'Can I get back to work now?'

'Don't get all high hat with me, missy. You might be a scientist but you're still a girl and I'm responsible for the functioning of the machinery.'

I stepped close enough to him to poke a finger in his chest. 'If you don't scram right away and let me do my work in peace, I will call security.' I spun away from him and acted engrossed while I listened for noises of his departure. For a minute, all I heard was the sound of his breathing. Then, I heard his feet shuffling away as he mumbled, 'You dames are all alike.'

I was out of bed before dawn on Thanksgiving morning, dressing as quietly as I could, trying not to disturb Ruth's sleep. She'd gone to bed in a blue mood the night before. Poor thing had never been away from home on Thanksgiving and like most of the Calutron girls, a trip home wasn't possible because of the time to travel and the gas needed for the journey. She'd be having dinner in the cafeteria with her sister.

I hadn't found the contamination source yet but I had a number of analytes to process. If all went well, I could accomplish that over the weekend. This morning, I'd use my physics background more than my knowledge of chemistry to try to find something suspicious.

The quiet within the Calutron building was spooky. The huge machinery cast tall shadows in the dim lighting and the absence of employees made it feel like a ghost town. I needed to look inside so I disassembled a portion of the exterior housing of the massive machine. Every little clink of a tool against metal echoed throughout the building adding to the eeriness of the atmosphere. I compared what I found inside the machinery to the engineering specifications.

Nothing seemed amiss – every nook and cranny of the equipment appeared to be in compliance with the diagrams. Still, there was a problem, which possibly meant a flaw in the design itself. I pulled out a silver wire wound electromagnet, turning it around to view its construction from every angle. I was about to reinstall it when a question popped into my mind: would more space between the wire eliminate the shorting? I didn't have much of an engineering background – certainly not enough to know how to test that theory. I had studied electricity in the context of chemistry and physics, though, and that knowledge indicated that the electricity would naturally arc and cause a short when the coiling was wound too tight.

Was that the solution to the problem? If so, could it be repaired on site? Or did the whole machine need to be rebuilt? And how much time would we lose? Enough to fall behind in the race with Germany to build a new bomb? Asking that question of anyone, even Charlie, could send me packing in a heartbeat. I strongly suspected that was the goal of this work. No one had told me that I was involved in the production of a bomb but the logic of deductive reasoning does not lie. There was no other possibility. Would this new bomb fall on Germany? Or would the Allies drop it on the escalating conflict in the Pacific? Would it end the war? Was any single weapon capable of stopping the conflict in its tracks?

I looked up at the clock on the wall and realized I was running out of time. I quickly took samples of pieces of ore, a couple of vials of oil for testing and swabbed the electromagnets, interior walls, anything that seemed to be a possible source of contamination. I secured all the samples in the lab and hurried out of the building. The war would have to wait for tomorrow. This afternoon, I'd feast at the Bishop home. My mouth watered, my stomach rejoiced as I hurried out of Y-12 to the dormitory to dress for dinner.

NINE

Seated around the Bishop family Thanksgiving table, I wanted to share my theories with Dr Bishop, but I didn't dare speak about any of the problems happening at Y-12. He knew all about the issues they faced but after learning I'd been in the facility that morning, he quickly changed the subject.

Working with the scientists and managers at Y-12, Ann knew from the stressful atmosphere and whispered consultations that something was wrong, but she had no idea of what it was. Mrs Bishop was totally in the dark – she knew next to nothing about her husband's work. She was aware that he worked in a laboratory contributing to the war effort and brought home a pay check. Beyond that she didn't seem to have the slightest interest in learning more. To me, it was incomprehensible that anyone could be that deficient in curiosity. Did marriage kill that quality in women?

There was no doubt, though, that Mrs Bishop could work miracles. How she managed to come up with all the fixings for a traditional Thanksgiving dinner in the midst of strict rationing,

I could not imagine. I enjoyed every bite even though she interrogated me throughout the meal.

'Whatever made you go off to college, Libby? Did some young man break your heart?' she asked.

'No, ma'am, it just seemed to be a wise plan for my future to further my education.'

'There are those who say a few years at college can make you a better mother but I've done just fine without it, haven't I, Ann?'

Ann rolled her eyes and said, 'Yes, Mom, you've been a good mother.'

'But you're such a cute little thing, Libby. It's hard to believe that you're a scientist like my husband, Marc.'

'I'm not exactly a scientist like him, ma'am,' I said with a smile. 'He earned a doctorate; I only have a master's degree.'

Dr Bishop said, 'Don't say "only", Libby. It's an amazing accomplishment for a woman, especially considering you also had a double major in physics and chemistry in your under-graduate studies. That's not something I accomplished.'

'Thank you, sir,' I said, feeling a bit self-conscious.

Turning to his wife he continued, 'And Libby is the only woman scientist in all of Y-12, Mildred.'

'That must be very lonely for you,' Mrs Bishop said. 'Then again, it does introduce you to a lot of potential husbands.'

'I do work with a lot of single men,' I agreed; it felt rude to argue with her while devouring the wonderful food she prepared.

'You'll have to introduce some of the nicer ones to Ann – she's not had much luck picking out good ones so far.'

'Mother!' Ann moaned.

I assumed that she was objecting to a criticism in her dating history. Mrs Bishop, however, had a different interpretation. She said, 'Oh, I wouldn't expect Libby to introduce you to anyone she had an interest in, Ann.' She turned to me and said, 'I certainly wouldn't want Ann to steal away someone you were sweet on, Libby. So, is there someone special who's caught your eye?'

'No one in particular, Mrs Bishop, but credit me with some common sense. If there were, I wouldn't introduce him to Ann. Your daughter is too pretty by far.'

'Both of you girls are pretty enough to be picky. Don't say "yes" to the first man who proposes. If you choose a fickle man, he'll break your heart for the rest of your life.' Turning to her husband, she added, 'Isn't that true, dear?'

'Of course,' he said without looking up from his plate.

'Don't worry, Mrs Bishop, there are plenty of little fishies swimming in our sea,' I said.

'Oh, I just love that little fishes song, don't you?' Mrs Bishop said, then broke into song, '"And they swam and they swam right over the dam." Let it be a reminder to you that your mother knows best and there are sharks out there just waiting for girls like you, Ann.'

I jumped at the opportunity to help Ann carry the dinner plates into the kitchen – a short reprieve from Mrs Bishop's questioning was a relief. 'I am so impressed with your mother for getting together everything for this wonderful meal,' I said.

'Don't be. I think she would have left Oak Ridge if she couldn't have pulled this off. It meant far more to her than it should. But why haven't you said anything outrageous?'

'Outrageous?' What did Ann want from me? An explosion of Y-12 secrets at the dinner table?

'You know, how you feel about marriage and babies and men. I was hoping you'd shock her speechless, making her choke on a mouthful of potatoes. And here you are acting polite.'

'This is the best meal I've had in six months, Ann. I want your mother to ask me to return for another.'

Ann sighed. 'I guess that means I'm going to have to wrangle more dinner invitations for you, get you to the point where it's not a big treat. When it doesn't mean so much you can then tell my mother some of the things you've told me; she'll never be the same.'

'But I like her just the way she is,' I protested.

'That's only because she's not your mother.'

As I worked in the lab the next three days, worried that all the testing would be futile – maybe I'd never find the source of the contamination. Then, on Sunday, I ran the oil that lubricated the Calutron. The lines on the graph made it clear – all of the impurities found were in that product. We needed a higher quality, purer lubricant – much higher, much purer – to solve the problem. That should be easy to fix.

Monday morning, I showed Charlie Morton the test results

and told him about my theory regarding the wrapping of the electromagnets. He responded with head nods and non-committal verbal responses. I didn't think he was making any attempt to process the information I provided before he changed the subject.

'What did you say to Mr DeVries?'

'DeVries, the engineer?' I asked.

'Yes, you certainly got him angry. He spoke to his department head, who came to me about his complaint. DeVries said you were uppity.'

'Ah, applesauce! I simply defended my authorization to be in the Calutron area when he tried to stop me. I suppose he thought I should scurry off. But I stood my ground so that I could do my job.'

'You shouldn't jump on your high horse so quickly, Libby. A lot of men are unwilling to accept the existence of professional women or even working women – unless they're nurses or teachers. Try batting your eyelids instead of being difficult. It'll make it easier to get what you want.'

I was furious but I did not trust myself to respond. It was so frustrating when men like Charlie, who did respect women's intelligence and ability, still thought we should bow and scrape to those males who regarded us as inferiors. Why couldn't men like Charlie understand that professional women would never get universal acceptance and respect by playing those little schoolgirl games?

To make matters worse, his unresponsiveness must have meant that he found fault with my conclusions. If he thought they were credible, I doubted that he would have diverted our discussion. I pondered and reexamined my thinking but could not think of anything that didn't fit the situation at hand. I even ran the analysis in the oil again but found no flaw in the original results.

In early December, without warning, the racetrack shut down completely. And, of course, no explanation was forthcoming. Suddenly, there were a lot of workers and no work. Managers scrambled to keep them busy with motion picture showings, games, lectures, classes. I attended a couple of lectures but spent most of my time gathering more samples from the Calutron, running tests on them and contemplating theoretical matters. Still I could find no flaws in my conclusions. I needed to ask Charlie to show me where and how I was wrong. Days passed, though, without an opportunity to corner him away from others.

On the morning of December 15, the buzz of voices in the building reached such an intense volume, I was pretty sure I could have heard it even if the noisy racetrack had been running. Charlie poked his head out of the door to our laboratory, ducked back and said, 'I knew it. He's here.'

'Who's here?' I asked.

'G.G.'

'Who?'

'General Leslie Groves. I knew he'd come about the racetrack problem.'

I peered around Charlie to look down the hall. It was easy to pick General Groves out of the crowd. Everyone milled around him. He cut an imposing figure in his star-bedecked khaki uniform. A bristly mustache over straight, grim lips, a prominent nose and firm chin like a general from central casting.

As the group approached the analytical chemistry lab, I backed up and returned to work at my station.

In a moment, General Groves' frame filled the doorway. 'Morton,' he said.

'Yes, sir,' Charlie responded.

'Which one is that brilliant young scientist with all those brilliant theories?'

That sounded a lot like sarcasm to my ears. I swallowed hard. Please don't let it be my theories. But Charlie pointed back to me, making me want to disappear. 'There she is, sir. Elizabeth Clark.'

'A woman?' Groves said. 'Interesting. Miss Clark, would you please step out here. I don't think we all can fit in your laboratory without damaging equipment.'

I followed orders, hating every moment of what was ahead. Today, I would lose my job. Public humiliation, then dismissal. Why couldn't Charlie have let me go quietly? Why did he want to shame me, too?

'Where did you go to school?' the general asked.

'Bryn Mawr, for my undergraduate work, and the University of Pennsylvania for my master's degree, sir.'

'Did you major in chemistry?'

'Chemistry and physics, sir.'

'And your postgraduate work?'

'Analytic Chemistry, sir.'

'That explains your ability a little better. Now, tell me: what are your theories about our production problem here.'

'Sir, I wouldn't dare to—'

'Yes, you would because I told you to do so. Speak.'

'Because of the impurities in the end product, I was concerned that it might be possible – at least theoretically – that the oil that cools the machinery was adding impurities during the processing.'

I looked back in the direction of the lab, hoping to find an escape hatch but instead saw that the doorway was filled with faces of the other scientists. I looked down the hall beyond the pack around the general and there I saw a tall, thin man with an intense, but otherwise ordinary face, nodding his head. Something about him looked familiar but I couldn't figure out why. I could only hope he wasn't too important, I was already praying that the earth would swallow me up whole where I stood.

'Colonel Mickels,' the general said turning to a man standing immediately behind him. 'Can you tell us all what our experts found when they checked out Miss Clark's theory?'

'Yes, sir,' Mickels said. 'They found dirt particles, copper contaminants, rust and miscellaneous debris.'

Groves turned to Morton. 'When did Miss Clark tell you about this theory, Morton?'

'The Monday after Thanksgiving, sir.'

'Oppie, when did the so-called experts figure this out?'

'Three days ago, G.G.,' the familiar-looking man said as he flashed a soft, barely perceptible smile in my direction.

Oppie? Was that Robert Oppenheimer, the brilliant theoretical physicist, smiling at me? I'd read every paper of his I could find. Dazzled by the possibility that I was in the presence of Oppenheimer, I barely heard what the general was saying at first.

'You were right, Miss Clark. If the experts had taken your work more seriously, we could have saved two lost weeks. Now, what was your other theory?'

Startled by his question, I pulled my focus back into the conversation. 'I think it's possible that the wires have been wound too tightly.'

'Mickels, what exactly did I say to you when that question was asked yesterday?'

'Sir, you said, "The damned bands are too close together. Who in blazes is responsible for that?"'

'Now, where do you live, Miss Clark?' Groves said.

Why does he care? I wondered. 'In one of the dormitories, sir.'

'Is your roommate a scientist?'

'No, sir, she's a Calutron girl.'

'Does she ask you questions about your work?'

'No, sir. Ruth Nance respects the boundaries of my required secrecy.'

'What about the other girls on your floor, in the building, do they ask questions?'

'All the time, sir.'

'And what do you tell them?'

'That I'm sorry but I cannot answer their questions.'

'Does that make them angry?'

'Sometimes, sir.'

Groves spun around and looked at the gaggle of suits and uniforms gathered around him. 'Does that make sense to anyone here?'

No one said a word. 'Fine. I want her in individual housing before Christmas.'

'Sir,' one of the community administrators, spoke up, 'that is against policy. Single individuals do not get their own homes.'

'Do you think I don't have the authority to override policy?'

'No, sir, but—'

'You've got a whole mess of those little flattops going up. Put her in one of them immediately.' Turning to me, he said, 'Come with me, Miss Clark,' as he headed up the stairs to the racetrack.

I fell in with the massive entourage. Feeling totally out of place, I loitered on the edge while Groves fired off questions and growled his dissatisfaction. Some people in the crowd glared at me. I tried to become as invisible as possible.

When Groves turned away from the equipment, he placed a hand on my shoulder. I hoped he couldn't feel me trembling. 'I want to thank you. And I want you to let me know personally if your housing situation is not remedied immediately.' He took off down the stairs. I was excited but I was also confused.

Did he really mean it? Would I actually have my own home?

I'd miss Ruth but a moment of privacy at the end of the day sounded like heaven. No feet pounding overhead. No more communal bathrooms. Somewhere that I could brush my teeth without waiting in line at the sink? Where I wouldn't need to struggle to concentrate over the noise of babbling voices? Would they follow the general's orders? Or would the civilian management company figure they could ignore a military command?

TEN

I hesitated to mention the day's events to Ruth. The general's orders for a change in my housing situation seemed to be just a nebulous possibility. And if it did occur, I certainly did not expect that it would happen any time soon. But the day after Groves' visit, I was surprised by the receipt of a letter informing me that I'd be moving in a couple of days.

'Ruthie,' I said as I entered the room.

'What's wrong, Libby? Bad news from home?'

'No, it's—'

'You look awful. Like you just had the shock of your life.'

'No, Ruthie, I'm just dumbfounded that—'

'Sit down, sit down. Do not say another word until you sit down. Can I get you a glass of water?'

'No, Ruthie, but—'

'Anything, Libby?'

'Ruthie, you need to sit down.'

'Me?'

'Oh no! Is it my family?' she wailed.

'Sit, Ruthie . . .'

'I couldn't bear it if something happened to my family, especially my sister Irene . . .' she said, easing down onto her bed.

'As far as I know, Ruthie, your sister is fine.'

'Then what . . .?'

Holding my index finger to her lips, I said, 'Sssh! Listen to me.'

Ruth furrowed her brow and held her breath.

'I'm moving out.'

'Did you quit?'

'No, Ruthie . . .'

'Were you fired?'

'No, Ruthie, I still have my job.'

'Have I been a horrible roommate?'

'No, Ruthie, you've been wonderful. Just let me start at the beginning. Did you hear about General Groves' visit yesterday?'

'Oh, yes, that's all anybody's been talkin' about.'

'I talked with him,' I said.

Ruth's mouth dropped open and her eyes widened, 'No! You didn't. Really?'

'Yes,' I said and told her about my encounter with the general. After that I explained the contents of the letter in my hand. 'I have to be packed and ready to move my belongings at 0700 hours on Saturday morning.'

'That's just two days!' Ruth protested.

'I know but it's not as if I have a lot of belongings. I'm just surprised because I didn't think it would really happen.'

'Where is your house? Is it one of the flattops?'

'Yes, it's at 384 East Drive.'

'I can't wait to see it. Do you want to go walk past it now?'

'Sure,' I said, delighted by her excitement. 'It's dark but I bet we can find it.'

As we walked down the boardwalk, we talked about what the change would mean. 'I think it's super that you'll have a place of your own, Libby. I hope you'll ask me over to visit sometime,' Ruth said.

'All the time. You're always welcome at my place. I'm counting on you to be a frequent visitor. I wonder who you'll get for a roommate.'

'I don't know. I was thinking about asking if my sister Irene could move in – she's in a dorm room with two other girls right now. They'd all be happy to have a little more space.'

'Speaking of your sister, why have I never met her?'

'I've asked her to come by and meet you but she never seems to have the time. She barely has a minute for me. For a while, she was going out with a different fella nearly every night. The next day, we'd meet up at lunch in the cafeteria and she'd tell me all about her date. She was crazy about most of them. Seemed like every week she was in love with a different one of them – a soldier one week, a young scientist the next. Lately, though, she's mostly been seeing one fella in particular but she won't tell me what they do or where they go. I often stop by her room right after work and talk to her while she's changing clothes for another night out. I keep asking her questions but all I've gotten out of her is that his name is Bill and he's a scientist and is a little older than most of the other guys she dated. I pressed her on that one but she won't tell me how old he is.

'Then, the other day, she started to say something about his family obligations but stopped and threw her hand over her mouth. I wanted an explanation but she tried to say I misheard her. When I wouldn't give up, she turned away from me and mumbled something about an elderly mother who was sickly.

'I didn't like the way she said that 'cause there was that little catch in her voice she had when she was little and I caught her in a lie. I got a real sick feeling in my gut and I just went ahead and asked, "Is your boyfriend a married man?" She puffed all up and said, "How dare you ask me that?"

'And I said, "You're not answering my question, Irene. Are you a home-wrecker?" And all she said to me was "You can leave now, Ruthie. I'm all grown-up and what I do is none of your business." She thinks I don't understand her. She says she wants to have fun – doesn't want to be an old maid, stick-in-the-mud, stuck in the sticks, Wallflower Queen like me. Maybe she's right.'

'Nonsense,' I said. 'I've seen you cut a rug. You're a quick learner, a natural dancer. You've really gotten the knack of the Lindy Hop. You impressed all the boys at the dance.'

'Thank ya, Libby. But to Irene, I'm just the boring older sister. I'm hoping she'll room with me when you move out, so at least I can keep an eye on her like a big sister should.'

'I sure hope that works out, Ruthie. Well, looks like this is it, doesn't it?'

The square little bungalow with its flat roof sat on a small rise. A newly constructed stairway, still smelling of sawdust, rose from the boardwalk to a landing at the door. We went up the steps and Ruth shone the flashlight inside but the light reflected off the glass and without it, it was too dark to see much of anything.

'Two days, Libby and this is all yours. I'm so excited.'

'Me, too, Ruthie. But I'm sure going to miss you. You must come over often so I don't miss you too much.'

*   *   *

On Friday at the lab, I didn't tell anyone except Ann Bishop about my upcoming move, but Ann apparently had a firm grip on the grapevine. In a matter of minutes, everyone knew. I was dismayed at the reactions I got. A few of the men treated me just as they always had, some with a smidgen more respect because my theories had been proven right. But the rest of them were another story.

They all lined up in two camps. One group became overly deferential as if I were capable of influencing their fates. Worse, was the surly segment who resented what they called special treatment. They made nasty insinuations about what I must have done to get it. They either snubbed me or whispered insults loud enough for me to hear every time they saw me in the halls. All I ever wanted was to be treated as an equal – respected for my education and analytical ability. But even the best of them, the ones who believed in principle in the equality of the sexes, still seemed to carry the attitude that I was a good scientist for a woman, but . . .

Saturday morning, just minutes after Ruth left for work, two soldiers arrived to load up my boxes in the back of a small truck and deliver me and my belongings to the flattop. When they pulled up in front, one of the soldiers handed me a key. I hurried across the boardwalk, past the coal box and up the steps of the small rise to the tiny front porch. I slid the key into the knob and held my breath in anticipation as I eased open the door.

Entering the living/dining room, there was a sofa on the left, stretched under a bank of four windows, set high on the wall. Caddy-corner from it, an overstuffed chair looked like the picture of comfort. On the front wall, a wooden table set below a larger window. The air inside was cold – colder, it seemed that the outdoors.

I looked to my right and saw the kitchen. I ran my hands across the curves of the white refrigerator. A long counter with two sinks ran under another bank of windows that sat down a little lower than the ones in the living room and above them smaller cabinets were attached to the wall.

Opposite was a four-burner electric stove with an oven. A cast iron skillet sat on its surface. I could cook my own meals. I could even bake a cake if I could get my hands on some sugar. My kitchen. My very own kitchen.

One of the soldiers, entering the front door carrying a box in one arm and a full coal scuttle, said, 'Sorry about the chill in here, ma'am. I'll get a fire started right away. You know how to work a coal stove?'

'Yes,' I smiled, remembering my dad's tricks for building and keeping the embers going during long hours away from the house.

'Roane-Anderson will keep a good supply in your coal box – leastways, they're supposed to,' he said with a grin. 'Well, there's just a couple more boxes to bring inside.'

I felt dazed as I drifted through the living room to the small bathroom. A sink, a toilet and a shower – oh, how I yearned to soak in the large claw-foot tub Aunt Dorothy had in her home. But even without a bathtub, it was my personal bathroom – a definite improvement over the communal restrooms in the dormitory.

I went into the last room – the bedroom. It had a dresser and two single beds. Ruthie could spend the night any time she wanted and we'd each have our own bed. As soon as the soldiers were gone, I pulled the sheets out of a box and made the beds. I only had one blanket and one bedspread so I put one on the first bed and the other on the second. I'd have to get one more of each and some more sheets. I felt the chill of the house, and amended my thinking – I'd have to have two blankets for each bed.

I sank into the cozy armchair with a sigh of delight. My place. My place. In one week, I would celebrate Christmas in my place. No matter how anyone treated me at work, I could come here. My shelter from any storm. My place. No one would come in unless I invited them. I felt the warmth of the fire blending with the glow in my chest. I couldn't remember ever being happier.

I looked around my tiny abode, feeling like royalty. 'My place,' I said out loud, savoring the vibration of the two words on my tongue and lips. 'My place.'

ELEVEN

The morning after the move, I started the day by attending a service at the Chapel on the Hill.

I returned home full of Christmas spirit, and rushed in to find the six glass ornaments I'd packed so carefully before leaving home. I hung them on drawer pulls and cabinet knobs around my little home. My home. I still found it so hard to believe.

In the kitchen, I made a peanut butter sandwich for lunch, wishing that I had some jelly to spread on the other piece of the bread. But sadly, I knew that I might not see any jelly or jam until after the war. I'd taken the first bite when I heard a knock on the door.

Ruth stood on the porch, clutching a small valise. She was flanked by two men in uniform holding large cardboard boxes. 'What's this, Ruthie?'

'C'mon in, boys, and set the boxes down on the floor,' Ruth said before flashing a grin in my direction. 'Got a surprise for you, Libby.' To the soldiers she said, 'Thank you, boys. See you at the next dance.'

'Glad to be of service, Ruthie,' one man said.

'Don't forget to save a dance for us,' the other one added as they walked out and closed the door behind them.

'Ruthie, what's going on? What's in the boxes?'

'Just look, Libby,' Ruth said, dropping to her knees and pulling apart the criss-crossed flaps on the top of one box.

I peered inside. 'Blankets?'

'Yes. And some sheets and two pillows.'

'Where did all this come from?'

'I went all over the dorm asking for donations of extra bed linen. Lots of girls who had more than they needed were glad to get rid of them since they were taking up space they just didn't have in those teensy rooms.'

I kneeled beside her, overcome with gratitude. 'You did all this for me.'

'Well, yeah, but it was a little selfish, too. You said I could spend the night whenever I wanted and I sure didn't want to spend it shivering.'

'Thank you, Ruthie,' I said, leaning forward to give her a hug.

When we had the contents of the boxes either spread on the beds or tucked away, Ruth said, 'Bundle up, Libby, it's mighty cold up in those woods.'

'Woods?'

'Where else would we go to get a Christmas tree?'

'A Christmas tree? I don't have an ax, do you?'

'Yep,' Ruth said, turning her suitcase on its side and clicking open the two latches. She pulled out a small hand ax in a leather case. 'Borrowed it from Willie. He was one of the two fellas who carried in the boxes.'

'You think we can cut down a tree with that puny thing.'

Ruth spun around, looking at the room. 'Libby, look at this place. Do you think you have the room for a regular sized tree? Shoot, it would be so close to the coal stove, you'd probably burn the whole house down. We'll get a little one – one that can sit right on that table over there,' she said pointing to one by a window.

Ruth bent back down and pulled two paper sacks out of her valise and shook them, making the contents rattle.

'Beans?' I said. Was Ruth planning on cooking beans tonight?

'No, silly,' Ruth said with a giggle. 'Whoever heard of putting beans on a Christmas tree? I brought some popcorn. We can pop it up and string it into garlands with the needles and thread I have in this other bag.'

Even though I was living alone far from family and friends, thanks to Ruth, I'd have a real Christmas after all. 'Look, Ruthie, look,' I said as I grabbed a gaudy red and white glass ball from off of a knob. 'I've got ornaments. Only six of them but . . .'

'Six is plenty for our little tree – with the popcorn wrapped around it, it will be beautiful. And we can cut a star out of one of those cartons and tie it to the top.'

We both scurried out of the house and up the hill to the wooded ridge. As we hurried out in search of a tree I was so caught up in the exuberance of the moment that I didn't notice the cold and wind. Finally, we located a suitable candidate on the edge of a clearing. It was small but it had an acceptable amount of foliage particularly in comparison to the others we'd seen.

It took much longer than it should have cutting down the little tree as we took turns swinging the ax, laughing as our clumsy strokes went far off the mark and embedded in the dirt. At last, I struck the final, fatal blow and Ruth hollered, 'Timber!' The three-foot-high tree plopped on the ground.

The walk back seemed to take a whole lot longer than the journey out. I didn't know if it simply took that length of time for the cold to seep through my clothing and for my nose, cheeks and earlobes to start aching from exposure or if now that the task was accomplished, I finally was paying attention to how cold it really was.

Once inside, we improvised a tree stand using a big pot from the kitchen that we filled with rocks to stabilize the evergreen in an upright position. After popping the corn, we settled down by the coal stove to string the garlands. I turned on the radio, spinning the dial until I found Christmas music.

Bing Crosby's voice filled the room singing 'White Christmas'.

'I do love that man's voice,' I said.

'Me, too,' Ruth said. 'I think if I ever heard him in person, I'd just swoon. Have you heard his new one?'

'You mean, "I'll be Home for Christmas"?' I said and had to squeeze my eyes tight to fight off the threat of tears.

'Oh, I shouldn't have mentioned that, Libby. I'm sorry. Me and Irene are going home but you're stuck here. Please forgive me.'

'Nothing to forgive, Ruthie. I like the song a lot, too. It's just that it usually makes me cry.'

'Should I turn the radio off?'

'No need for that. Tell me about growing up in Lynchburg so I can think about something else.'

'Life there isn't too exciting, Libby. Tell the truth, the only big thing that ever happened was my pa gettin' killed.'

'How did that happen?'

'Pa was out on the tractor plowing a field. He went up a hill that he'd gone up hundreds of times and never had a problem. This time, he musta done somethin' different 'cause that tractor tipped over and pinned him underneath it. Don't know how long he was layin' out there and don't know how long it took him to die. When he didn't come home for supper, Ma went looking for him. She found him flattened out in the field with his blood soaking into the ground. She built a fence around that spot and buried him right there. It was a peculiar service with the preacher and everybody else dressed in nice clothes trompin' out over clods of dirt and through the furrows he'd dug 'fore he died.' Ruth sighed. 'Poor Ma. For a while she went out there every single day, rain or shine. Nowadays, she still goes most Sundays right after church. What about your pa? He died in a fire?'

'When my aunt and uncle's farmhouse caught fire, my brother and my cousin got trapped inside. My dad ran in after them even though everyone told him it was too dangerous. When they finally put out the fire, they found him laying face down on the floor with an arm around each boy. They said that they all died of smoke inhalation but for a long time I had nightmares of them catching fire and burning alive.'

We sighed in unison and sat silently for a while. We both clutched a needle and thread in one hand but neither of us worked on the popcorn garland. I was lost in my painful memories of the fire and I imagine Ruth was remembering the day her dad died, too. But when Bing crooned 'Silent Night' on the radio, Ruth broke the spell.

'What are we doing here?' she asked. 'It's Christmastime and we're talking about dying. If we cry on the popcorn, it won't be no good for stringing.'

'Turn up the radio, Ruthie. I'll fix us a pot of tea.'

The volume went up and just then the song we both needed filled the flattop with its perky rhythm – 'Jingle Bells' sung by Bing and the Andrews Sisters. We sang along at the top of our lungs. By the time the tune ended, our spirits were up and our fingers flying on the garlands.

On Christmas morning, I opened my eyes and started thinking about work before I even had time to yawn. The ultimate goal had troubled my sleep that night as it quite often did. I now was certain that an atomic fission bomb was the end result and wondered if it would end the war or just unleash a new monster on the world.

I pushed those thoughts away, remembering that it was Christmas and I was alone. No time for morose thoughts. I did have a tinge of regret that I wasn't in the dorm on this morning. Most of the time, I loved my little flattop home but on this morning, I longed for the easy camaraderie of dormitory life, even though I was usually more of an observer than a participant.

I shrugged off the covers, ignored the warning of my frigid nose and slid out of the warmth of the bed. I slipped into my robe and slippers, and hurried out to the living room. I stabbed at the embers in the coal stove, and was delighted to see a core of glowing red. I tossed in more coals, stirred up small blue flames, closed the door and opened the flue a little wider.

The plywood walls of my home, devoid of insulation, provided little protection from the coldness of a winter night. I wrapped my arms tight around my body as I shuffled across the blue-green linoleum floor and into the kitchen. I daydreamed about a real cup of coffee as I tossed the ground chicory into the tin pot and turned on the stove. I warmed my fingers over the burner before sliding the coffee percolator onto it. I pulled a cup out of the plywood cabinet and set it down on the silver-specked white countertop. At first, I huddled close to the warmth of the stove as I waited for my hot cup of bitter brew.

Then I moved over to a window and scraped off a patch of icy crystals that had formed on the inside overnight. In the early morning sunlight, the ice-covered tree branches twinkled as if stars had fallen from the night sky and embedded in the bark, turning the frigid reality of the outdoors into the vision of a magical fairytale setting.

My nose scrunched in protest as I took the first sip of the harshly bitter dark liquid. I went into the living room and sat on the floor by the tabletop Christmas tree, a smile on my face as I recalled the tree-cutting adventure with Ruth a weekend earlier.

I'd deferred opening my Christmas packages until this morning to add a little festivity to the lonely day. Looking at the packages, I felt a flash of annoyance. The tattered, retaped edges bore silent witness that each one had been opened, inspected and rewrapped by a stranger's hands before being delivered. It didn't seem right that someone else had learned the secret of their contents before I did. They were my presents – not the government's.

I doubted I'd care for whatever it was my mother had sent so I opened it first, saving the best for last. I felt a lot of guilt for that sentiment when I discovered a tin of coffee – real coffee! – inside the box. How did Mother get hold of that? She must have raided my stepfather's supply; he would have never given his permission. He couldn't have known about it at all. I'll have to keep my thank you note vague to keep Mother out of trouble.

For a moment, I clutched the tin to my chest as I savored the anticipation of that first sip of the real thing. Then I jumped to my feet and hurried back to the kitchen. I poured the chicory drink down the sink and prepared a fresh pot of actual, real ground coffee.

I swallowed down the first cup too fast, scalding my tongue. But I didn't care – it was so good, so right, so welcome. I poured a second cup and returned to the living room and the package from Aunt Dorothy.

Four different gifts awaited in that box: a copy of the new best-selling novel, *The Robe* by Lloyd Douglas I'd been wanting to read; a hand-knit cardigan sweater, which I slipped on right away – oh, so thick, so warm, so comfortable – a perfect gift for my living conditions; and wonder of wonders, a Fifth Avenue candy bar! I had thought it was impossible to get one of those unless you were a soldier shipped overseas, but here it was – chocolate, and it was all mine. Real coffee and real chocolate – all on the same day.

The fourth present in the box was wrapped in white tissue paper and had a note attached that read: READ BEFORE OPENING. I removed and unfolded it:

> Dearest Libby,
>   I was shopping one day and discovered the latest in fashion for intimate garments. It made me chuckle. I asked the clerk about what I saw and she said that elastic was very difficult to procure. Thus, we have panties without an elastic waist. I thought you'd get a good laugh out of them, too. Is nothing sacred? No sacrifice too great to defeat the Fuhrer!
>   With Love, Aunt Dorothy

I unwrapped the package and there, lying in my lap, were a pair of panties with little tiny buttons on the side. I laughed as I dropped the ones I was wearing and pulled them on. A perfect fit, but how long would it take me to get used to the feel of the lump of thread on the back of the buttons rubbing against bare skin?

I went back into the kitchen for a third cup of coffee and got out a knife. I was careful not to damage the wrapper as I sliced a piece of it away from the chocolate and cut off about a fourth of the bar. I folded up the end sealing it shut with a creased fold to keep fresh for later. Curling up in the chair in front of the coal stove, I savored that chunk of chocolate, pressing it against the roof of my mouth with my tongue, allowing its delicious flavor to melt and ooze across my taste buds for as long as possible. I must have looked like a simpleton getting so much joy from that small pleasure but I didn't care. That's one thing war taught me – every moment was a gift.

When I finished rhapsodizing over my bite of chocolate, I noticed the unusual silence outside. The world was muffled by the ice but it was more than that. The bustle and noise of a place in a constant state of construction, I almost didn't hear the cacophony any longer. But now the absence of it roared with a fury. It seemed louder than the rumbling trucks, squeaking cranes, pounding hammers, yelling voices. For the first time since I arrived here at Clinton Engineer Works, the world was still.

And that made me curious. A walk was in order. I left the house, bundled up against the morning cold, reminding myself to be cautious on the ice. Stepping out on the stoop, I pulled the wooden knob to shut the door. I instinctively reached for my dirt-caked galoshes, but then realized that cold had hardened all the mud, making it easier to navigate. If there was too much ice on the boardwalk, I could detour onto the street without the fear of sinking into the muck.

I walked past a temporary monument to our usual living conditions, a stuck car with its rear wheels mired in the frozen mud halfway up its hubcaps, the newest victim of the numerous potholes on the dirt and gravel road. Strolling through my community of flattops, I was surprised to see that there were dozens more of them erected since I'd moved in a week ago, although most of them still looked empty. They were bound to fill up quickly after the holiday. The sun had already started melting the thin coat of ice on the boardwalk. Where it warmed the bare wood, I could smell the scent of fresh sawn lumber still wafting up beneath each of my steps inspiring a feeling of kinship with the pioneers who headed west and built towns out of the wilderness. They, too, had sniffed that newness in the air, lived with the rawness, the mud and the downed trees of a new world being born. They coped with isolation and deprivation. The early settlers, though, did it without bulldozers, cranes and graders, without electricity or running water, without the government aid to meet their immediate needs. They did it all with their bare hands and a spirit of community.

Much of that same spirit lived here in this new outpost. Like the frontiersman of old we, too, struggled for survival. We didn't battle with the day-to-day, hand-to mouth challenges that they did but we were in a battle for a way of life. If we did not stop Hitler in Europe, how long before he goose-stepped across the Atlantic? With their ally Japan applying pressure on the west coast, how long could we withstand the onslaught? How long would it be before the heel of oppression flattened our whole continent?

My dark thoughts were weighing too heavy on this special day. I shook them away and focused on my immediate surroundings. Ice glistened like tiaras on the branches overhead, icicles hung from the eaves of houses like icing dripping down the sides of a glazed cake, the spikes of frozen dirt rising up from potholes looked like jagged, forbidding mountains in a horrid nightmare.

Even the sounds of the place seemed enchanted on this day – the plink of melting ice falling to the ground like a gentle rain, the loud crack and rumble as warmed chunks of ice broke their grip on trees and buildings and plummeted to the earth below, the distant squeals of children at play. I moved toward the voices, walking into the area of the larger cemesto homes. The size of the home you were assigned was based solely on the number of people in your family, creating a diverse neighborhood where PhD scientists lived side by side with carpenters and other tradesmen. Not something you'd see in the regular world.

It was here I saw the first signs of human life this day – children bouncing balls, riding bicycles and tricycles or simply running aimlessly through each other's yards. Although Santa Claus had provided them all with a lean year and parents had all seemed troubled by the restrictions due to rationing and inadequate supplies that meant fewer gifts under the tree, the kids didn't seem to care. Doing without didn't seem so bad when everyone else was just like you. And the older children seemed to embrace the spartan situation with patriotic fervor.

I walked past Ann Bishop's house on Magnolia Road. Closing my eyes, I could remember the smells and tastes of the turkey, stuffing, gravy and pumpkin pie I had enjoyed the month before. Now, though, the house was dark – Ann and her family had travelled to her grandmother's home in Nashville for the Christmas weekend.

At the shopping center, I peered into shop windows, blocking the light on either side of my eyes with curved hands. The shelves in the drug store looked sparse. In the market, the 'no meat today' sign still hung on the counter. Hunger pangs hit me then as I thought of the magnificent break from canned salmon and spam I had waiting at home. A small meatloaf made by Mrs Bishop – meat that Ann's mother could have used for her own family and yet she gave it to me as if it were no big deal.

Although Ann and I had little in common she, like Ruth, had become a good friend. Ann couldn't wait until the war was over and she could stop working, get married and have babies. For now, I couldn't imagine that life for myself. After the war, though, would I feel differently?

Would the global conflict ever be over? Would the work that we were doing really make a difference? And if it did, would it change the world into an unrecognizable place? A place where marriage and children weren't the normal condition of women?

I was so deep in thought, I started at the realization that I'd returned to my street without realizing it. And there was my little flattop with its flat roof, squatting like a toadstool on the rise. It was plain and square but it was a beautiful sight. I couldn't wait to see how nice it would look in the spring when flowers were blooming and the trees crowned with green.

The thought of warmer weather to come made me shiver and quicken my pace. I had a coal stove to tend and a new book to start reading before it was time to heat up my Christmas dinner.

DECEMBER 27, 1943

'A woman is like a tea bag: you never know how strong it is until it's in hot water.'

Eleanor Roosevelt

TWELVE

I was glad that Monday's work in the lab didn't require any deep theoretical thought. I kept busy at the scales and on the mass spectrometer, weighing, extrapolating and analyzing data – making heavy use of the left hemisphere of my brain, skirting away from the store of the emotional issues that dominated the day before.

At lunchtime, I rushed to the hospital to see Ruth. The guard was still there but he no longer blocked the entrance. He sat in a chair by the open door and nodded when I walked past. Ruth was groggy and nothing she said made a lot of sense.

She asked, 'Did Irene make it home?'

I patted the back of her hand. How many sedatives had they pumped into her? 'Don't you worry about Irene right now, Ruthie. We just need to get you home first.'

Ruth drifted off and when her eyes popped back open, she asked again, 'Did Irene make it home last night?'

'Sleep, Ruthie. I have to get back to work now. But don't you worry about a thing.' I stopped at the nurse's station on the way out to ask about Ruth's prognosis and was told, 'We have no more orders for sedatives from the doctor.'

'Could I take her home after work?'

'I'll find out from the doctor, but as long as she won't be alone tonight, it'll probably be all right. We'll let you know what the doctor says when you come back.'

Walking to the hospital at the end of the work day, I was tired but satisfied with what I'd accomplished in the lab. I'd made good use of my time even though the production line was still shut down. I was worried about Ruth and hoped she remembered the tragic events about Irene now.

I stopped at the nurse's station and received the go ahead to take Ruth home. The guard was gone now and Ruth was sitting on the edge of the bed in her street clothes. She looked alert but was still very pale.

'I didn't think you'd ever get here, Libby. They told me you'd
be comin' by for me two hours ago and I've been edgy ever
since. Nobody will tell me nothin' about Irene. I've gotta call
Ma but I don't know what to tell her.'

'Let's get out of here first. Then we'll try to figure it all
out.'

Outside of the hospital, Ruth said, 'Thanks, Libby. I can make
it back to the dorm by myself.'

'I'm sure you can. But we are going to the dormitory together
to get your things.'

'Get my things?'

'Yes, you're coming over to stay at my place.'

'But what if someone comes with news about Irene? I need
to be there for her.'

I doubted that anyone would bother, but bit my tongue. No
sense in being more pessimistic than necessary. 'We'll leave a
note.'

'I don't know, Libby.'

'I do. I know. The nurse said that you needed to stay with
someone tonight.'

'OK, Libby. You're probably right. I'd just drive myself crazy
in that place all alone,' Ruth said.

Arriving at the dorm, we found the door of Ruth's room
hanging open. The linens on both beds were disheveled. Drawers
looked hastily shoved closed but not completely shut.

'She's been here,' Ruth said. 'Irene's been here. Look at the
mess she made.' Ruth looked under her bed. 'And she took my
Jack Daniels, too.'

I so wished that was true but I couldn't let that falsehood stand.
I owed Ruth honesty. 'The police took your bottle and they
searched your room. It wasn't Irene. We saw Irene under the
bleachers – remember?'

Ruth's shoulders slumped. 'I guess I just wanted to forget . . .'

'I know,' I said, feeling a sympathetic lump of pain in my
throat.

'Why did the police search my room? Will I be in trouble for
the Jack Daniels? Why did they have to make such a mess?'

'Just grab a bag and throw together the things you'll need.
And I'll make the beds, OK?' I finished with the beds, then
pulled a piece of paper out of the desk and wrote a note. 'To

whom it may concern: Ruth Nance is staying with Elizabeth Clark at 384 East Drive.'

'Look OK to you?'

Ruth nodded her approval and I stuck it between the door and frame as we left. On the boardwalk, I asked, 'What happened after I left you at the bleachers?'

'First a police officer came and told me I had to get out of there. I was just laying there next to Irene, holding her hand. I ignored him. Then he yelled at me saying he'd come in and get me if I didn't get out of there right now. So, I did. Then he told me I had to go to the police station with him. And I said, "I will not. I'm not leaving my sister here on the ground." Then, two jeeps full of soldiers pulled up. One of them was a colonel. And there was a guy in a suit who pulled up in another car. They told me to come with them. I told them I would as soon as my sister was seen to. Then it got really strange. The soldiers all lined up so I couldn't see Irene and that man in a suit told me that Irene wasn't there and I needed to go home.

'Then I kinda went a little loco. I tried to get back to Irene but they wouldn't let me. Then, I felt something stick in my arm and the next thing I remember, I was in the hospital bed. What's going on, Libby?'

'I don't know, Ruthie. What did that man in a suit look like?'

'He had a nice height and short hair,' she said with a shrug.

'Did he have blue eyes?' I asked, thinking of the man I met in Captain Wilson's office.

'I don't know if I noticed. Oh, wait a minute,' she said stopping and closing her eyes. 'Yes. Yes he did. I remember when he looked at me and told me Irene wasn't there. His eyes were blue – not blue like Irene's, not that soft, pretty blue – but a cold, icy blue that makes you feel like an ant.'

The rest of the way back to my flattop, we were quiet. I imagine Ruth was as lost in her thoughts as I was in my own. What should I do now? What and who should I believe? Were the police lying to me? Were soldiers moving bodies? Were there any other possibilities? Could the killer have returned and taken the body? But how could that be possible – Ruth would have seen him if he'd gotten there before the police and soldiers arrived. And I can't quite imagine someone waltzing up and walking away with the body right under their noses. Police don't move bodies. And they wouldn't let anyone else do that. Not before investigating the scene. And they don't find bodies and pretend they didn't exist. Or do they? But why? Nothing made any sense.

The evening was tumultuous. Ruth alternated between sorrow and remorse, wondering what she should have done differently. I comforted her as well as I could. When she seemed calm enough to handle it, I pulled out the little blue fawn pin and asked, 'Ever seen a pin like this before?'

Ruth gasped. 'Where did you find that?'

'In the athletic field.'

'She was there. Irene was there. She got that for Christmas. She pinned it to her coat. This proves she was there. If we show it to them, they'll have to admit it, won't they?'

'I don't know. I just don't know, Ruthie. Right now, I don't know if giving it to them is a good idea. Once they have it, they can deny ever seeing it.'

Ruthie slumped in her chair, looking even more morose than she had before.

'Hey, why don't we see what's on the radio,' I said as I turned on the set. We tried to listen to a program but my thoughts kept drifting away from the story and, glancing over at Ruth, it didn't seem as if she was able to concentrate on the storyline, either. When I finally turned the radio off, I couldn't even remember which program had been airing.

I tucked Ruth into bed a little later. I didn't expect to sleep well and, unfortunately, I was right. My slumber was haunted by chase scenes. Once I ran off a cliff, another time off the top of a building. Both dreams startled me awake in the middle of a fall. Before I realized they were figments of my mind, I'd felt a surge of bile in my throat as my hands desperately slapped out for purchase on the mattress. Each time, I had to stare at the ceiling for an hour or more before I could slip away from consciousness. Just two days ago, I could look down the road to the future and see nothing but sunny skies and happiness. Now I sensed a brewing storm and feared it would sweep in without warning and carry me away.

THIRTEEN

I was out of eggs so we went down to the central cafeteria for breakfast the next morning. When we got back home, I perked a pot of coffee and we sat down in front of the coal stove.

'I feel as if I am living in a nightmare – a long, dark, horrible nightmare. I don't even know if I can trust my own eyes any longer,' Ruth said. 'We did see Irene under the bleachers, didn't we?'

'Yes, Ruthie, we did.'

'But where did she go?'

'I wish I knew.'

'If she was there, what did they do with her? And why would they lie about it, Libby?'

'I don't know. But I do know she was there. And I do know someone moved her body.'

'What if we were wrong, Libby? What if she got up and left as soon as I crawled out from under the bleachers? What if she snuck away? Who knows where she is now!' Ruth jumped to her feet and paced the small room.

I had to remain calm, for Ruth's sake, if not my own. Ruth was right about one thing: this was a total nightmare. I placed a hand on each of Ruth's upper arms, and said, 'Ruthie, please. I'm so sorry. I wish I could tell you that there was a chance that Irene was alive. But that would just be delaying your pain. You have to accept it and move forward. I know it's hard.'

Ruth lifted her chin and looked straight into my eyes. 'Are you sure you're not as confused as I am?'

'I am confused, Ruthie. I've never been more confused in my life. But I know that Irene was murdered. The signs were evident. And I know I can trust what I saw – what *we* saw. I know you don't *want* to believe it, but that doesn't make it any less true.'

Ruth stepped back and slumped into the chair. 'You're right, Libby. I don't want to believe Irene is gone. My mind keeps trying to come up with a way to make it not true.'

'It's a natural reaction, Ruthie.'

'I've only seen one other dead person before. It was my grandmother. I went in one morning to bring her a cup of tea – and there she was in bed. It was like her life just faded away. It seemed nice, peaceful. But Irene . . .' Ruth doubled over, sobbing.

'I am so sorry,' I said, patting her back before retrieving my coffee cup and returning to the opposite chair. 'Any time you want to talk about Irene, I'm here. Or anything. You can talk to me about anything. And it all stays right here with me.'

'Oh I know you can keep a secret,' Ruth said, laughing weakly. 'We've all been trained to do that. Who knew you could get this many women together in one place and still keep a secret?' Ruth sniffled and forced a smile.

'We all do that every day now, don't we?' I said, plastering a smile on my face.

We settled back in uneasy silence. After a few minutes, Ruth said, 'Thank you, Libby.'

'You think nothing of it, Ruthie. I'm your friend now and always. We best be getting to work. Your shift starts in ten minutes.'

When I pulled the door open, I gasped. A uniformed soldier stood on my stoop, one fist raised up in front of his face as if he were about to knock.

Without any greeting or introduction, he blurted, 'I'm here for Miss Nance. Miss Ruth Nance.'

'Miss Nance is here. But we're running a little late for work.'

'I'm just here to pick up Miss Nance and take her to the police station.'

Ruth's face turned ashen and her hands trembled. 'What is it? Did you find my sister?'

'I don't know anything about your sister, miss. I was just told to transport you to the police station.'

'Libby, come with me,' Ruth pleaded, her eyes rimmed with tears.

'Of course, Ruthie.'

At the police station, we sat in chairs by the front desk. I asked to use the phone and called Charlie to let him know that I was involved in a serious personal problem and I'd be in as soon as I could. I was relieved that he didn't press me for more information because I didn't know what I was allowed to say about the situation.

Finally, we were ushered back into the captain's office. 'Please have a seat,' he said gesturing first to one chair, then the other. 'I have some bad news, Miss Nance. Your sister's body has been found.'

Ruth wailed, doubled over in the middle and placed her face in her hands. I wrapped an arm around her shoulders and handed her a handkerchief. Ruth sobbed, rocking back and forth in her seat.

'Where did you find her?' I asked.

'Well, we didn't, actually. The Knox County sheriff's office did. The deputy here will take you to Knoxville to identify the body.'

Looking up, I noticed a man in a brown uniform standing in the corner. He nodded at me and said, 'A couple of boys fishing this morning found her body on the riverbank, not far from the Solway Bridge.'

'Thank you,' I said, then turned to Captain Wilson. 'Are you and the sheriff's department going to work together to figure out how her body got from the bleachers to the riverbank?'

'Ma'am, as I told you before, there was no body at the bleachers. There was no body found inside of the gates. The body was found outside of our area in Knox County. No crime happened here. It is not our case.'

'So you're going to do nothing?'

'It's not in our jurisdiction.'

'Liar!' Ruth shrieked.

I knew he was lying, too, but I didn't want to alienate the deputy so I kept my mouth shut. I stared at Wilson and willed him to read my mind. He wouldn't even look at me though, and I was sure if he did, I'd see shame in his eyes.

The man with the cold, blue eyes stepped into the office. 'Is there a problem here, captain?'

'Miss Nance is just a bit upset,' he said.

'Upset. You bet I'm upset. He's lying to me. You lied to me. You're all lying,' she said flaying her arms about wildly. 'Whaddya think? I'm a German spy or an agent for Hirohito?'

'I suggest that you calm down right now, Miss Nance,' the man said. 'We have some patience with grieving family members but it is not limitless.'

Ruth spluttered but before she could say anything further, I wrapped an arm around her again, 'C'mon, honey, let's go get this over with.'

During the drive, I comforted her as best I could and tried to prepare her for the ordeal ahead. 'Do you understand what we're going to do?' I asked.

'Maybe it's not Irene.'

I didn't know what to say to that. Mistakes do happen. What if it was some other person? Would it mean they may never find Irene? 'Deputy?' I said.

'Yes, ma'am.'

'How did you know it was Irene?'

'Can't say I did, miss. They gave me an envelope, said it had her identification badge in it and sent me out to your police department to find someone to identify the body. I didn't know she had family here. I'm sorry I had to do this.'

'Were you out to the spot where they found the body?'

'No, miss.'

'Do you know what they found?'

'No, miss.'

'Did you know that Miss Nance and I found the body yesterday morning by the high school?'

'Miss, I'm just a lowly deputy – newest one in the department. They've told me I have no need to know so many times, I'm beginning to think it's my name. They don't tell me anything about any investigations. They just tell me what to do and I do it.'

Seeing his eyes in the rear-view mirror, it seemed as if he was telling the truth. 'Deputy, will the sheriff be there when we arrive?'

'I doubt it, ma'am. He doesn't spend a lot of time in the office.'

I turned back to Ruth. 'Listen, when we get there, you grab hold of my hand and you just squeeze as hard as you want.'

Ruth nodded and leaned on my shoulder. I felt slight tremors rocking her body while she cried.

We followed the deputy into the morgue. It seemed with every step, Ruth got more wobbly. I gripped her harder, praying she wouldn't pass out. The smell in the air in the morgue wasn't helping – a swirling odor of antiseptic and underlying rot that made me feel light-headed and nauseous. I imagined its impact was even worse on Ruth. I stifled a gasp at the sight of a series of tables bearing sheet-draped shapes that I didn't want to believe were bodies.

The deputy directed us towards the closest one. A man in surgical scrubs, quietly and gently pulled down a sheet, taking care not to uncover Irene's throat. Either the scarf was still there or he didn't want to reveal the angry welt left in its place.

I eased Ruth up to the table, glad to see someone had shut Irene's eyes. An intense surge of pain blasted up my arm as she nearly crushed my hand. Ruth emitted a shrill shriek that sounded more animal than human as it reverberated in the utilitarian room. I winced as I tightened my grip on Ruth. I struggled to push the rising images of my father, brother and cousin's charcoaled bodies out of my mind. I could not allow myself the distraction – Ruth needed me.

She fell forward, wrapping her arms across her sister, laying her warm cheek next to the cold one. I gave her a moment and then tugged on her shoulders. 'C'mon, honey, c'mon. Let's get out of here, OK.'

'But Irene, Irene . . .'

'I know, Ruthie, I know. Let's go. We need to call your family.'

Outside of the morgue, the deputy helped us find a phone in one of the offices in the sheriff's side of the building. Ruth said, 'Hello, Ma . . .'

While she talked, I pulled the deputy to the side. 'I want to speak to an investigator.'

'I'm sorry, ma'am. I can't do that. I was given strict orders. Pick you up and take you straight back. No detours. In fact, I might get into trouble for letting her make this call.'

'Well, why don't you take Miss Nance back and I'll just stick around in town.'

'No, ma'am, I can't allow that. I was told to bring you back – both of you – and under no circumstances . . .'

I waved him off as Ruth set down the receiver and rushed back to her side.

'Oh, Libby, that was the hardest thing I've ever done in my whole life. Ma was heartbroken.' Ruth put her hand over her mouth and made a choking sound. 'I talked to my brother Hank, too. He enlisted when he turned eighteen this month, but doesn't report for another week. So he can drive up here to get me to take me back for the funeral,' Ruth said, her voice cracking on that last word. 'Funeral. It's such an ugly word. So final. So ugly. I just wanna die.'

Back at my house, I made sure Ruth had everything she needed before I left for the lab for the rest of the day. I returned home late and we sat up until well past midnight. We slowly nibbled away at the rest of the Fifth Avenue candy bar, trying to figure out what to do next. I had to keep working, even though Ruth would not be expected to report for duty under the circumstances. She'd meet her brother at the gate with a pass when he arrived the next day. Then, Ruth and Hank would go talk to a security officer about the problem with the police.

'Ruth, I was wondering, do you think Irene's boyfriend could have been a local?'

'I don't know. She said he was a scientist – an important one – but I guess he could have been born here. Does it matter?'

'It might. I don't know, either. But you know how much some of the locals hate all of us. Did Irene ever go outside the gates?'

'Most Monday nights she took the bus into Knoxville to shop. Other than that, I don't think she went outside till we went home for Christmas. I think I would have known if she had. She would've told me.' Ruth's brow furrowed and her mouth twisted at an odd angle.

'Just trying to make sense of it, Ruthie. Don't mind me. It all puzzles me so. Nothing is making sense – and I don't like that.'

'That's the scientist talking, Libby. And I know that science stuff is important to you but it's the friend in you that I'll never forget. I couldn't have made it through all this without you by my side.'

'You'd have done the same for me, Ruthie.'

'I sure would like to think so,' she said with a rueful smile. 'I'll probably be gone before you get back from work, Libby. But I'll leave you a note about what happened.'

'And, please, Ruthie, let me know what I can do while you are away. If you have any problems when you and your brother talk to security, let them know where to find me.'

'Are you sure you want to stay all mixed up in this?'

'You try and stop me.'

FOURTEEN

All day while I worked, I worried about Ruth and wondered about the meeting that she and Hank had with security. Walking home, I couldn't stop the smile on my face that still happened the moment when my home came into view. Tonight, though, I was startled by the car parked by the segment of boardwalk that ran past my house. And there was a light shining from inside my house. I walked as fast as I dared without risking another pratfall into the thawed mud.

I opened the front door to find Ruth and a man I assumed was her brother Hank standing in front of the coal stove with steaming cups in their hands. 'Ruthie?' I asked filling the one word with a dozen questions.

'Oh, Libby, I didn't think you'd ever get finished at work,' Ruth said.

'I've had longer days,' I said, smiling at her.

'Oh and this,' Ruth said holding up her cup, 'it's chicory. I didn't use your good coffee.'

I was a bit ashamed that I felt so grateful that my little stash of coffee was still secure. Abashed, I said, 'Ruthie, you are welcome to my coffee. Why are you still here?'

'Well, things didn't go quite as planned,' Ruth said.

'But we have a new plan,' Hank added.

'Oh, sorry, Libby. This is my brother, Hank,' Ruth said.

I nodded at him but turned right back to Ruth, anxious to hear about her day.

Ruth plunged into her story. 'See, I told them everything about finding the body and the strange way the police were acting and what did they do? They called the police and asked them. Then they turned back to me and said, "There was no body found by the high school."

'I got a little aggravated then. I told them that I didn't imagine it, that there was a scientist with me and she saw the body, too. So, they wanted your name – I hope that's OK.'

'I already told you it was, Ruthie. Then what happened?'

'I told them that they needed to investigate Irene's murder and they said it was out of their jurisdiction – it was on civilian land and it was up to the authorities in Knox County. And I said that they were wrong. The murder of my sister happened here. Someone who lived here was responsible.

'That's when everything went bad. They starting asking about how often Irene went down to the hutments. And that's when Hank snapped his cap.'

'He was insultin' my sister,' Hank said. 'Irene didn't spend time down there with those colored folks and I knew he was implying somethin' even worse. I could tell by the leer on his face. My sister had a decent upbringin'. She didn't socialize with coloreds. She was not that kind of girl. She was a little wild but she wasn't bad.'

I recoiled from the racism blazing in his statement but didn't object to it. A grieving man was not receptive to social commentary or a change of attitude. 'But what happened?'

Ruth sighed. 'Hank lunged at the officer. A couple of MP's grabbed a hold of him and tossed him outside. That made me pretty mad. They didn't have to be so rough with him. Anyway, I told them that I didn't understand why they were doing my family wrong like they were.

'And this guy wearing a lot of brass who hadn't had anything to say up to that point, spoke up and said, "What if I told you it was a matter of national security?" And I said, "I'd say that you're lyin'."

'He kept staring at me as he stood up and walked out of the room without sayin' another word. Then they started in on me with one question after another, trying to get me to promise I wouldn't say anything, saying that all the scientists loved their country and my scientist friend would shut up and not back up my story. And if I didn't forget about this, I would regret it.

'Well, that's when I took it too far – it didn't seem that way to me but it sure did to them. I told them I can't forget about my sister. She was murdered and I would do everythin' I could to find out who did it and get him put in jail. And that's when the main officer, the one behind the desk said, "What do you mean, you would do everythin'?"

'And I said that means everythin', anythin'. I'll talk to anyone, any time. I'll tell them about every secret I know about this place

– but, Libby, you know I don't really know any secrets, I don't even know what I'm doing watchin' those dials, I just follow instructions.'

'I know, Ruthie,' I nodded.

'Well, he didn't. He pounded a fist down on his desk and said, "That's it. You've said enough. You are no longer employed here. You no longer work here. You are dismissed in the name of national security. And if you even whisper a word about the work we are doing here, you'll be charged with treason. Now go, pack up your personal belongings and don't try to take anythin' else, you will be searched before you can go through the gate."

'That really ticked me off and I just gave him the evil eye. And he said, "Go now. Get your things and say your goodbyes. If you are on the grounds tomorrow, you will be arrested."'

'Oh, good grief. What a mess. What can I do, Ruthie?'

'Did you really mean it when you said you wanted to help?'

'Of course.'

'OK. Me and Hank, we have this idea—'

'Plan,' Hank interjected. 'We have a plan.'

'Idea, plan? What difference does it make?' Ruth exclaimed.

'A lot. A plan sounds like we thought it through. An idea is just like the lightbulb in the funny papers,' Hank said.

'Still, Hank, it can't be a plan until she agrees to do it.'

'But a plan sounds like we're serious—'

'Please,' I said, interrupting the little bout of sibling rivalry, 'just tell me what you want me to do.'

Ruth sighed again. 'We can't be here, Libby, or we'd do this. Somebody has to find out what happened to Irene. We were hoping you would do that for us.'

'I could try, Ruthie, but I just don't know—'

'Ruthie told me how smart you are, ma'am,' Hank said. 'If anybody can, you can. And if you agree to do it, I'll leave my car here so that it's easier for you to get out and talk to the sheriff and all.'

'Your car?'

'Yes. I leave next week to report for duty. I imagine I'll be going to Europe or the Pacific – don't know which one – just know I won't need my car wherever I'm goin'. And I've got these gasoline ration coupons,' he said, pulling them out and handing them to me.

'How are you going to get home?'

'We already took care of that. Ruthie and me will take the bus into Knoxville and stay there overnight. In the morning, we'll go home on the train – the same train that's taking Irene home to her restin' place.'

Ruth moaned, 'Oh, Irene.'

My eyes welled up in sympathetic tears. 'I'll try. I'll do my best. I just don't know . . .'

Ruth wrapped her arms around me. 'Libby, your best is all we can ask for. We need to know what happened to our sister and you're our only hope.'

The burden of that sentiment settled heavy on my shoulders. I felt the stomach-churning lump of the fear of failure that haunted me throughout my university years and during my first few months working in the Clinton lab. Now it grew exponentially larger making my chest feel tight and my throat clench. This was a far greater responsibility than anything I'd faced before. It involved a human life – now gone – and the grieving heart of a friend. Ruth's faith in me was reassuring but her expectations hung as heavy as a freighter-sized anchor on a row boat for two.

FIFTEEN

On the morning of Wednesday, December 29, I ran a sample through the spectrograph. As soon as I reached the point in the developing process that I could turn the light back on, I slipped out of the smaller lab to return to my main work station. I had some time before I had to take the photographic plate out of the sodium thiosulfate solution. I was just about to go back to do that when a soldier walked into the doorway and barked, 'Elizabeth Clark.' Instead of looking straight ahead, his eyes were focused on the ceiling. I followed his gaze upward, saw nothing there and realized he probably was concerned that he'd see something he shouldn't and never hear the end of it.

'Is there an Elizabeth Clark here?' he repeated.

'Yes, I'm here.'

'I need you to come with me, immediately.'

'Where are we going?'

'To the security offices, miss.'

'Why?'

He lowered his chin, his eyes opening wide. Obviously, he'd expected me to obey without question.

'I have no idea, miss. I was simply instructed to accompany you there immediately.' His chin went back up to its original position and he stared again at the ceiling.

'Right now, I am in the middle of a procedure that I need to complete before I can leave.'

'I'm sorry, miss, I have orders to bring you back immediately.'

For some reason his serious demeanor struck me as funny. I laughed and checked the clock – two minutes until I could remove the plate. To buy a little time, I tried to divert his attention, hoping I could get him to loosen up. 'Soldier, are you telling me I should desert my post when I am performing a vital task for the war effort?'

'Miss, I don't know what you do here and I don't want to know. I just want to follow my orders. I do not want to use force.'

'You would forcibly remove me from my work?'

'Miss, I really do not want to do that.'

'Tell me, soldier, where are you from?'

'I can't be taking time for idle conversation. I have a job to do.'

'Oh, c'mon, you can answer a simple question. Where is home?'

'The eastern shore of Maryland, miss. Near Salisbury. Really, Miss Clark, we need to go.'

Just one minute more. 'Do you jitterbug in Salisbury?'

'Miss?'

'Jitterbug. You know, dance?'

A grin crossed his face. 'Yes, ma'am, I cut a rug with the best of them.'

'Do you ever go to the dances here at the Recreation Center?'

'I've been a time or two.'

'Next time, look for me. I'm pretty good myself.'

'Will do, Miss Clark. Can we go now?'

'Just a minute,' I said, dashing off to the spectrographic lab over the soldier's loud objections. I pulled the plate out of the solution, placed it under running water and set the timer for thirty minutes. Back in the main lab, I asked Gregg to finish up the process if the timer went off while I was gone. Turning to the soldier with a smile, I said, 'Yes, let's go,' offering him my elbow.

'Miss, I don't want to be rude or anything, but I don't think on-duty soldiers are supposed to be linking arms with persons of the opposite sex.'

I laughed as I walked off quickly, leaving the soldier struggling to catch up with me.

The laughter was really more for my own benefit. I was fairly certain that the timing of this summons was no coincidence. It had to be connected to Ruth and her sister Irene's death. They'd probably try to bully me just as they had done with Ruth.

The private pulled up in front of the administration building that everyone called the castle on the hill. After opening the jeep door, I looked down. The gap was too wide for me to jump across it to the boardwalk – particularly not in front of this building, where it was said others had sunk up to their hips in the mud.

'Hold on, miss. Don't move.' For a moment, he disappeared from view. When he reappeared, he clutched a long board under his arm. He used it to bridge the space between the jeep and the boardwalk. I thought he'd want me to walk across it but he held up a finger and said, 'Wish me luck,' before stepping out on it. He bounced a couple of times and when it didn't crack or dislodge, he reached into the jeep. 'Pardon me, miss,' he said as he scooped me up out of the seat.

I squealed involuntarily as he swung me up and over to the solid surface of the walk. I started blushing even before I was back on solid footing. I felt the muscles of his arms tense as they wrapped under my legs and the bare vestiges of stubble on his chin as it brushed my cheek. I smelled a faint aroma of tobacco and a strong male scent. It was a giddy, stimulating moment and then it was over, leaving me with a sense of disappointment.

'Well, that worked well, didn't it? Hope you weren't offended but I've seen some of the others do that and I thought I'd give it a shot.'

'T-thank you, private,' I stammered. 'That's was very kind.'

He led me inside and to the office of Captain Smedley. I stood in front of his desk, waiting for an invitation to take a seat. It was not forthcoming. I was offended by his rudeness when he looked up and said, 'We understand that you are involved in a situation questioning the authority and competence of the Oak Ridge Police.'

'May, I have a seat, sir?' I said, using Aunt Dorothy's dignified and proper tone of voice, hoping I'd knock him off balance and force him to return to more chivalrous behavior.

When he turned red from his neck to his ears, I couldn't help but smile. 'Please, miss. Where are my manners? Yes, please, have a seat.'

'Thank you,' I said as sweetly as possible, taking as much time as possible making my descent. I ran my hands beneath my skirt, smoothing it as I settled down in the chair. 'You were saying?'

'Miss Clark, your former roommate, Ruth Nance, was in here yesterday making crazy allegations about her sister's death. Are you aware of this?'

'I am aware that Miss Nance came to the security office for help but I was not aware that she said anything crazy.'

'She claimed that the two of you found her sister's body under the bleachers at the high school and the police moved the body to cover up their involvement in the crime.'

'She said that?'

'Yes, miss.'

'She used those words?' I pushed, knowing she hadn't.

'Not exactly,' he admitted. 'But that was the general meaning.'

I stared at him as I made deliberate moves, crossing my legs and folding my hands on the raised knee. 'I suspect, sir, she did not use the phrase "cover up" and I also doubt that she accused the police of being responsible for her sister's homicide.'

'Well, that might be, but—'

'And yes, Miss Nance and I did find Irene's body under the bleachers. Then the police and some army folks went there, and, poof, the body was gone. We don't think it was an act of magic and we do not know who moved the body outside of the fence. Whoever it was did not want the body found either in that location or that time. Doesn't that sound logical to you?'

'No. Yes. I mean it sounds logical but there's no truth in it. I have talked to the police. There was no body under the bleachers.'

'Follow this train of thought, sir. Miss Nance and I arrived on the scene, discovered the body and I went for the police. We were the first ones there, aside from the person who committed the crime. Therefore, we saw the scene before anyone had the opportunity to tamper with it.

'The police arrived second, after both of us touched the body, thereby altering it in at least a microscopic way. Our previous presence alone gave law enforcement a scene not as fresh as the one we had. Are you following me, sir?'

'Yes, miss.'

'And yet you are telling me that instead of believing the people who observed most accurately what that scene looked like, you want to believe the people who only had a secondary, later look. Does that sound logical to you?'

'No. But that is not the view we are taking here in the security department. You and Miss Nance did not see the scene you are alleging you saw. It did not exist. It never happened. We do not know if you two are fabricating this story. Or if in distress over Miss Nance's sister, you both had a mutual hallucination. We do not know. But we do know this: Miss Nance did not accept our version of events – the real version of events – and she was sent home. She will not be returning to work. Is that clear, Miss Clark?'

'Perfectly clear, captain,' I said, rising to my feet. 'I am surprised I am not being sent home, too.'

'General Grove's actions during his last visit here made it clear that was not an option.'

'Oh, really? Interesting that who one knows is more important than who one is. Ruth Nance is at least as trustworthy as I am, maybe more. May I get back to my work now? Every minute lost is an advantage to Germany.'

As I suspected, a call to patriotism brought an immediate, positive response. I did believe in the importance of our work here but it saddened me to see how easily platitudes could be used to manipulate others. I was ashamed of myself. The ends do not always justify the means. It's hard to remember that in a time of war.

Every day that I went to work, I grew more certain that the goal was a nuclear bomb. The quicker I worked and the better I worked, the sooner people would die. It was difficult to accept and even harder to live with that knowledge. One thing kept me going: somewhere in Germany, scientists were working to the same end and my country needed to get there first.

The rest of the week crawled along slower than a toeless sloth. I often worried about Ruth going through the funeral for her sister and coping with the loss of her job. I also thought a lot about the conversation in the security office. I had to keep my promise to Ruth and no one should be able to dictate what I did in my free time. No matter what the colonel said, questioning authority was part of being a good scientist and I was determined to ask those questions until I found the truth. Saturday, I'd drive to Knoxville and hope the sheriff could offer some answers.

SIXTEEN

I hadn't driven a car for months and I'd never driven one on the dirt, gravel, mud and pothole-filled streets of Oak Ridge. I was very apprehensive when I climbed behind the wheel on the Saturday morning. During the past week, I'd thought about driving it to the A&P or to work but I worried that I'd use up the gasoline ration coupons Hank had given me and wouldn't be able to get any more.

Hank's car was old – a 1932 black two-door coupe with a rumble seat. It appeared as if he'd taken excellent care of it but its boxy roof made its age apparent. The newer cars had rounder, almost voluptuous lines in comparison.

I started the car, said a prayer, made a wish and eased the vehicle away from the curb. I didn't want to do any damage on my first trip out. I breathed a sigh of relief once I passed through the Solway gate and reached the state-maintained road without getting stuck or running into anything.

The twenty miles of countryside looked a lot like the rolling foothills of the Blue Ridge Mountains back in Virginia. I imagined this piece of Tennessee would be as beautiful as Virginia in the spring when the trees budded out and the ground turned green. Still, although the limbs were bare and the grass was brown, it was nice not to be surrounded by anything but the bare dirt of a new community under construction.

I got confused about where I was going and stopped at a restaurant for directions. Following the turns provided by a waitress, I finally found the sheriff's office. The old building smelled a bit musty compared to the fresh scent of construction I'd become used to in all the structures behind the fence. My nose wrinkled up in objection as I walked up to the front desk. I greeted a woman whose steel-gray hair was pulled so tightly back from her face, it looked painful. She was reading a document on her desk and didn't seem to notice I was standing in front of her.

'Excuse me, ma'am.'

'Can't you see I'm busy,' she snapped.

So much for southern hospitality. I mustered the patience to wait without further interruption. As I did so, I watched the uniformed deputies moving in and out of the front room, picking up forms, dropping off completed documents, stopping to exchange a few words with another officer. It seemed to be a busy place.

I was startled when, at last, the woman spoke. 'I'm sorry. That was rude of me. But I'm doing the work of three people. Every time I get a new girl trained to help me, she gets a job out there on that government project. More than aggravating. How may I help you?'

'I'd like to see the sheriff, please.'

'The sheriff? You got an appointment?'

'No, ma'am. I was hoping to catch him in the office.'

'Let me see if I can set you up an appointment next Monday or Tuesday,' she said pulling out a calendar.

'I'm sorry. I can't come back on a weekday. I have to work.'

'Don't we all? Well, maybe I can get the sheriff to stop by and see you. Where do you work?'

'I don't think that would be possible.'

'Why not?' the woman asked, then her eyebrows shot up. 'Oh, I get it. You're from out there, aren't you?'

'Yes, ma'am.'

'What in heaven's name are you doing here? You have your own police department and your own security force. Go see them. You've got no business here.'

I wrapped my fingers around the edge of the counter and

leaned forward. 'Please, ma'am, the body of my friend's sister was found in Knox County.'

'Still, Sheriff Lawrence doesn't like to mess with you people. You're nothing but trouble.'

'Please?' I begged.

The woman exhaled hard. 'I'll go ask. Ain't making any promises. If he has any sense, he won't see you.' She shuffled out as if she had all the time in the world. But in a moment, she was back. 'I forget to ask: what's your name?'

'Elizabeth Clark, ma'am.'

The woman harrumphed as if my name were an affront and waddled into the back. When she returned, she pushed open the gate in the counter and said, 'C'mon. It seems he's in a real good mood today. Despite my advice, he'll see you.'

The secretary stopped at a doorway marked with 'Charles R. Lawrence, Sheriff, Knox County' in gilt lettering on glass. She rapped on the door and threw it open. 'Sheriff, here she is.'

'Miss Clark,' he said. 'Come on in and have a seat. What can I do for you today?' With his cowboy-style hat, sharp nose and dimpled chin, the sheriff brought to mind Tom Mix, one of my childhood matinee favorites.

'Sheriff, I wanted to talk to you about Irene Nance.'

'Who?'

'The woman whose body you recovered out near the Solway gate last weekend.'

'Oh, right. We found one of those identification badges that y'all use.'

'She was my friend's sister.'

'I'm surprised her sister isn't here with you then.'

'She's gone home for the funeral, sir,' I said.

'Whereabouts? Up north somewhere?'

'No, sir. She's a Tennessee girl – from Lynchburg.'

'But you're not a Tennessee girl.'

'No, sir.'

'You almost sound like a Yankee – but not quite.'

'I was raised in Virginia, south central Virginia. I moved up to my aunt's home in Philadelphia after my father died.'

'Next best thing to a Tennessee girl is a Virginia girl. We're nearly neighbors,' he said, smiling for the first time since I entered his office.

'The important thing is not me. It's Irene. I wanted to know what you observed where her body was discovered.'

'Really?' he said, furrowing his brow as he rested his forearms on his desk and leaned toward me. 'And why would you want to know that?'

'I suspect that you saw no evidence to indicate that she had been killed at the spot where her body was found.'

'And why would you suspect that?'

'Because, sir, I saw her body at another location the day before those boys came across her on the riverbank.'

'Where was that?'

'Under the bleachers in the athletic field at the high school.'

'The high school at Clinton Engineer Works?'

'Yes, sir.'

Lawrence leaned back in his chair and steepled his hands on his chest. 'Well, then, it's not my case. It's out of my jurisdiction. I'll close the book on it now.'

'Sheriff, please don't. No one is investigating her death. Her family—'

'Not my case, miss. Now, if you'll excuse me, I need to get back to work,' he said, rising to his feet.

I refused to take the hint. I stubbornly nestled down firmly in the chair. 'Sheriff, I need your help. Irene needs your help.'

'Well, you're going to have to find it from your people, not from me.'

'I don't understand why you won't help.'

'It's pretty simple, actually. First of all, I don't want to meddle in an investigation that will bring me to the attention of the federal government – it's not healthy in a time of war. Secondly, I can't say I care for you people or what you have done.'

'Irene's done nothing to you. Irene's family has done nothing to you. I've done nothing to you.'

'That's all true. But none of you'd be here causing problems for us if you hadn't rolled in and stolen our land.'

I stood then and stepped close to his desk. 'Sir, we were informed that all that land was bought and paid for by the federal government.'

'Sure, it was paid for,' he said. 'But it's not like any of us had a choice in the matter. It's not like we could name our price.'

'You lost property?'

'My parents' farm – gone. You've probably walked over their land and not even known or cared that it mattered to somebody.'

'I'm sorry – it's the war, sir. We're doing important work to defeat the Axis powers.'

'And what exactly do you do?'

I felt the warmth of color rising in my face as I answered, 'I can't tell you that, sir. I'm sorry I—'

'Thought so. You're all the same. All sorts of strange rumors are floating around these parts. You're our neighbors but you don't act like it. Not a word to put our minds at ease.'

'Sir, I can't—'

'I know you can't. It's just pretty frustrating. Let me tell you about my Uncle Henry. He had it even worse than my parents. He used to run a business up in the mountains. Old Teddy Roosevelt came in and claimed his property as part of the Great Smokey Mountain National Park – all a part of our national heritage, he says. Henry set up a business in a new place. Along comes Franklin Delano Roosevelt. He takes that from him for the Tennessee Valley Authority – to bring electricity into the rural homes for the good of everyone. Then you all come along and take the third place he set up his business for that secret installation you got out there. And you say it's to win the war. Well, my Uncle Henry pretty much thinks you all are out to get him. And I can't say I blame him. There are a lot of people out there like my uncle. Don't expect any of us to be looking for a way to do you a good turn.'

'Sir, I don't know what to say. I'm sorry about what happened to your family but I didn't—'

'Yes, you did. You would not be here taking up my time if you all hadn't dispossessed my Uncle Henry. Can you find your way out?'

'Sir, I would have thought murder would be important to someone in your position.'

'Let me tell you something, miss. Sometimes you've got to decide your priorities. Now if we were talking about a nice young woman who never did a thing wrong in her life, I could get all excited about this case. But we're talking about a tramp here.'

'Sir, you didn't even know Irene. How can you say that?'

'Because I saw the autopsy report, miss. That Irene Nance was carrying a child when she died – pregnant and unmarried.

That's some kind of floozy in my book. Now, are you through wasting my time?'

'Yes sir,' I turned away to leave. I doubted that Ruth knew that Irene had been expecting. That added complication provided an additional reason for her murder.

Before I reached the door and stepped out of the office, the sheriff added, 'And don't bother coming round here no more.'

Once I was outside of the city limits and didn't have to concentrate on navigating the streets, I reflected on my experience with the sheriff and was humbled by my apparent naiveté. How could I possibly think an outsider would want to help? I'd heard the stories about the hostility out in the community. I should have known better.

No help would be forthcoming from the inside either; I'd have to be sneaky to get what I needed. 'The ends justify the means' rolled through my head, taunting me. I ignored it. I didn't need to get a search for the truth about Irene all mixed up with a big philosophical question. I'd think about that later.

The closer I got to the Solway Bridge, the better I felt. It would be a relief to get back on familiar territory – to return to the place where, despite the obstacle of my gender, I'd found some measure of acceptance and friendship. Someone would help me – I just had to find the right person.

But once I crossed that bridge, my day grew even worse.

SEVENTEEN

I was humming 'It Had to Be You' as my tires rolled up to the gate. I rolled down my window, flashed my badge and was puzzled when I wasn't waved right through to the property. When I first arrived with Dr Morton that was what happened then. But this time, the guard took my identification, walked several steps away, and turned his back to me as he pulled out his two-way radio. At first, I imagined it was just a new security precaution.

The guard quickly disabused me of that notion. He returned with shoulders back, his walk stiff and a stern expression on his face. He reached down to the handle and flung open the door. 'Please step out of the vehicle, Miss Clark.'

The machine gun and tanks pointing in my direction suddenly felt even more menacing than they had before. 'Is there a problem?'

'No problem at all, ma'am, if you will step out of the vehicle.'

I swung out my legs and stood on the ground beside the car. 'OK. I'm out of the vehicle. Can you explain the problem to me now?'

He wrapped a hand around my elbow and propelled me over to the other side of the road. 'Just stay right here. Someone will be picking you up in a few minutes.'

'Picking me up? Whatever for? I can drive wherever I need to go.' Was there some rule about having a car inside the gate than I violated without knowing it?

He turned away and walked back to the car.

I started to follow him but he spun around. 'Ma'am, I do have handcuffs. I'd really rather not use them.'

I backed up. Is this man crazy? 'Handcuffs? What is wrong with you? Handcuff me? Have you lost your mind?'

'Miss Clark, we normally do restrain car thieves, but since—'

'Car thief? Are you calling me a car thief?'

'Yes, ma'am, as you probably should have expected, the owner has filed a stolen vehicle report.'

'He did not. He loaned me this car.' Did Hank report his car stolen? And why?

'Yes, ma'am, that's what they all say,' he said as he walked back to the other side of the road, slid behind the steering wheel and leaned over to rummage in the glove compartment.

'This is absurd. I have not stolen this car. I have the owner's permission . . .'

The guard turned his head around and asked, 'Do you have it in writing?'

'Of course not. If this is a prank, it doesn't seem very funny right now.'

The guard shrugged. 'Someone will be coming by to transport you into town. Now if you'll just stand there quietly, I'll take care of my job over here.'

Another vehicle came across the Solway Bridge, stopped at the gate and showed identification. The guard looked at the badges of all three people in the car and allowed them through. The woman in the back seat stared at me as they drove past. I was mortified.

A jeep pulled up to the guard station. A private stepped out, saluted the guard and said, 'I'm here to transport Elizabeth Clark.'

I looked over to the guard. When he nodded, I climbed into the passenger seat. The private executed a U-turn and took off at a speed that made every bump in the road send me bouncing up and down.

'What's your name, soldier?' I asked.

'Private Leland, ma'am,' he answered without looking at me.

'Where are you taking me?'

'To the administration building.'

'Do you know why?'

'No, ma'am. Can't say that I do. Everythin' is on a need-to-know basis and nobody figures I need to know anythin'.' He looked at me with a grin. 'That's why they call us privates, I reckon. Keep everythin' private from us.'

He pulled into the rut-filled lot and parked.

'What now?' I asked.

'I'll be escortin' you in, ma'am.'

I followed him through the large front doors, up a flight of stairs and down a hall to a door marked: Lieutenant James Cooper, Commander, Military Police. He knocked on it, turned the knob and pushed it open. I walked inside and Private Leland pulled the door shut behind me.

Lieutenant Cooper's chiseled face appeared harsh, sour and unforgiving. I thought with a smile he'd be rather handsome but without it, he had the look of an angry hawk. His prominent nose, thin lips and dark brown eyes without a trace of warmth gave him the look of a predator. He rose from between the two flags standing sentinel behind his desk. The brass on his jacket gleamed as it caught the light with every movement. 'Please have a seat, Miss Clark,' he said, gesturing to a straightback wooden chair that looked about as comfortable as a new pair of shoes soaked in saltwater.

I perched on the chair's edge, adjusting my posture to conform to the military rigidity of the lieutenant and the two other officers in the spartan room. In contrast, there were also four men in business suits, slumped against the walls. I felt surrounded by hostile forces. The soft breath of unspoken threat hung in the air.

The lieutenant eased back into his chair, placed his forearms on his desk and leaned forward. 'Where have you been, Miss Clark?'

'I went to Knoxville, sir.'

'What was the nature of your trip?'

'I had personal business to attend to, sir.' My mouth suddenly felt dry. I swallowed quickly to generate some moisture.

'You are a scientist, Miss Clark. We are at war. You have no *personal* business. Everything you do is subject to our examination.'

I refused to be bullied. I straightened my back a bit more and stared straight ahead without responding.

'Miss Clark, we know where you have been. We received a call from the sheriff. We know you told him that you and Miss Ruth Nance found the body of Irene Nance at the high school. In doing so, you violated the security of this facility and thereby, the security of this nation.'

'That, sir, is an outrageous allegation. The death of one young woman who worked reception at the guest hotel is not a matter of national security.' The sheriff had reported me? Why? He made no attempt to hide his disdain for everyone here. Was that all an act?

'How many times have you seen that billboard with the message: "What you see here, stays here", Miss Clark?'

'I did not reveal any information about the work we do. I simply wanted to talk to local law enforcement about the death of a friend's sister. I have an obligation to the family.'

'Then you should be happy for the family that their loved one's body was found outside the fence. They'll get a death certificate and the parents will be able to bury their child.'

'What are you saying, sir?'

'On this side of the gates, death certificates are classified information. If you were run over in the street, your mother would not get a death certificate. If you slipped, fell down the steps in front of your house, banged your head and died, your mother would not get a death certificate.'

Was he threatening me?

'Do you understand me, Miss Clark?'

I nodded.

'Do you understand that your obligation to your country outweighs your obligation to any *one* or any *thing* else.'

'Sir, a young woman is dead – murdered. I cannot comprehend how that is a matter of national security.'

The man in the brown suit against the wall behind Cooper's

desk stepped forward and slid into the chair beside me. 'Miss Clark, people are not murdered here. There is no crime here. People are safe here.'

'Most people are, I suppose,' I said, making a heroic effort to tamp down my bubbling anger.

'We – and that means everyone in this room, including you – have an obligation to make sacrifices to win this war. The price of defeat is far too high. You, like all the scientists here, are working to make that happen every day. But you have a responsibility to more than just the science of this project. You also have a moral responsibility to help us protect the emotional health of our little community, to create an environment where you can do your work unimpeded. We expected you to do all you can do to keep up the morale among the workers. It is a heavy burden that we all share and take very seriously.'

'And how does this impact a proper investigation of this murder?' I asked.

The brown-suited man sighed. 'Miss Clark, I believe you are very sincere in your belief. But if you persist in spreading this story, it will have a deleterious effect on our community. Can you imagine how the anxiety will elevate if they believed your little tale? How would the married scientists be able to focus on their work if their wives are at home, quaking in fear? How will the Calutron girls be able to get to work every day if they are fearful of walking the streets? And to say it happened at the high school! Are you trying to frighten the children, too?'

'Perhaps they should all know so that they can safeguard their own lives,' I retorted.

The man sighed, looked to the lieutenant with raised eyebrows. Cooper leaned back in his chair and looked over to another man in a blue suit wearing a wide boldly patterned tie. That man pushed off the wall and walked in front of me, easing his rump down onto the front edge of the desk. 'How often did Irene Nance go down to the hutments?'

He had a much more intimidating presence than the lieutenant. The military man appeared capable of maintaining control at all times; this other man looked like losing it would be his idea of fun. I struggled to hide my budding fear. 'What? What does that have to do with anything? Her body was found at the high school.' I jutted out my chin in a gesture of a bravado I did not feel.

'Her body was not found at the high school. No body was found at the high school. You are mistaken.' He raised his arm and pointed his finger in my face, its tip just inches from my nose. 'Is that clear, Miss Clark?'

I wanted to shout him down but doubted I would leave that room employed unless I agreed with him. It galled me to do it but I made a jerky nod, while my eyes focused on the floor.

The blue suit rose and sauntered across the room, resuming his position on the wall. He had a smirk on his face that stirred up an urge in me to say something to shock him out of his smug self-satisfaction. I pinched my lips shut to keep the words from escaping.

'Miss Clark,' the lieutenant said, 'consider this a warning. We do not always give warnings but we understand that many consider you an irreplaceable asset and that your work has been noticed by G.G. – uh, General Groves. Be grateful that your value has been noted. If there is a next time, I will personally advocate for your removal. Is that understood?'

'Quite,' I said through my clenched jaw.

'Private!' the lieutenant shouted.

The door opened in response. 'Yes sir,' Private Leland said with a salute.

'Escort Miss Clark back to her car. Tell the guard that the stolen vehicle report was a simple misunderstanding.'

'Yes, sir.'

'Miss Clark,' Lieutenant Cooper said with a dismissive nod.

I returned his gesture and rose to my feet and turned around to face the door. With all the dignity I could muster, I walked out of the room, eyes straight forward, shoulders squared.

EIGHTEEN

My limbs felt as stiff as wood as I stepped into the jeep and stared straight ahead. A scream formed in my chest and thrust up into my throat, making me clench my jaw tighter to prevent its escape.

Private Leland grinded the vehicle into gear and took off with a jolt. 'Miss?'

I heard him but said nothing. Right now, I didn't want to talk to anyone.

'Miss?' he tried again. 'Miss, I heard most of what went on in that room.'

I blinked rapidly as the kindness in his voice brought tears close to the surface. I refused to look at him and focused on quelling the onslaught of emotions that battled with my self-control.

'Miss, I need to talk to you.'

Still I did not respond.

'Miss, I was seein' Irene for a bit a couple of months ago.'

That statement forced me to react. I turned in his direction. He still looked like a child – a dusting of freckles danced across his cheekbones and the bridge of his nose. His blue eyes appeared as earnest as those of a boy scout.

'I don't think this is right, miss,' he continued. 'But I think you need to drop it. No good'll come of it.'

'Drop it? Forget about Irene's death as if she didn't exist? I made a promise to her family, soldier. You want me to break my word?'

'I don't like that either, miss. But maybe, after the war . . .'

'After the war? After the war? Do you know how sick I am of hearing that phrase? After the war. It disgusts me. Irene's death has nothing to do with the war.'

'Miss, I am not sayin' any of this is right but I am sayin' that innocent people might be hurt if you continue.'

'What do you mean?'

'Remember when they brought up the hutments?'

'Yes, what about it?'

'If you keep pushin', this is what I think they'll do. They'll go down to the hutments and grab a few colored boys who they already labeled as troublemakers. Then they'll haul them in and finger one of them for the crime. Maybe they'll turn him over to the sheriff. Maybe the sheriff will conveniently lose track of him when the lynch mob comes callin'.'

'Are you telling me they would convict and maybe even kill an innocent man?'

'An innocent *colored* man? Yes, miss, I am.'

'I realize we are in the south, soldier, but most of the managers here are from the north. We don't treat our coloreds like that.'

'Right. You don't. You're a lot more subtle. You elevate a few token Negros to make you feel good but the rest of them – most of them – what do they do? Join you for tea? Nah. They haul your garbage, clean your house, carry your bags. You're just like us except you're bigger hypocrites.'

I was stunned by his forthright, but brutal, honesty. There was so much truth in what he said and yet I'd never really considered the hypocrisy.

'And if you think the Yankees in charge here are doin' the colored folks any favors, you should see how they make them live in the hutments. Men and women are segregated – even husbands and wives can't live together. They're just all jumbled together – women in the female huts, men in the male huts. And they don't have any indoor bathrooms and no hot water. If that's equality, I'm the president of the United States.'

Chastened, I sat still for a moment absorbing the reality of what he said. 'Perhaps, I should go down to the hutments and see for myself.'

'Oh, no, ma'am. You don't want to be doing that. People will get the wrong idea about you.'

'I don't particularly care what a bunch of racists think about me.'

'I'm not just talkin' about them, Miss Clark. I'm talkin' about the Negros, too. White folks go down to the hutments for two reasons only: to engage in somethin' illegal or to arrest somebody for doing somethin' illegal. They will not even consider that you might have good intentions. They'd all assume the worst about you.'

Recalling the leer on the faces in the room when a reference was made linking Irene to the hutments, I knew he was right. 'But what about you, private? You're a Tennessee boy, aren't you?'

'Yes, ma'am. Sure am.'

'Your attitude toward the coloreds seems out of character for someone born and bred in this state.'

'Well, ma'am, as a kid, I worked the fields with colored folks, right alongside my daddy. Now, he was a preacher on Sundays and he always taught me that in the eyes of God, we were all colored. God was wondrous and pure white from the brilliant light that shone all around him. He said that we might call ourselves white folks but that was just our arrogant pride trying to make us feel like God.'

The theology seemed a bit odd but it certainly explained Leland's viewpoint. Understanding, though, did not make the dilemma go away. Leland had just made my decision even more complicated. Keeping my promise to Ruth would not just put my career at risk, but it would also threaten the lives of unknown men in the hutments.

Private Leland pulled to a stop by the guard house. 'Miss, you just stay here till I talk to the guard. Don't want him gettin' all worked up before he knows the score.'

A couple of minutes later, Leland jogged back to the jeep. 'He's callin' in to confirm what I told him. Once he does, he will give you your car keys and you'll be free to go.'

'Thank you, Private Leland.'

Leland grinned making him look even younger. 'You're welcome, miss.' The smile slid from his face. 'Please promise me you will think about what I said. I don't think it's right. I think Irene deserves justice – her family needs it – but right now, I can't see how it can be found, no matter what you do.'

I explored the openness of his face. I could not make a commitment to turn my back on Irene and Ruth, but I could promise to think about what he said. In fact, I doubted I could avoid it. I'd probably have trouble stopping my mind from turning it over and over long enough to be able to get any sleep that night. I nodded my agreement.

At a wave from the guard, I got out of the jeep, retrieved the keys and climbed into Hank's car. Driving home, I couldn't help contemplating the restrictions on my freedom; the liberty I once took for granted. I expected limitations working as I was at a secret installation. I knew I had to watch my words about my work, and of course, I'd accepted doing without the typical abundance of American life. Those restrictions, those sacrifices had all seemed for the greater good. But now I had doubts. Was it all as necessary as we'd been led to believe?

JANUARY, 1944

'I'll bring my sons and daughters
I'll bring my heavy waters
Titanium Uranium
Dance around my atom fire'

Woody Guthrie

NINETEEN

On Sunday, I tried to put my ethical dilemma out of my mind by listening to shows on the radio but, no matter how hard I tried to focus on other things, my thoughts swung like a monkey through the tree tops alternating between trying to make a logical decision and running away from it all.

Perhaps a walk would clear my head. For a few blocks, I mentally wiped my slate clean and then started over making a fresh assessment of the current situation.

On one hand, I'd made a promise to Ruth and her family to investigate Irene's death. If only someone in a position of authority would do their job – it didn't matter who: the local police, military security or even the Knox County Sheriff's Department could tackle the murder investigation and relieve me of that obligation. But clearly no one would. As long as that didn't change, how could I not live up to my commitment?

But if I did, what then? Did I have any chance to succeed? I had no experience and the forces of the government were lined up against me. If I moved forward, would they arrest and convict an innocent colored man? If that happened the double burden of not finding the person responsible for Irene's murder and ruining the life of someone I'd never met would be crushing.

Would that false arrest then lead to my dismissal? Would I be considered a troublemaker or worse yet a traitor? The world was at war and lives were at risk all over the globe. But before now, I'd never considered the dangers that lurked stateside in the middle of the country, far out of reach of kamikaze pilots and U-boats.

I'd sworn to uphold the secrecy at this installation. I had no problem with that; I understood and accepted that I could not talk about my work, the projects underway, or even the identities of the people living here. But this was a personal crime – this was not part of the war effort. Did they honestly believe that it was a security risk or were they simply trying to cover up the truth? And why? Because they feared the effect on morale of the civilians as the men in suits indicated? Or was there a darker purpose? Were they protecting the perpetrator? If so, who could be that important?

I mentally ran through the list of scientists I knew who were in the positions of greatest responsibility. Ruth had said that Irene's boyfriend was a scientist named Bill. I could think of four or five men named William or Bill in the management group. Bill. My only clue. But where would it lead?

Until I resolved the moral questions, I could not spare a thought for suspicion or investigation. It was one of the biggest decisions of my life. I jerked to a stop when I realized my mindless ramble had taken me behind and above Towncenter and now I was approaching the high school. Did my feet have a mind of their own? Perhaps there's wisdom in the subconscious drive that brought me here. I continued moving forward to the football field.

I stared over the empty expanse searching for answers but finding none. Where should I go from here? I needed to talk to the one person who had helped me with all the major decisions in my life since I was twelve years old. Even if I could find a telephone to use, all the calls were monitored. I had to get Aunt Dorothy to Tennessee. But how?

Ann Bishop might be able to help. I didn't want to draw unwanted attention by seeking her out at her desk, so I waited until an opportune moment. When Ann walked in with messages for Charlie, I intercepted her. 'Ann! Got a minute?'

Her shoulder-length blonde hair swayed as she turned towards me. 'Sure, Libby, if you'll tell me who that new guy is in the back of the lab.'

'Spare your energy on that one, Ann. I found him crying the other day 'cause he missed his mom.'

'What a waste of good looks,' Ann said as she looked at him again and sighed.

'You have a phone in your house, don't you?'

Ann darted her eyes right, then left, and whispered, 'Mom doesn't want me to tell people, but yes, we do.'

'Do you think she'd let me use it to make a call to my Aunt Dorothy?'

'I don't know, Libby. She's afraid she'll get overrun by people wanting to make calls. I know she likes you but . . .'

'How about if I brought her a gift? Would that make a difference?'

'I don't know. She seems to get most everything she wants one way or another. Oh, but there is one thing . . .'

'What?'

'An eye of round roast. She's craving one like crazy and she never seems to get to the market at the right time. If you can get your hands on one of those, she'd let you make a call and wouldn't care if it was all the way to China.'

'Meat? I can bribe your mother with meat?'

'There's a war on,' Ann said with a giggle. 'But not just any meat – the eye of round. She's craving it. I think mainly because she can't get her hands on one.'

How in heaven's name would I locate an eye of round roast? How many days would I have to stand in line just to find one there when I reached the counter? Mr McMinn. He was from Lynchburg, Tennessee, just like Ruth. He'd set aside some yummy pork chops for Ruth once and we'd cooked them on a forbidden hot plate in the dorm room. Maybe he would help me.

After work, I rushed home, grabbed my ration coupon book, grateful that it was the first of the month and I had plenty stamps. It would mean nothing but spam and canned salmon for weeks, but it would be worth it. Now, if only Mr McMinn would help make it possible.

At the market, I went straight for the meat counter. The 'No Meat' sign stood tall behind the glass but I hit the bell on the counter anyway. A white coated man hurried over from produce.

'Ma'am, we have no meat – see the sign.'

'I know, sir. I just want to speak to one of your butchers, Mr McMinn.'

He put his hands on his waist and scowled. 'No one here will accept bribes. We follow the rules. Don't sell anything under the counter. And besides, we have no meat.'

'You are presumptuous, sir,' I said in the most imperious voice I could muster, hating the sound of the words as they left my mouth. 'I need to speak to Mr McMinn about a family from his hometown.'

The produce man raised both palms up in the air. 'I am sorry. And you are right. I should not have jumped to that conclusion.

I think Mr McMinn is doing paperwork in the back. Let me see if I can find him for you.'

What was I becoming? A liar? A rule breaker? There was that 'ends justifies the means' thing again. It seemed to pop up every day. It never seemed to be a problem before the war, now it seemed to haunt every corner of my life.

The hefty Mr McMinn lumbered out from behind the meat counter with a furrowed brow and an unspoken question in his eyes. The tie of his clean, white apron strained at his waist. 'Yes, ma'am?' he said, squinting his eyes.

'Mr McMinn, I don't know if you remember me or not but Ruth Nance introduced us a few weeks ago.'

The furrows in his brow grew deeper and then flashed smooth. 'Hey, yeah, you're that scientist lady. Ruth's roommate.'

'Yes,' I said, nodding and smiling.

'Is Ruth here with you?' he asked, his neck craning around as he scanned the store.

'No, Mr McMinn.' I stepped forward and lowered my voice. 'Ruth was dismissed and sent home.'

'No! What happened?'

'She was very upset about Irene and she said the wrong things to the wrong people.'

McMinn hung his head and let it sway side to side. 'That was just awful. Do they know what happened to Irene? Do they know who did it?'

'That's just it, Mr McMinn. No one seems to want to know. Ruth asked me to try to figure it out.'

'What can I do to help?'

'Well, I'm not sure what to do, Mr McMinn. I really need to speak with my Aunt Dorothy to figure it all out but I don't have a phone.'

'Sorry, but I don't either.'

'I didn't think you would. But I know someone who does and I'm sure she'd let me use it if I came bearing an eye of round roast.'

McMinn shrugged. 'Right now, I don't even have a scrap of meat big enough for a pair of dogs to fight over. But if you can wait till Wednesday, I'll have at least one side of beef coming in. I'll cut an eye roast and set it aside for you. Just make sure you come by after work Wednesday and bring your ration coupons. I can't hide it for long.'

'Thank you, Mr McMinn. I'll see you then.'

On the way back home, I felt a jagged energy generated by the thrill of bending the rules and stepping out of line. I was ashamed at my jubilance. I shouldn't be so excited by my shady little plans but I couldn't deny what I was feeling.

I had no problem leaving work a little early. We'd been spending a lot of time just doing work that was as mind-numbing as the endless practice of piano scales. But there wasn't much else to do since the flaws in design of the Calutrons were uncovered and the equipment was shipped back to the manufacturer. I had plenty of assignments to keep me busy but none of them arrived with any sense of urgency, in contrast to the intensity that had been November and early December. Half the time when I went upstairs to get samples, the Calutron girls were sitting around playing cards. Each day I felt more nervous. We'd never stop the war if we couldn't get production flowing again.

Despite my early arrival, the line in front of the meat counter stretched a block long outside of the store. I hated waiting in lines and often did without rather than waste all that time. Today, though, I had no choice. I queued up with strangers and neighbors, nodding and smiling at the people I recognized.

After an hour, I finally stepped inside the store and felt the wonderful and welcoming warmth on my chilled nose and cheeks. At first, it stung my skin but felt good all the same. I pulled off my gloves and rubbed my fingers together. In another half hour, I was close enough to the counter to spot Mr McMinn, his white apron now streaked with dried blood.

I caught his eye and he nodded. When I reached the counter, Mr McMinn pulled out a package wrapped in butcher paper and tied with cotton string. 'That will be forty-eight ration points and a dollar and seventy-seven cents.'

I handed over five ten-point coupons and two one-dollar bills. He returned two ration tokens, two dimes and three pennies. Mr McMinn gave me a wink and we exchanged quick smiles before I walked away. When I got out of the store, I breathed a sigh of relief. I half-expected that someone would call me out and ask unwelcome questions about my purchase. But I got away without incident.

I walked over to Magnolia Drive and knocked on the Bishops'

front door. Ann jerked the door open. 'What took you so long? My dad will be home soon and we always sit down to dinner as soon as he gets here.'

I grimaced. 'There was a line . . .'

Ann sighed. 'Of course there was. C'mon in.' Ann turned toward the kitchen. 'Mom! Libby is here to see you.'

Mrs Bishop came to the foyer, her golden blonde hair pulled back in a bun, her smile blazing bright red. Around her waist, she wore a pink flowered apron with a ruffled edge. She must have bought that before the war – no ruffles were allowed in apparel manufacturing now.

'Hello, dear. What can I do for you?'

'I brought a present, Mrs Bishop,' I said stretching out my arm with the white package.

'For me?'

'Yes, ma'am.'

'May I open it now?'

'You should, Mrs Bishop.'

'Let's go in the kitchen,' she said, leading the way. She pulled out a pair of scissors, snipped the cord and folded back the paper. 'Oh my! Look at this!' She ran her hand over the oval of red, bloody meat. 'This is glorious. An eye of round? I can't believe it. How did you ever? I might swoon.' She patted the roast affectionately. 'I'll make this for dinner tomorrow night. Oh, Libby, you must join us. I have some potatoes – I'll mash them and I'll make gravy, too. And what else will we have? Oh, green beans. Do you like green beans, Libby?'

'Yes, ma'am, I do.'

She grabbed my elbow and tugged me toward a cabinet. Flinging open the door, she said, 'Look! Look at this.'

Inside, gleaming jars of green, orange and yellow filled every shelf, making me think of my mother sweating over the stove, home-canning vegetables every summer for weeks on end. Mrs Bishop stuck her hand in the cabinet and pulled out a jar of preserves. 'Here take this back with you. They are really good.'

'I can't take that, Mrs Bishop, but I would like to use your phone to call my Aunt Dorothy if that would be OK.'

'Oh, dear, are you homesick?'

'Yes, ma'am.' It was true – it wasn't the reason for the call – but still, it wasn't a lie.

She grabbed my hand and pressed the jar of preserves into it. 'Here, you take this and go right ahead and make the phone call, too. You can't believe what your surprise gift meant to me. I must seem awfully silly but it really is more meaningful than the meat itself. It's like the whisper of the old life gone by,' she said and sighed.

'Thank you, Mrs Bishop,' I said as I picked up the black phone receiver.

'And Libby?'

'Yes, ma'am?'

'You can stay for dinner tonight, too, if you like.'

'Thank you, ma'am, but no thank you, I need to be getting back to the house. I will be here tomorrow.'

I dialed Aunt Dorothy's number, imagining the secret person listening into my conversation, deciphering the number from the spin of the rotary dial.

I heard a click and then, 'Clark residence.'

'Aunt Dorothy?'

'Libby? Is that you?'

'Yes, ma'am.'

'What a delightful surprise. I trust everything is going well.'

'Yes. Well, except for this one thing. I really need to talk to you.'

'What's on your mind?'

'Aunt Dorothy, I just don't feel comfortable talking on the phone.'

'Do you have a problem, Libby?'

'Yes. Well, it's about a boy,' I lied, resenting the censors who made it necessary.

'A boy? I never thought I'd find you flummoxed by a boy.'

'It's not the usual thing. I really need to talk to you. I was hoping maybe you'd be somewhere near me and I could come meet you.'

'Well, Libby, it is your lucky day. I've got my assistant working on my schedule for the recruitment trip I am making for the graduate school. I told her to work in the University of Tennessee as one of my stops. I was going to send you a telegram as soon as the date was determined. I should know when by the end of the week.'

'Oh, I can't tell you how much that means to me.'

'Whatever is troubling you, Libby, just remember that decisions made in haste are decisions that we regret all too soon.'

'I'll do nothing until I talk with you. Thank you, Aunt Dorothy.' I carefully set the receiver back in its cradle as unshed tears moistened my eyes.

'Is everything OK at home, dear?'

'Yes, ma'am. Aunt Dorothy will be visiting the university soon and I'll be able to see her.'

'That's wonderful, dear. I'm not your mother or your Aunt Dorothy, Libby, but if you ever need an older woman to talk to . . .'

'Thank you, Mrs Bishop. I really need to run. I'll see you tomorrow evening.'

What a relief. Aunt Dorothy would not tell me what to do but she would listen carefully and walk me through the maze of conflicting responsibilities and help me set priorities. It still wouldn't be an easy decision but at least I wouldn't have to make it alone.

TWENTY

I was working on a report when Ann Bishop breezed into the room. She walked past me without a glance, dropping a folded-up piece of paper on my desk without a pause. Every pair of male eyes followed Ann as she travelled the length of the lab and out the door at the other end. I could tell by the way she walked that she was aware of their stares and loving every minute of it.

I opened up the note and read: Washroom. Five minutes. Don't be late.

Whatever did she want now? I liked Ann but sometimes she seemed such a silly girl and although I was only three years older than her, the difference in maturity often made my teeth ache.

I finished the paragraph I was writing and followed Ann down the hall. Did this summons have anything to do with tonight's dinner? Did she think I knew something about her that her parents didn't know and she wanted to warn me not to mention it? I pushed open the washroom door.

'Lock it,' Ann hissed.

'Lock the door?'

'Yes.'

'Why?'

'Do it.'

I flipped the catch. 'OK. Now, what's so urgent?'

'What have you done?'

'What?'

'You heard me. What have you done?'

'I don't know what you want to know, Ann. Is this about dinner tonight? Don't you want me to come?'

'Oh, no, I want you more than ever. I can't wait to see how Dad acts while you're there.'

'Ann, you aren't making any sense,' I said, feeling like I'd stepped into the middle of a book without a clue about what happened in the first half of the story.

'You really don't know, do you?'

I shook my head.

'You're in big trouble and you don't even know it?'

'Big trouble? What are you talking about? Please, Ann, start from the beginning.'

'Last night, we'd finished dinner and Mom and I stood up to clear the table. Before we could step away, there was a loud, pounding knock on the door. Dad pushed back his chair and went to answer it. Mom and I hurried into the kitchen to set down the dishes and then rushed back to see what was happening.

'There were four uniformed soldiers at the door. And Dad was in a bad mood. He doesn't like the military one little bit. He would put up with the solitary private that used to come with messages or to summon him to the laboratory or a meeting somewhere, but he didn't like it. That's one reason why he insisted that we get a telephone and raised Cain until we got one. We haven't had many uniforms at the house since. But this time there were four of them and Dad was not happy. After they left, he called it an invasion.'

'OK, OK, Ann, get to the point.'

'Oh, right. Well, the reason they were there was because of you.'

'Me?'

'Yes. They wanted to know what you were doing at our house. Dad said he didn't know you'd been there, which isn't exactly true because Mom told him about the roast. But sometimes he doesn't really listen so he probably wasn't lying.

'Mom said you were calling home and told them they should know that since they listened in to all our phone calls. The lieutenant got all huffy about that and gave her a speech about her patriotic duty, war time and all of that. Mom got huffy right back at him, talking about her sacrifices and the mud.

'Then the lieutenant said you were talking in code on the phone. And Mom said he was a crazy man. She said you were just a poor, sweet girl who was homesick and having boy problems.

'And the lieutenant said it was all a ruse. And my mom said that she was calling the administrators and asking them to build an asylum on the grounds because obviously that's where he needed to be. Then the lieutenant got ugly. He threatened Mom for covering up for a spy. That's when Daddy hit the roof and ordered them out of the house. The lieutenant said they'd be watching all of us and then they left.'

It was difficult to grasp the essence of the situation but it had to be about Irene. What had Irene done to make them so determined to hide her murder? 'What was the lieutenant's name?'

Ann wrinkled her nose. 'I don't remember.'

'Could it have been Cooper – Lieutenant James Cooper?'

'Yes. It might have been.'

'Brown hair. Blue eyes. And an expression on his face that looks like he just smelled something bad.'

'Yes. That's him.'

'Oh, dear.'

'So what have you done, Libby?'

'I've done nothing wrong, Ann. I swear it.'

'Then, why . . .?' Ann began.

'He just doesn't like me,' I said.

'Oh, he made a move on you and you put him in his place, didn't you?'

Not only did Ann accept my improvised answer at face value but she expanded on it. I certainly didn't want to deceive her but I didn't want to elaborate either. 'I hope your parents weren't too upset.'

'Well, when you left, Daddy told me that I shouldn't be spending anymore time with you. It wouldn't look good. Mom lit into him like you wouldn't believe. She said you were a wonderful young woman. That you set a good example for me. Dad asked her if that was what she wanted for me – if she wanted me to be a career woman. Mom said that of course she didn't want that. She wanted me married. She wanted grandchildren. But for now and until the war was over, I had to have my little career and learn responsibility and I could learn it all from you. And then she said that you were a sensible girl who could help me find the right kind of man instead of making the same mistake that a lot of women do.'

'A piece of meat did all that?' I asked.

'Well, no, Libby. She liked you before that. She felt real bad for you at Christmastime, all alone and everything. While we were away, she kept fretting about you, regretting not inviting you to come along. After Christmas, she said that not having you with us in Nashville was one of the biggest mistakes she'd ever made.'

Terrific, she must think I'm pathetic; a pity case. 'I guess I shouldn't be coming to dinner tonight then.'

'Oh, you better. That's when she told Daddy you were coming for supper. When he said that was not a good idea, Mom said, "Oh, you're going to let a few little soldiers push you around. Are we going to have to run and hide again?"'

'What does that mean?' I asked.

'I don't know. I asked Mom later and she told me it was just an expression and then said that it was rude for me to eavesdrop on their conversations. But they were talking right in front of me, Libby. What did she expect?

'Anyway, Dad turned bright red when she said that and stomped out of the house without a coat or boots or anything. We heard him stomping around the outside of the house. In five minutes he came back in and said, "Is there anything for dessert?" Mom said, "It depends." And Daddy said, "I'm looking forward to seeing that nice Clark girl tomorrow evening. She's a hard worker, a quick thinker and a very pleasant young lady." And that was that. I sure don't know what's gotten into Mom. When I was growing up, no matter what Dad said, she'd always go along with it. "Yes, dear. Whatever you say, dear." Now, it's just the opposite. Dad doesn't say the same words but he acts just like Mom used to.'

'Do you think their marriage is in trouble?' I asked.

'Oh, no. Nothing like that. They get along just fine. It's just that I used to think Dad was in charge but now it seems like Mom is.'

'Maybe you just see things differently because you're older,' I suggested.

Ann shrugged. 'Maybe. I tried to talk to Mom about it but she just said, "Never you mind, young lady. Some things are just between you father and I. When you're married, you'll understand about that." Of course if this war doesn't end soon, I'll be an old spinster and never get married.'

'So are you sure I should come tonight?'

'Oh, you have to come. I promised I wouldn't say a word to you. If you don't come they'll know I broke my promise.'

'Ann, you shouldn't have,' I said in mock protest.

Ann giggled and said, 'We girls have to stick together. Gotta get back to my desk before I'm missed. See you tonight.'

I leaned back against the sink. Things were getting messier and messier. I didn't want to cause any problems between Ann's parents. I'd really have to make sure I didn't let any of them know what was up until I talked to Aunt Dorothy and sorted everything out. I'd go to work, go home and do nothing else but the bare minimum of shopping.

The military had made a mistake with that overt action – now I was forewarned. If did find answers to Irene's murder, they'd stop at nothing to shut me down. All day at work, the conversation with Ann kept running through my head, threatening to stir up my fear. But that emotion was debilitating – I was determined not to become afraid.

After work, I caught the bus and disembarked just two blocks from home. I walked fast to keep the deepening cold at bay. When I went up the steps, I spotted a small potato sack sat on the landing. I scooped it up and went inside. I set it on the table while I got the fire going.

I stoked the embers, tossed on more coals, pulled off my gloves and warmed my hands over the fire. Slipping out of my coat, I carried the bag to the kitchen counter. Inside was a pair of hand-knitted green mittens with yellow stripes. They'd come in handy if there was a snow. With these, I could help the kids next door build a snowman. But where did they come from?

I spotted a piece of paper in the bottom of the stack and pulled it out. 'I have my eyes on you.'

I jumped back, dropped it as if it were a hot coal and watched it drift to the floor. My heart thudded painfully. I picked the note up and read it again. Who left it on my porch? Lieutenant Cooper? The man who killed Irene? I ran into the living room, opened the door to the coal stove and threw the mittens inside.

That was probably a mistake. I was just being paranoid. All this secrecy and warnings about spies had made me too wary – too jumpy. Maybe it was nothing more than a secret admirer who had no idea that his simple words could be twisted into such a dark meaning. Still, I could not shake my feeling of unease. I grabbed a kitchen chair and rammed it under the knob of the front door.

'I've got my eyes on you.' After the war, I'd laugh about this moment. Maybe. It all depended on how the war ended – and with the production line for the uranium sitting idle, hope of a good outcome had stagnated. How would I be able to sleep ever again?

TWENTY-ONE

Walking to the Bishop home, I was on edge. Was I being followed? Or was it the phone call that captured the attention of the authorities? I squirmed and fought the constant desire to look over my shoulder as I walked. If I started behaving furtively, and someone was watching, it would only make matters worse.

Ann answered the door with a grin and whispered, 'Good luck' into my ear as she helped me out of my coat. Dreading the sight of Dr Bishop, I plastered on a smile and stepped out of the small foyer into the living room where the fireplace was blazing.

He pulled a pipe out of his mouth and rose as I entered saying, 'Good evening, Miss Clark. Come closer to the fire and warm your hands.'

'Thank you, sir,' I said, stepping forward to absorb the heat.

'Has there been any excitement in your life lately?'

A lump formed in my throat. Was he making conversation? Was he spying on me for the security department? Or was he just nervous about having me in his house? 'You probably know more about the situation at Y-12 than I do,' I answered. 'But on the personal front, I just finished reading a fascinating book I got for Christmas, *The Robe* by Lloyd Douglas. Have you read it?'

'No. But it seems everyone else has. We have a copy here somewhere. I believe Mrs Bishop has read it. What else is happening in your life?'

To my great relief, Mrs Bishop stepped into the living room with a more exuberant greeting than her usual cheery welcome. Was it because of the roast? Or out of curiosity about my trouble with security?

'Dear Libby! What a joy to see you,' she said. Placing a hand on each of my arms, she leaned forward and brushed a kiss on my cheek. 'Dinner will be ready in five minutes.'

'Let me help,' I offered, eager to escape Dr Bishop's gaze.

'Oh no, dear, you're company, I couldn't allow that.'

'Of course you can. When I'm in your home, I feel like family – and family *always* helps out.'

Mrs Bishop beamed. 'Well, come along then. I'd love to have your help.'

At the dinner table, Dr Bishop sliced the roast in nearly paper-thin pieces. The result was mouthfuls of roast beef that seemed to melt on the tongue. I accepted seconds but balked when Mrs Bishop offered me a third serving. 'Not another bite,' I said. 'That was delicious, Mrs Bishop. You prepared that meat to perfection. Thank you. It's definitely the best meal I've had since Thanksgiving.'

'It's not just what I did, dear. The taste had a lot to do with how Mr Bishop sliced it – he's a magician with that carving knife. But even more importantly, if it weren't for you, we wouldn't have had this luscious eye of round to prepare and enjoy. Thank *you*, Libby.'

'Miss Clark,' Dr Bishop said, 'since you feel like family here, I am thinking you would not mind if I asked you a personal question.'

I forced a smile and said, 'Of course not.'

'Could you tell me why security came by here to ask about you last night?'

'No sir, I can't.'

'Have you been discussing your work with anyone?'

'Not anyone outside of my laboratory, sir.'

'Are you sure about that?'

'Absolutely.'

'Then why would they have any interest in you?'

'I–I–I think it might have something to do with the roommate I had while I was in the dormitory. She was let go right after Christmas.'

'Was she betraying her country?'

'No sir. No. Not Ruth. She doesn't even know anything worth telling anyone.'

'Sometimes, Miss Clark, the most innocent comments told out of school can do unimaginable damage.'

'Sir, it had to do with her sister. Her sister, Irene. She was murdered. Ruth made a few unwise comments when she was very emotional about the loss of her sister.'

'I must say, Miss Clark, I am very concerned about security's interest in you. But more importantly, I am disturbed that the issue has been brought into my home. Can you give me any reason why I shouldn't be worried about this development?'

I opened my mouth but words failed me. I closed and opened it again.

In a high-pitched voice, Mrs Bishop piped in, 'I made a special dessert for tonight. I broke into my sugar supply and baked a jelly roll.' She pushed her chair back from the table.

Ann popped to her feet. 'Stay seated, Mom. I'll be right back.'

'But the dessert plates – you'll need help with those,' Mrs Bishop said, rising to her feet.

I lurched up out of the chair, eager to grasp at the opportunity to escape. 'Sit back down, ma'am. I'll help Ann.'

I couldn't get into the kitchen fast enough. I stepped through the swinging door and leaned against the counter. 'Phew!'

'You're telling me,' Ann said. 'I couldn't stand another minute of that. Ssssh! Listen.'

I barely breathed as she strained to hear the quiet conversation in the other room. I couldn't pick out any distinct words but the tone was apparent. Mrs Bishop was chastising her husband. He argued back with her. Then he raised his voice, 'OK, Mildred, OK! You've made your point.'

After a moment of silence, Ann said, 'Coast is clear. Let's go.'

Ann picked up the plate with the jelly roll and I grabbed the dessert plates and forks. I smiled and nodded as Mrs Bishop engaged in nearly non-stop chatter about the weather, her frustrations with bureaucrats and the anticipation of spring.

My nerves jangled like the bell on a besieged shop door. I could barely wait for enough time to pass before I could excuse myself without appearing rude. When the moment seemed right, I thanked Mrs Bishop again and bid a good night to the family.

'Wait a minute, Libby,' Mrs Bishop said and turned to her husband. 'Marc, darling, it is absolutely frigid out tonight. Why don't you give Libby a ride home?'

My chest tightened. I couldn't let that happen. I couldn't bear to be alone with Dr Bishop. He was bound to begin the interrogation in the car before he even slipped it into gear. 'Oh no, I couldn't impose like that on Dr Bishop. I'll walk. It's not that far.'

'Nonsense,' Mrs Bishop said. 'Marc, go warm up the car.'

'No, really, Mrs Bishop. I want to walk. After all I've eaten tonight, I need to walk. If I don't, I'll never be able to get to sleep – my stomach is too full.'

'But it is terribly cold out—' Mrs Bishop began.

'You are being rather foolish, Miss Clark.' Dr Bishop joined his wife's entreaties.

'Daddy that's rude,' Ann admonished.

Dr Bishop frowned at his daughter, then at me, and turned to go back into his study. It certainly felt as though I'd been dismissed and I wasn't sure how welcome I'd be again in the Bishop household. Dr Bishop clearly felt I caused more trouble that I was worth, and right now I wouldn't have blamed him.

Mrs Bishop furrowed her brow. 'Well, if you're sure . . .'

'Absolutely! A brisk walk through the cold night is just what the doctor ordered.' I pulled on gloves as I talked and headed for the front door. 'Thanks again for a wonderful dinner and a lovely evening.'

Halfway back to my house, the pain in my nose and the numbness in my toes filled me with regret about my decision. But what choice did I have. At least, now, with no one else out walking on the blustery night, I knew I was not being followed.

When my home came into view, I picked up my pace but halfway up to the steps, I froze. An envelope was wedged between the side of the door and the jamb, reminding me of the mystery gift of mittens and my suppressed dread. I rushed up to the door, grabbed the envelope, went inside and flipped on a light. It was a Western Union envelope which meant a telegram. I ripped it open.

'Wednesday, January 13. Dinner. Andrew Johnson Hotel.'

Six days. Six long days. Could I stay calm and not draw any more suspicion till then?

TWENTY-TWO

All that week, I kept busy on meaningless work, hoping that the rumors from the manufacturer, Allis Chalmers, were true. Supposedly, the new Calutron units were built and being loaded onto railroad cars for shipping south. Maybe soon we could return to the important work for the war effort that brought us all here. I'd also heard that the scientists and engineers in the mysterious K-25 building were laboring round the clock. I didn't know what they were doing, but the fact that they were busy made me want to join them.

I kept my weekend deliberately uneventful, leaving the house only for necessary errands. I avoided talking to anyone about anything. A nod, a smile and a quick escape were all that was on my agenda. I dared not do anything that raised suspicion.

That Monday, we celebrated in the lab as the rumor became the official announcement. Not only had the new components for the racetrack left Chicago but they actually were sitting in freight cars in the rail yard waiting to be unloaded and moved into Y-12 for assembly.

Measuring samples at my work station, my scalp prickled as if I was being watched. I tried to shake the feeling – to pass it off as senseless paranoia – but it clung to me like the tendrils of early morning fog that drifted through the nearby mountains. I looked up and discovered it was not all in my imagination.

A man with black hair and brooding, bottomless brown eyes stood in the doorway, one shoulder resting on the jamb. He stared straight at me from under a pair of heavy eyebrows. His mouth was tight. His jaw twitched. He looked vaguely familiar but I couldn't place him. I looked quickly away – but it was not quick enough. He'd raised a brow at my stare but he did not flinch.

I picked up a piece of scrap paper and walked over to the next work station to Gregg Abbott. Laying the page in front of him, I said, 'Gregg, would you look at this for me?'

He picked it up and looked down at the scribble of notes and nonsensical doodles. 'What's this?' he asked.

'Look back down at the paper, please, and pretend like you are interested in it.'

He lowered his head and pointed a finger at an oblong shape with stripes. 'What's going on, Libby?'

'There's a man in the doorway who has been staring at me,' I said placing a finger to the left of his.

'Well, you're not a bad looking girl. You ought to expect a few ogles.'

'He is not ogling me, Gregg. It's more like he's giving me the evil eye. Do you know who he is?'

Gregg looked up and back down. 'He looks familiar but I can't place him. And you are right – he certainly doesn't look like he's carrying a torch for you.'

'And he's wearing a wedding band.'

Gregg sneaked another glance. 'Yeah, he is. That's something you want to avoid. He definitely can't have honorable intentions.'

'Trust me, Gregg. *That* is not a look of seduction.'

'Wait. I know where I've seen him before.'

'Where?' I asked.

'Remember when G.G. was here and he talked to you?'

'Of course.'

'Wasn't he one of the men in that group around the general?'

'Maybe. That could be why he looks familiar.'

'Maybe he took exception to you figuring out the racetrack problem – maybe that was his responsibility?'

'I guess that's possible,' I said, 'although it seems a scientist doing work this important and timely would want a solution – any solution – even if it came from a Calutron girl. Does he work here in Y-12?'

'I don't know,' Gregg said shaking his head. 'You know how those big deal scientists are. They all use phony names. How can they possibly think we'd fall for it? I mean, really, that Eugene Farmer is so obviously foreign with his accent and mannerisms – at least they could have given him a code name that was a bit more realistic. Did they really think that none of us would recognize a prominent scientist like Enrico Fermi at first glance? That's all wet.'

A shout rang out in the hall. 'Hey, Dr Smith!'

The man in the doorway turned around, stretched out his arm and shook the other man's hand. Except for the end of one limb, that other man remained out of sight. The two walked off together.

'Ah, horsefeathers! See what I mean. Dr Smith? Please.'

'Well, Smith is a common name,' I said.

'Libby, you don't seriously . . .?'

'No, not really.' Who was he and why was he intently staring at me? Could he be Irene's married boyfriend? Her killer? Had he somehow found out about my investigations?

'Are you OK? Your face is as pale as a fish belly.'

'It's nothing, Gregg. I'd better go sit down. I feel a little woozy.' I turned away and walked toward my station.

'Can I get you anything? Glass of water? Anything?'

'No. Thank you, Gregg. I'll be fine.'

I placed my hands flat on the surface of my work counter, trying to still the tremors that seemed to give my fingers a life of their own. It was only a look. But the fear it transmitted loomed larger than the headline 'WAR!' that had blazed on the front of the newspapers more than a year ago.

How could I figure out who he was? We weren't supposed to ask questions about secret identities. Should I even try? Two days. Two days and I'd see Aunt Dorothy. My insides felt as if they'd been dipped in liquid nitrogen and were crumbling with every breath I took.

Not knowing what I was going to do next was the worst part. Talking to Aunt Dorothy would enable me to make a decision. Once I did that, I would have a plan. Perils might abound in whatever course I took but awareness of the path ahead would make it manageable. If I approached the problem as if it was a lab experiment – one careful step at a time, everything moving forward in a linear fashion – ultimately it would lead to a solid conclusion.

Two days and I'd know the parameters of the experiment that lay ahead.

The time passed in a fog. I jumped at every unexpected sound, peering around every time I sensed a nearby presence. Always on the look-out for that Dr Smith who stared with such malicious intent. I didn't see him again that week, but he never left my thoughts.

I drove the car to work on Wednesday so that I could leave immediately for Knoxville when the day was done. My hands started to tremble as I drove up to the Solway gate. Would they stop me again?

It was a different guard. He looked at my badge, asked when I expected to return and waved me forward. I crossed the bridge holding my breath, praying he would not have second thoughts. When I reached the other side of the span, I exhaled loudly. I'd made it out. I now focused my thoughts on my memories of the woman who had most shaped my life – Aunt Dorothy.

TWENTY-THREE

I'd enjoyed my aunt's visits to the farm as far back as I could remember. My mother often referred to Dorothy as a 'modern woman', using the phrase as an insult. When my father said it, though, it was with pride – his sister's education and accomplishments were laudable in his mind.

Dorothy Clark, with her exceptional education and prominent position at Bryn Mawr, was a formidable role model. She always visited at Christmas bearing gifts and every year one of her wrapped packages was a new book or two for me.

Aunt Dorothy grew even more important to me when tragedy upended my life. I was only ten years old when my father died in a house fire in a valiant but failed attempt to rescue my brother. The burden of running the farm fell largely on me, as Mother withdrew into the shelter of willing helplessness. I took on responsibility for both of our lives, at times staggering under the oversized load.

Six months later, Mother made an unfortunate decision, marrying Ernest Floyd. He'd lost his own farm when the impact of the Great Depression hit rural Virginia and he proceeded to run our flourishing homestead into the ground, too. When the finances grew too pinched for comfort, he fired the farmhand and forced me to drop out of school to work full-time caring for livestock and the land. Aunt Dorothy came to the rescue, spiriting me to her home near Philadelphia to continue my education.

I couldn't fathom the bleakness of the life I would have led under Ernest's thumb – uneducated, stifled, devoid of any hope in the future. I shuddered at the thought. I felt a lot of animosity toward Mother for not standing up for me and not protecting me from her second husband. I was grateful for Aunt Dorothy's intervention. It was a debt I could never repay.

Pulling up to the Andrew Johnson Hotel on Gay Street, I slipped off my muddy galoshes, replacing them with a pair of black pumps decorated with black-eyed susan bows, tucked a black envelope purse under my arm, and stepped out of the car. I brushed off the wrinkles in my skirt and walked into the lobby of the hotel.

At the front desk, the clerk called up to Aunt Dorothy's room and said, 'Miss Clark will be down in a moment.' I stood by the elevator waiting for her arrival. Aunt Dorothy stepped out in a pinstriped suit that I didn't remember. After exchanging a hug, I asked, 'New suit?'

'Yes, it's the latest in patriotic fashion,' Aunt Dorothy said with a chuckle.

'Patriotic?'

'The newest rage, my dear. Plunder the attic for your father's old suits and turn them over to the seamstress who turns it into a woman's suit with scraps of fabric left over for making quilts. I bought one of those, too. You won't believe how warm they are with all those squares of worsted wool. After using it for a few cold nights, I put my name on the waiting list for another one to send down to you.'

We didn't say much until after we were seated and had placed our orders. Then, Aunt Dorothy said, 'I imagine what you want to discuss with me is not fit for a public forum. I thought we could save that for after dinner in my room and just catch up on other things.'

'I don't know what I could possibly talk about in my life that doesn't touch on the big issue. So, please, tell me all the news from back home and how your new graduate school of social work is going.'

Dorothy talked about my old friends from the neighborhood and school – most were still at home, waiting for boyfriends or husbands to return from the war, but two of them were now nurses working in the Pacific theater. I silently said a quick prayer for the safety of those now in harm's way. I listened to her description of the progress she'd achieved at the school but had to struggle to focus and prevent my thoughts from drifting to the matter in the forefront of my mind.

'Now, Libby, surely there is something about life in general in your new home that you can tell me about. For example, how are you doing for food?'

'Well, I eat a lot of spam and canned salmon but I am so happy to be able to make my own dinners. The food in the cafeteria was atrocious. Vegetables are cooked to death and loaded up with fatback. And chicken is usually fried to a crisp – all very southern cooking, much like my mother's. But I've gotten so used to Mrs Schmidt's cooking that it was a real shock to go back to the way I used to eat.'

'Is it difficult to get the food and other things you need?'

'Sometimes. Unlike the women with husbands and children and no jobs, I don't have whole days to stand in line. I do it when I know it's something I need but I don't have the time to join mysterious queues and hope there's something worthwhile at the end.'

'People do that?'

'Oh, yes,' I said and laughed. 'Remember me writing to you about my friend Ann?'

'Is that the girl who had you over for Thanksgiving dinner?'

'Yes, that's the one. I was so impressed that her mom was able to pull together everything for a traditional meal that day, I talked to her about how she did it. Mrs Bishop said she'd always keep an eye on her front window. If she saw a group of women heading down toward Towncenter, she'd grab her purse, follow them and get in line. She didn't know what they were selling but when she got to the front of the line, she'd buy whatever it was. She figured if it was something she didn't need, she could trade it with someone for something she did want.'

'What a strange way to live. Life is peculiar for everyone right now with the rationing but it certainly seems a bit worse down here.'

'Yes, it is. But at least we have some shops now. When I first got here, the only store was Williamson's drugstore and it was nothing more than one glass counter with cosmetics, aspirin and things like that set up in the corner of the cafeteria. There's one item, though, that's pretty easy to get here – easier than most places, I would imagine.'

'What's that?'

'Stockings. I can get all I want whenever I need them.'

'Are you serious?'

'Oh, yes. How do you think I could send you three pairs at Christmas?'

'I couldn't imagine how difficult that was at the time. But now, you're saying it's easy. How's that possible?'

'There's a hosiery manufacturing plant right outside of the gates in a town called Clinton. Inside the fence, there are several women who have family working there. They make a little money on the side by selling them to the rest of us.'

'Lucky you. Feel free to send me stockings every birthday and Christmas for the duration of the war.'

With dinner eaten and all the conversation fit to be overheard done, Aunt Dorothy requested coffee for two in her room. As we ascended in the elevator, I ran over the important points I wanted to make, apprehensive about her reaction to it all.

TWENTY-FOUR

I tried to deliver the facts of the situation and keep my emotions in check but sometimes my voice caught in my throat, betraying me. I explained about meeting Ruth's sister, Irene, for the first time on Christmas night, the search for Irene the next day, and the discovery of the body under the bleachers at the high school football field.

Although horribly tragic, those facts marched straight and true to the drumbeat of reality. Aunt Dorothy murmured and nodded in response as I ticked off the details.

Then I had to veer away from the typical thread of a tale of murder to a place where everything became distorted like a step through Alice's looking glass into an alternate universe where facts were incidental and truth was variable. I knew this part of my story would be the most difficult for Aunt Dorothy to accept at face value.

'The police insist there was no body under the bleachers. The military agreed with them. So who moved Irene's body from where I'd seen it with my own eyes to where it was later found on the other side of the Solway Bridge?'

Aunt Dorothy's face grew long and pale as the story twisted into something unrecognizable. I told her about the promise I made to Ruth and Hank, my frustrating encounter with the sheriff, my confrontations with army officers and civilians, and the military's inquisitive visit to Ann's home.

Two things I kept to myself were the mittens with the menacing message and the unsettling stare from the mysterious Dr Smith. I wasn't sure they were related to the big problem and I didn't want to make Aunt Dorothy worry anymore than she already was.

After I finished, we sat in silence for a few moments. Then Aunt Dorothy said, 'So as I understand it, your dilemma is between a promise to a friend and the insistence by the authorities that revelation would be detrimental to the war effort. Is that correct?'

'Yes, ma'am.'

'Do you have any reason to suspect that Irene was involved in anything nefarious?'

'You mean, like spying? No. She was nothing more than a fun-loving girl looking for good times and a husband. Nothing more serious than that ever crossed her mind. I'm certain of it.'

'If that's true,' she said, 'then there would be no official reason that she needed to be silenced.'

'Silenced? You think our government would do such a thing? Kill a civilian?'

'Worse things have happened in time of war. If she saw something she wasn't supposed to see, whether she understood the importance of it or not, who knows? When the stakes are this high, some men will stop at nothing.'

I tried to process this possibility but it conflicted with my notions about my government. 'How could that be possible?'

'The people have given up so much in the name of this cause. I have. You have. I believe our mission is just. I believe this war is necessary. But no matter how valiant the effort and how willing the populace, we no longer have freedom of movement throughout this country. We no longer have ready access to goods and food. We no longer have any assumptions about privacy in our correspondence. No matter how great the cause, there are always scoundrels around – men in power who will use this trying time and these extraordinary circumstances to seek their own advantage. That's one possibility. Another is that this unknown boyfriend is someone whose work is vital to the war effort and no one wants to interfere with his progress. The last possibility I can imagine is that you've been told the truth. They are genuinely concerned about the morale and they fear what would happen if the residents lost their sense of safety and security. And then, of course, there is the possibility that it is a combination of the above or something that hasn't even crossed my mind.'

'Poor Irene, a simple country girl dazzled by her new life, she didn't deserve to be discarded as if she didn't matter. And now the authorities are willing to destroy her memory by alluding that she was up to no good at the hutments.'

'The hutments?' Aunt Dorothy asked.

I described the primitive living conditions in the colored area of the community. 'I don't know how our government can treat human beings that way.'

'It's deplorable how the poor are treated the whole world over, Libby. I've been working to change that all my life.'

I was lost in despairing thoughts about the intransigence of poverty until Aunt Dorothy spoke again. 'Before you make your decision on your course of action, Libby, make sure you are certain that there is no possibility that Irene did something that made her a target. If she's in the wrong, you do not want to join her.'

'Irene worked in the guest house, Aunt Dorothy. She was never near any of the labs. Nothing that I can understand, or even imagine, would make Irene a threat to security.'

'You're probably right. And the first question is: who moved the body? Was it the same person who killed her?'

'I don't think it could have been her killer. Irene was there until the police and military arrived and I can't imagine them standing idly by while the murderer whisked away the body. It had to be the army or law enforcement that moved the body or someone working under their auspices.'

'Are you sure she was seeing that married scientist exclusively?

Are you certain she wasn't seeing someone else at the same time and when that man found out about the scientist, he flew into a jealous rage? Maybe that man was a policeman and the department wanted to protect one of their own. Or maybe a soldier – or even an officer, a high-ranking one possibly – whom the military thought was too essential to the mission.'

'She'd dated all of the above,' I had to admit. 'But Ruth believed that her sister was only seeing the one man right before she died. I suppose, though, that one of her former dates could have killed her in anger because she ended their relationship.'

'Jealous rage is a strong motive, you can't overlook it. Sometimes the line between love and hate can run precariously thin. For the sake of argument, let's say you decided to keep your promise to the Nance family. What do you think would be the first thing you should do?'

'I'd say the most productive first step would be to determine the identity of that married scientist named Bill.'

'I agree: that is logical.'

'But how can I do that, Aunt Dorothy? I'm being watched. I know it. I have to be careful. I can't put an announcement in the newspaper. I can't ask everyone I see. And to make it even more complicated, all the top scientists have code names and I don't know if "Bill" is his real name or an alias.'

'You're not an investigator. You can't do this on your own. You need allies. So who would be your best choice? The women in the dorm who knew Irene?'

'No, except for Ruth who's now back home, there's no one there who really trusts me. They hold me at a distance because I'm unnatural. I'm not waiting for the war to end so that I can get married and make babies, because my work is more important to me than a happy little home in the suburbs.'

'What about the young scientists you work with? Now that I mention it, that does sound best. You scientists naturally question authority and seek meaningful answers. Wouldn't that be the best place to turn since you're looking for one of them?'

'That's just it, Aunt Dorothy. I don't fit in there, either, because I'm not a man.'

'You've got to play the hand you're dealt, Libby. Don't waste time hoping for the impossible. There is a special power in being a woman and you've been gifted with more than just good looks. You're intelligent, educated and full of common sense. You're a strong woman, Libby Clark. You've demonstrated that all of your life.'

'But Aunt Dorothy that takes me back to the first and most basic question: is it right for me to pursue these answers?'

Dorothy leaned forward and grabbed both of my hands and looked into my eyes. 'Let's start with what you know for a certainty. You know you promised Ruth that you would find out what happened to her sister, right.'

'Yes,' I said, nodding my agreement.

'You accepted a car from her family in order to help you keep that promise, correct.'

'Yes.'

'You've been told that keeping that promise would be a violation of the nation's security, right?'

'Yes, but not specifically why – it was so vague.'

'That's right, Libby. You don't know for a fact that it is an honest claim because you have not been given details and because those who told you are possibly involved in Irene's murder or in the cover-up of that crime. If they are involved, it would be irresponsible and immoral for you to allow them to get away with it.'

'Agreed.'

'So tell me madam scientist, when you put those two opposing viewpoints on the scale, which side wins?'

'My promise. But if I do what is right, I could lose my position here. I could be sent home in disgrace. I could embarrass you.'

'If you stand up for your principles and do what you think is right, I will never be ashamed of you and I will always stand by your side with pride. You must look for answers unless or until you uncover something that tells you that you are endangering the nation's security or crippling the war effort. If that happens, stop long enough to think it through and re-evaluate the situation – make sure what appears to be is actually what is. Then, if it is, take that knowledge and move in that direction, even if it means putting it all into reverse.'

I closed my eyes in a vain attempt to stop the tears seeping through my eyelashes. 'Am I strong enough, Aunt Dorothy?'

'Absolutely! But beyond that, you have to be clever. You need to think carefully about who your allies should be and then pursue them in any way you can. And if you make a mistake along the way, learn from it and move forward to your goal.'

'Irene deserves justice – who could deny that? That goal should not be dismissed by anyone in this country.'

'You are right, she does. Seek the truth and find that justice – not just for Irene and her family but for all of us. We are not working to defeat the Axis just to destroy ourselves along the way.'

TWENTY-FIVE

A t the Solway gate, soldiers stopped my car and made me get out of the vehicle and wait on the side while they searched it, paying close attention to the glove box and the trunk. When they finished, one of them asked, 'Where were you?'

'The Andrew Johnson Hotel.'

'Why were you there?'

'To visit with my aunt who is travelling through the area on business.'

'What is your aunt's name?'

'Dorothy Clark.'

'Wait right here,' he said then walked away and talked into his mobile radio. He waited in silence with his back rigid. I knew this delay was not the typical treatment for returning workers. Other residents would not be scrutinized in this way. But if they thought it would discourage me, they were wrong; it merely made me more convinced that I was right and firmed up my determination to find the truth.

The radio squawked. He spoke into it, his words indiscernible from the distance. He marched back and stood in front of me. 'Your story has been confirmed, Miss Clark, you may pass.'

I was seething at the injustice as I stepped back into the car wondering who was behind it all. I could probably make a long list of the possibilities. I needed to think about who I could trust. The first person that came to mind was Gregg Abbott. I had some doubts about him, too, but I would have to take some risks or give up without trying.

The lab was in a state of high energy when I walked in the next morning. The new Calutron was being installed. It was only a matter of days before we'd actually have some product from it and be able to get down to serious work. We all tested and retested equipment, checked supplies, and did all we could to make sure we'd be ready when the racetrack was up and running.

Mid-morning, I slipped over to Gregg's station and asked, 'Think I could tag along with you at lunch?'

His eyes scanned my face as if, by doing so, he could find a reason for my request hidden there. Then he asked, 'Something on your mind, Clark?'

'Yes, Abbott.'

'Something serious?'

I nodded.

'OK,' he said. 'We'll need to be the last to leave so that everyone is already seated and less likely to join our table.'

I agreed and went back to my work station. At lunchtime, I watched as one by one, the others drifted out on their way to the cafeteria. I cleared up my area and acted busy in order to leave the moment Gregg gave the word. Finally, he approached and said, 'Ready?'

'Yes,' I said, grabbing my coat. At the door, we slipped off our good shoes and slid into our galoshes to trudge down the street.

'I've noticed you've seemed preoccupied lately, Clark.'

'Yes, I have been. By the way, I wouldn't mind if you called me Libby.'

'I wouldn't mind that either,' he said with a grin. 'I always use your last name at work because I wanted to deliver the message that I considered you an equal.'

'I appreciate that, Gregg. You may be in a minority, though.'

'No, there are a few dinosaurs in the lab but most of them are smart enough and progressive enough to understand that a woman can be as smart – or smarter – than the rest of us. The others just make us look bad. Is that what this is about? Is one of the chemists giving you trouble?'

'No, Gregg. I wish that were the problem, but it's far more serious.'

Gregg pulled open the cafeteria door and said, 'Let's get something to eat and find a corner where we can talk without being disturbed.'

After we settled at a table, Gregg said, 'I don't know if you noticed but as we walked back here, a few guys waved at me, trying to get me to join them. I pretended as if I didn't see them but it's bound to stir up some talk.'

'You mean about us?' I asked and Gregg nodded. 'I don't mind. I stopped paying attention to idle chatter a long time ago.'

'So what's your problem?'

'Before I start, I need to know that if you don't want to help, you'll keep what I tell you in confidence.'

Gregg furrowed his brow. 'Does this have anything to do with the war effort, Libby?'

I swallowed hard before I answered. 'I've been told it does, Gregg, but I don't believe it. I think I'm being pressured to drop the matter under a false pretense.'

'You've been threatened?'

I nodded.

'Even though you were singled out by General Groves?'

'Yes.'

'Nonetheless, you're confident it is not a matter affecting national security?'

'Gregg, I've been over it in my mind looking for anything that might have a bearing on our war effort. I can't find it. If you see something, I want you to tell me what I'm missing. At this point, I can only conclude that someone is pulling strings for his own personal benefit – using the security threat to protect himself from criminal prosecution.'

'That's a serious charge, Libby.'

'And I don't make it lightly.'

'I never suspected that you would. It's serious enough that if your arguments make sense to me, I will agree to help you and, if I don't I will agree to keep everything you say in confidence.'

'Thank you, Gregg. Well, here goes. The best place to start is to explain about the people involved first.' I outlined my history with Ruth and her sister Irene, the discovery of the body and the events following Irene's murder.

Gregg listened with an open mouth and exclamations of surprise. 'It is difficult to believe. But I don't doubt what you're saying. Libby, if it is a massive cover-up, whoever is behind it must be high up in the organization here.'

'Maybe, Gregg, or maybe it's just a simple matter of

Roane-Anderson or the military not wanting anyone here to know that a crime took place. They're always pushing the image of our safe, crime-free environment.'

Gregg laughed. 'Except for those occasional drunken scuffles.'

'But, they don't really happen, Gregg – they couldn't. We are in a dry county,' I said.

'Sarcasm noted. I know for a fact that the top-ranking officers and the management ranks have cocktail parties on a regular basis.'

'And if there's no one actually hiding a still on the premises, there are plenty of locals peddling Splo.'

'Well, aren't you one in the know. How did you learn about that name for the local home brew? I hope you're not imbibing it. That stuff can kill you,' Gregg warned.

'Don't worry, you won't find me with any Splo. I've seen it in the dorm, but no thank you.' I shivered at the thought of that stuff. 'Seriously, Gregg, would you be willing to help me get to the bottom of Irene's murder?'

Gregg chewed on his lower lip. 'The cautious side of me tells me to run as far from you as I can. But my inquisitive nature abhors questions without answers. I don't know how I could walk away from this, Libby. But I think the two of us will not be enough. We need a gathering of minds, pulling in data and applying logic to find the answers. I think this is a job for the Walking Molecules.'

I squinted at him, not sure if I'd heard him correctly. 'The Walking Molecules?'

'Yeah, it's a pretty silly name, I admit. But it's a group of us from the Alpha lab and the Beta lab who get together once a week to talk about scientific problems and solutions. We look at theoretical issues more than anything.'

'But, the Walking Molecules?'

'Yes, well, we walk, we're comprised of molecules and the night we came up with it, someone had unveiled their secret stash of scotch.'

'You get drunk and talk science?'

'Only occasionally,' Gregg said with a laugh. 'Usually, we wet our whistles with some weak Barbarosa beer in a back room at Joe's. Can't hardly get drunk on that barely improved water.'

'So what do you talk about?'

'A lot of the time, we discuss what we think will be discovered and developed once the war is over and we're not all focused on defeating the enemy. We start with the direction science was headed before Pearl Harbor and the path it will take when the world is at peace again. Sometimes, though, we veer into what was happening in Germany before the wall of silence came down as well as the hints we picked up in journals before the war about the experiements at the University of Chicago, Berkeley, Stanford and Princeton. We talk about what they were doing and, hypothetically, where it might have led.'

'Could be dangerous territory.'

'We're careful not to talk about our work here – after all, we are from two different labs and we can't know what the other lab is doing. One of the group brought along a new textbook one night: *Applied Nuclear Physics*. We've all read it and everything was pretty clear to all of us then. We all know it – we just don't verbalize it. Lately, we've been getting a little philosophical and, in all likelihood, a bit too close to our reality here. We try to check ourselves but in the heat of discussion, it's often difficult to find the brakes.'

'Aren't you concerned that your conversations will be reported to security?'

'Of course, we worry about that but we try to minimize that probability. We know spies have been recruited in all the labs – probably all over the place – some of us have been approached. We've tried to identify and exclude those people, no matter how much we like them or respect them as scientists. We tried to form a group whose commitment to scientific exploration and aversion to absolute authority and regimentation is strong.

'We all take an oath to keep everything said in the group within the group. I've told you more than I have ever told anyone on the outside. No matter how this goes, I need you to keep it all to yourself.'

'I have no problem with that, Gregg.'

'I can't guarantee we don't have any stoolies but the odds are good. Where our discussions have gone lately with the lull in real work has been a bit too near the edge, to my way of thinking. I think it would be good if we all focused on a question that could divert us for a while. Irene's murder might well be the perfect answer.'

'No problem, Gregg. What happens now? Do I just show up at your next meeting?'

'No. You need to be nominated by someone in the group first. I'll do that at the next meeting.'

'When is that?'

'Wednesday night.'

'And what? You just vote on me?'

Gregg hung his head and red spots appeared on his cheeks. 'It's not that simple.'

'Are you embarrassed?'

'Yes, this is the goofy part.'

'Goofy?'

'Actually, I never considered it goofy until just now. It's one of those ritual things that closed organizations tend to adopt.'

'You mean like an induction ritual?'

'More like seeing if you measure up.'

'I can understand that, Gregg. What makes it goofy?'

'Sitting here explaining it to a woman.'

'Really . . .' I objected.

'Well, I have two sisters, one younger and one older. They both gang up on me sometimes about the inadequacy of men.'

My lips twitched as I suppressed a laugh. 'And . . .?'

'I can hear my older sister Isabelle now. If I told her about this, she'd say: "For the life of me, I cannot understand why men get to run the world when you act like boys so much of the time."'

'She does have a point . . .'

'I can't argue against it. I just tell her, "Please, take over. See how well you handle it." And she says, "We're trying, little brother."'

'So, tell me, what is this ritual? Even if I think it is ridiculous, I'll have to do it, right?'

'Yes, otherwise you won't be seen as a proper member of the group if we make an exception for you. I'll propose you and if the majority agrees to allow you to take the test, we'll do it. Probably next Sunday.'

'What would I have to do, Gregg?'

'You have to go into Dossett Tunnel, the railroad tunnel up in the hills.'

'Is that all?'

'It's not as easy as it sounds.'

'And I'm a lot tougher than I look.'

'Look, maybe I could get them to make an exception.'

'Don't you dare! If I want their help, I need to prove myself. Don't even suggest anything less. Is that clear?'

'I don't think you know what you're getting into, Libby, but you sure sound a lot like my older sister.'

'As you said, Gregg, I have to do what I have to do or I will never be considered an equal in the group. I've been fighting for respect since I left the comfort of an all-female university and I'm not going to stop now.'

'OK. Thursday at work, I'll let you know what happens at the next meeting.'

For the next couple of days, I tensed whenever I saw anyone looking in my direction. I had that continuous, uncomfortable feeling that someone was always looking over my shoulder, following me down the street. Was it all in my imagination or was I under official scrutiny on a day-to-day basis? In an environment of hyper-security, it was hard to separate normal observation from special treatment.

Thursday morning, I held my breath as Gregg walked across the lab. 'We're on,' he said. 'It wasn't easy. Some objected to a woman in the group on general principle. A couple of us shamed them out of their backward, nineteenth-century attitude. But I need to warn you: there are those who are hoping you'll chicken out or fail.'

'I can handle that,' I asserted, my chin involuntarily thrusting upward. I'd faced bigger challenges growing up on the farm that anything these men could possibly offer.

'OK, then. We'll all meet up at the Elza gate at 0800 Sunday morning and hike through the woods to the tunnel.'

'I'll be there.'

Gregg looked down at my pair of navy pumps. 'I hope you have something better than those to wear on the hike.'

'I was raised a farm girl. For as long as I can remember, I've had a pair of Chippewa ranger shoes – they don't get much sturdier than that. So, don't you worry about me keeping up, Gregg.'

'I hope I don't regret this.'

'Gregg, I promise, I will not embarrass you.'

'That's not my worry, Libby. I know you won't act like a girl, oh man, I mean . . .'

I laughed at his distress. 'That's all right, Gregg. I know what you mean.'

'Sorry. But it's your safety I'm worried about, Libby.'

'Don't.'

'Can't help myself. The first time I saw the Dossett Tunnel, I wanted to run away as fast as I could.'

TWENTY-SIX

No one had exaggerated in their descriptions of the Dossett Tunnel – more than a mile long and a fearsome sight to behold. Huge piles of blasted black rock funneled into a dark, forbidding hole. Would it look less menacing in spring with the green leaves of kudzu cascading over its face? Probably. In the dead of winter, though, the bright growth was gone. All that remained was a skeleton of brown vines gripping the rocks in a stranglehold.

I stepped onto the tracks and walked closer, stepping on one railroad tie then the next. When I reached the maw of darkness, I could see a faraway, small shape of light. The light at the end of the tunnel; I'd heard that phrase many times but the reality of it was never as visceral as it was now, a tiny bead of hope at the end of an ominous emptiness.

My whole body felt peculiar – weary from the hike to the tunnel, invigorated by the fresh air, jittery with excited anticipation, nauseous from the surge of adrenaline. I heard the others breathing. Which of them hoped I'd simply take a look and walk away? Which of them imagined me bursting into tears? Did any of them really believe that I would succeed?

But I had to do it. I needed their help. To get it, I had to prove that I was just as good, just as brave, as they were. I sucked in a deep breath, inhaling the first traces of the acrid smoke that bellowed from the trains, lingered in the confines of the rock and drifted out into the trees. I sucked in another breath as if it would imbue me with courage. 'I guess this is it,' I said and took another step closer.

'You gotta go halfway or it doesn't count,' Tom said. With his thick hank of bright red hair, a sprinkling of freckles across the bridge of his nose, and a nearly perpetual sneer, he looked like a schoolyard bully. Although he didn't utter the playground challenge of 'double dog dare you', I felt the words hanging in the air. He had to have been one of the men who objected to the addition of a female.

Teddy, one of the scientists from the Alpha lab, handed me a flashlight. 'Good luck,' he said. With his dark, curly hair and sparkling blue eyes, he could easily be quite a charmer over dinner or on the dance floor.

Gregg reached out and touched my forearm. 'Just halfway, then turn around and come back.' His pupils floated in liquid fear. Was he more afraid than I was?

I forced a brave smile, then stepped into the tunnel. The stench of burnt coal tasted harsh in my mouth and felt tight in my lungs. I walked until the light from the entryway faded, the inkiness felt like a physical substance brushing against my skin, before I turned on the flashlight. The rock was so black it seemed to absorb the light, pulling it from the bulb and swallowing it whole.

I kept moving forward one step at a time. The flashlight shook in my hand. I successfully banished the fear of the approaching train only to have it replaced by a more intense terror at the thought of being crushed to death by the collapse of this manmade passageway. A slight shift in the earth and one boulder after another could tumble down, crushing my bones. First, I'd be pinned to the ground. Then, one by one, every bone in my body would break, my lungs would collapse, I'd be dead. Would they bother trying to dig out my body? Or would they all – like scared little boys – scurry back to town, vowing one another to secrecy, pricking their fingers, mingling their blood with an oath that was eternal.

My foot faltered as I slipped on a slick tie. I pulled in my gut to support my back and regain a sense of balance. I shook my head to drive out the morbid products of my imagination, filling the void with a recitation of the periodic table – Hydrogen, Helium, Lithium, Beryllium, Boron, Carbon, Nitrogen – one element for each step. Then I heard shouting.

'That's far enough.'

'You made it.'

'Come back.'

'Turn around'

'Come back now.'

I heard them yell but kept moving forward. To succeed in a male-dominated world, I couldn't just be as good as them, I had to be better. I'd make it to Iron, the symbol of strength, before turning back. Oxygen, Flourine, Neon, Sodium, Magnesium, Aluminum, Silicon, Phosphorous . . .

Their shouts grew more frenzied, a pleading tone echoed in the tunnel. Still I walked forward – one element, one step. Sulfur, Chlorine, Argon, Potassium, Calcium, Scandium, Titanium, Vanadium, Chromium, Manganese, Iron . . .

I paused, raised my arms in the air and pirouetted to face the path I'd traveled. Fear clutched my throat; the entrance looked so far away, the window of light too small. I started walking back, still reciting the periodic table to keep my terrors at bay. I shuddered when the element Arsenic passed my lips. Was there someone in the group aligned with the perpetrator of Irene's murder or with those who wanted to cover up the crime? If so, did he now pray to an evil God for the arrival of a train – a rushing, relentless monster of metal that would obliterate my life as if it had never been?

Maybe the whole group was being used by outside forces to silence me permanently. It would look like nothing more than a tragic accident. Once I was dead, the tunnel would become officially off-limits. Maybe they'd even post a guard.

Red lights flashed danger inside my head. The surging fight-or-flight response screamed at me to run but I refused to listen. I had to maintain my dignity to really pass the test and besides, the possibility of twisting an ankle on the ties or tripping and falling on the uneven surface was great.

Then, I felt the vibrations under my feet. Dread and disbelief exploded and raced through my limbs. My fingers went numb. I moved faster now, taking more risks. I heard renewed, even louder, shouting.

'Hurry!'

'Run!'

'Get out of there!'

I walked as quickly as I could, afraid if I broke into a run, I was sure to fall. I heard a roar echoing through the tunnel. I looked over my shoulder. I could no longer see the exit – just one round light piercing the gloom, moving closer. It was gaining on me, I had to move faster. I broke into a stumbling run. I was a few yards away from the end when a hand grabbed and pulled me faster.

When my feet tangled up, an arm encircled my waist, holding me up, propelling me forward. We broke into open air and kept moving, past the barrier of solid rock, tumbling to the side, into the dirt. A hand pushed down on my back. I lay flat, turning to look at who came to my aid. Teddy; he'd introduced himself to me on the hike up to the tunnel and he made it clear that he didn't resent my infiltration. I mimicked his actions – pursing my mouth tight, squeezing my eyes shut, putting my hands over my ears.

Still the noise was overwhelming; it vibrated in my teeth, rang in my ears. A rush of hot, vile air spewed out as if from the throat of a demonic dragon. It washed over me, filling my airways. Gravel pinged on my face. I pressed my nose into the ground and felt tiny, stinging attacks on the top of my head. For a moment, I did not believe I would survive.

Then it was over, as suddenly as a nightmare. I looked up, amazed. I pushed up on all fours and rose to my feet, my wobbling knees barely able to hold my weight. On the opposite side of the track, the others straggled towards us. No one spoke. Teddy's hand grabbed mine again, jerking my arm upward.

'The champion!' he screamed.

Across the tracks, the others erupted in a raucous cheer. I knew that some barriers still remained but I had taken a step closer to being one of them. Or, perhaps Teddy's act of bravery was nothing more than a smokescreen. A false front designed to trip me up, to put me in his debt, to be a stumbling block in my search for answers. As I looked at Teddy, though, a grin split his face, not a trace of duplicity marred his features. But if he were clever enough to come to my rescue with a dark purpose in mind, wouldn't he be sharp enough to craft an impenetrable mask?

I set aside those dark thoughts and reveled in the newfound camaraderie with my fellow chemists. I couldn't stop grinning as they patted me on the back and commented on my gutsiness

– 'pretty damn tough for a girl', 'Ought sic her on Adolph', 'Let her spit in the eye of the kamikaze'. The high spirits and banter continued all the way down the hill and into town, ending only when the men entered the Benton Hall and I continued on to my little flattop home.

After a shower and a bowl of soup, I went straight into bed. I was physically exhausted and emotionally drained; still, questions about the risk of trusting this strange little group of Walking Molecules kept me awake for more than an hour. When I finally drifted off to sleep, their faces haunted my dreams.

TWENTY-SEVEN

A special meeting of the Walking Molecules was called for Monday night to discuss my problem, propose theories and outline action steps. I was nervous. Sure I'd impressed them with my bravado on Sunday but could I dazzle them with logic in a calmer setting? I opted to eliminate emotion and focus on hard facts; a scientific explanation as if addressing a symposium.

'Before Libby starts, let's go around the table and give our names to refresh our newest member's memory. As you know, I am Gregg and this is Libby.'

The redhead next to Gregg said, 'Tom.'

He was followed by the sandy-haired bespectacled Joe; my rescuer from Dossett Tunnel, Teddy; the chubby, buck-toothed Gary; then Stephen, with the whitest complexion I'd ever seen.

'Rudy,' said a brown-haired, brown-eyed man who never seemed to put out a cigarette until he had another one lit. Next to him was Dennis, a tall, rangy guy with a face that looked like a stereotypical westerner. Finally, the man with a large, bulbous nose and a prominent Adam's apple said, 'Marvin.'

I summarized the problem first: my discovery of the body, its disappearance and the official version of events. I postulated theories to explain the sequence of events including the actions of a single person, the cover-up by police and administration and a conspiracy by the military. I concluded with a risk assessment.

'I have clearly been warned that the pursuit of answers in the mystery of Irene Nance's death could be detrimental to my career. As a scientist, I can't help but bristle when any authority tries to interfere with the finding of facts. As a human being, I am conflicted by my obligation to my country and my commitment to my friend. I have resolved these diametrically opposed needs by reaching the conclusion that the former is a false paradigm.

'It is up to each one of you to decide if you want to help me uncover the truth behind these events and, thus, put your careers in jeopardy. No one can make that decision for you. If you decide to back away, I only ask that you hold this matter in confidence as you all vowed you would any discussion occurring within this group. Thank you.'

I stared down at the surface of the table, unwilling to look any of them in the eye, fearing that they would all look away. For a couple of minutes no one spoke. The only sound in the room was caused by bodies shifting their weight in chairs, beer mugs sipped and set back down on the table and a host of erratic sighs and audible exhalations.

Gregg spoke up first. 'As you all know, I brought Libby into our group because I believed that she had a need to uncover facts and that we might possess the ability to help her do so. I, for one, will assist her in this project whether the group chooses to become involved or not.'

'Do you say that because you and Clark are stuck on each other?' Tom asked, a leering expression on his face.

Gregg jerked his head toward Tom's voice. 'If we were, so what? That wouldn't alter the problem under consideration. But here are the facts: Clark and I work together in the same lab. I have great respect for her competence in the lab and the nimbleness of her mind. Until last week, we had never met each other outside of Y-12. And then we had lunch together to discuss this same problem.'

'But, Gregg,' Tom said. 'She's a woman. You know how they overreact and exaggerate.'

Gregg leaned forward, his elbows resting on the table. 'How can you overreact to a murder? How can you exaggerate a murder? It was a murder, you know. That's not an exaggeration. The authorities admit it is a murder. The only dispute is over where it happened. Or do you disagree with that, Tom? Do you think you know more than the police, the sheriff's office and the military?'

'But you only have her word on that, don't you?' Tom taunted.

I held my anger at bay, sensing that any interference from me could possibly send some of the group out of the room and, thus, decimate any hope of cooperation. As long as others were defending me, I was safer simply observing.

'Oh, come on, Tom,' Teddy interjected. 'We've all heard that Irene Nance is dead. We've all heard about her body being found outside the Solway gate. We all heard the preachy message about the dangers that lurk out there among some of the disenfranchised locals.'

'Yeah, but before now, we never heard anything about a body being found in the high school bleachers, did we? What if she's making it all up to get attention?' Tom asked.

Joe, the archetypal quiet one, with his studious demeanor and thick, dark-framed glasses, cleared his throat. Every head turned in his direction. 'I find it quite offensive that someone would question the honesty and integrity of one of our scientific peers without cause.' When he paused, no one said a word or made a move, except for Tom who pushed back from the table and rolled his eyes. 'It seems obvious to me,' Joe continued, 'that the first step here is to determine who among us has ever dated the deceased.'

Gary, who seemed to follow Tom's lead, snickered. 'Who hasn't?'

Tom spoke up again. 'I really don't like speaking ill of the dead . . .'

I jerked my head up and snapped, 'Then don't!' I looked at the faces of the men gathered around me. 'Are you telling me that every one of you dated Irene Nance?'

The question was greeted with a mingled mutter of yeses and nos. 'How about a show of hands?' To my surprise, five of the nine men present raised their hands. 'My word. Well, I guess I shouldn't be surprised. Her sister said she went out every night of the week.'

'I regret saying this,' Joe said, 'but everyone who raised a hand is now a suspect. Perhaps we should discuss the nature and duration of your relationships with Miss Nance?'

Teddy's face flushed. 'It wasn't much for me. In October, I

took her to a dance in the cafeteria. Then a couple of nights later, we just went walking.'

'Where, Teddy?' Joe asked.

'I don't remember exactly where but we ended up at the football field at the high school.'

'On the bleachers, Ted?' Tom asked.

'Well, yes, actually we did. We sat down on them and looked at the moon.'

'Looked at the moon? Oh yeah, I bet that's all you did,' Tom said and guffawed.

'Look,' Teddy said. 'We did hold hands and I kissed her twice . . .'

'Was she a good kisser?' Tom teased.

'Shut up, Tom,' Gregg snapped. 'You were saying, Ted?'

'I thought we had something going,' Teddy admitted, 'but after that night, I asked her out four or five more times. She was always busy, always had a date with someone else. I finally gave up. I've only seen her in passing since.'

One by one, the other men who dated Irene described their brief fling with her. Not one of them admitted to getting any further with her than hand-holding and a kiss or two.

Tom blew out a long breath. 'And what have we got – a bunch of suspects who want us to take their word for what happened with no proof, no documentation.'

'That's really not a helpful attitude,' Joe said. He stared at Tom and used his middle finger to push the center of his glasses up higher on his nose. 'We need to trust one another unless and until that is shown to be unwise. Does everyone else agree with that?'

Murmurs of agreement went around the table. Stephen, pale as a worm and thin as a zipper, rose to his feet and paced the length of the table, his body leaning forward at a near impossible angle while he walked. 'Don't we need to start with an inventory, as it were? A list of all the scientists so we can know who is called Bill here at – uh, we can call this place Oak Ridge now, can't we?'

'Yes,' Gregg said, 'At least inside the fence. I don't think we're supposed to use the name if we go into Knoxville or any of the little towns around here.'

'OK, well, how can we get all those names?'

'I can ask Ann Bishop, I think she might give me a list,' I offered. 'But she's only going to have names for those in Y-12. We know work has started at K-25 but I, for one, have no idea if it's still in the basic construction stage or if scientists are at work in functional labs.'

'But, Libby,' Gregg said, 'if we don't know anything about or anyone working at K-25, how would Irene?'

'She worked at the guest house. She saw all sorts of people. She once described a man who was the spitting image of Enrico Fermi but she said his name was Eugene Farmer. Who knows who else she met there?'

'So it could be a resident scientist or a visiting scientist,' Stephen said. 'Does anyone have any contacts at K-25?'

The question was greeted by a shaking of heads. 'We need to start somewhere. Why not Y-12? That is what we know,' Teddy said.

'I hate to complicate matters even more,' Stephen said. 'But what if this Bill guy wasn't the one who killed her? What if someone else did out of jealousy or some other motive?'

'I thought about that, Stephen, and you're right,' I agreed. 'But we need to approach this problem in a linear fashion. If we discover data that points to another possibility, we need to retain that information for possible exploration, but we need to start somewhere and focus on the answer to one question before moving on to others.'

Nods went around the table. Everyone agreed to attempt to identify anyone they could whom they knew as Bill or who was hiding behind an official alias. They would meet again on Wednesday. At last something was being done. But my relief was short-lived as I tried to fall asleep. What if I had placed my trust in the wrong hands?

TWENTY-EIGHT

After work the next day, I stoked up the fire in the coal stove in the living room and put on a pot of water as soon as I walked in the front door. Hot tea was the perfect antidote to a nippy night, filling me with a delightful warmth with each swallow and driving the stiffness out of my fingers as I held the cup tight in my hands.

As soon as my digits felt limber, I picked up stationary, a pen and the letter I had received from Ruth the previous week. I reread the chatty correspondence, chuckling about the convoluted and subtle way Ruth had referred to her sister's murder. To the censors, it had to sound like nothing more than the nearly meaningless babble of a shallow young woman.

Ruth's craftiness in her composition was impressive. I would have never thought that my open, honest friend was at all capable of subterfuge. Nonetheless, there it was in her own handwriting – words veiled and cloaked but with an underlying meaning as clear as a glass of spring water to me. Ruth needed to know about her sister's death. She wanted to know if I'd made any progress in finding the culprit. The not knowing filled Ruth with an anxiety that magnified her grief. Her silent scream for justice lurked between every line.

I mimicked Ruth's nonchalant tone as I drafted my response, taking care not to use any specific names like Y-12 or Alpha or Beta laboratories. I hoped my meaning was as clear to Ruth as Ruth's had been for me:

Dear Ruthie,

The weather here continues to be dreadful – frigid, icy and only the smallest glimpses of sunshine. The silver lining in the cloud is that the colder it remains, the harder the mud freezes. I haven't heard of anyone losing a shoe in the mud all month. Ha! Ha!

I miss you a lot, Ruthie, and wish you were here. I often long for you to be here to talk over problems with me. But I have made a new group of friends – some scientists from my building. Yes, they are all fellas and I'm the only girl but NO, I'm not stepping out with any one of them.

I get together with my new friends and we discuss different problems and seek solutions. Of course, we cannot talk about work since we are from different areas, but you'd be amazed at how adept they are at applying scientific method to basic, everyday problems. If one gave them a mystery to solve, I'm sure, given a little time, they could solve the toughest one you could imagine. Maybe I should ask them to find out what is really in that loaf they serve in the cafeteria. Ha! Ha! But their conclusions could very well get them in hot water. None of them would care though – finding answers is more important to them than facing the consequences. That's one of the things I really like about them.

Keep warm, Ruthie, and the next time you have a sip of Jack Daniels think of poor, dry me.

Your friend always,
Libby

At 10:30 the next morning, I slipped away from the lab to speak to Ann Bishop. I found her at her desk pounding away on the typewriter. 'Hi, Ann,' I said. 'Got a minute?'

'Oh, do I! My mother just called and wanted me to ask you to dinner tonight.'

'Tonight? Really?'

'Yes. She's so excited. After endless days of meatless spaghetti, tuna casserole and vegetable mishmash, she was the first person in line at the grocery store this morning and got ground beef, ground pork and ground veal to make a meatloaf. She couldn't believe her good fortune and she wanted you to share it with us.' Ann laughed and said, 'Sometimes, I wonder if she thinks that working all day with a bunch of men puts too much temptation in your path and without a mother-figure in your life, you might forget the need to protect your reputation and your chastity.'

I tried not to show any dismay at that remark, hoping there wasn't any truth in it.

'Oh, don't look so shocked, Libby. I was just joking. Mom likes you, that's all. And she wants to have you to dinner.'

'That's very nice of her. Please tell her that I will gladly accept her invitation.'

'Swell! Now what brought you to my desk?' Ann asked.

'You know how it is with those men I work with?'

'Oh, yeah, they think just 'cause they're men, they're smarter.'

'You got it. You wanna help me get back at them?'

'Soitently, pal.'

'I need a list of all the scientists working at Y-12. Can you get that?'

Ann narrowed her eyes. 'What's this all about, Libby?'

'I'm saying that the most common male name in this place is
Bill.'

'You could be right. But it might be Tom.'

'That's what a couple of the guys say. Another one says
Charlie.'

'But what if I give you the list and you're wrong.'

'In that case, there would be a second part to the favor,' I
continued.

Ann cocked her head to the side, 'What do you mean?'

'You could leave off a name here or there and where would
they go to prove that I'm wrong?'

Ann grinned. 'Me?'

'And what will you tell them?'

'I'm not authorized to provide that information, sir. You'll have
to make a request through your supervisor.'

'Exactly,' I said, smiling at her quickness to fall for my scheme.
'That means they would have to go through the building getting
every single name. And with the racetrack about to be up and
running again, they're going to be far too busy.'

'Swell. I'll try to get it ready for you before lunch.'

'Don't take time from anything you need to be doing.'

'No worries, Libby. Nobody ever yells at me 'cause nobody
wants to have to explain why to my dad.'

Ann surprised me by providing a typed document. I'd expected
a hastily scrawled list of names that would be difficult to read.

'And you were right, Libby. If you count up all the men named
William, Wilbur, Wilfred – well, maybe we shouldn't count the
Wilfreds, people usually call them Freddie. But even without
them the Bills win.'

Now that I had what I wanted, I inwardly cringed at how easy
it had been to manipulate Ann. I ran down the list looking for the
men I knew were not married. That left a lot whose marital status
was unknown to me and even more I didn't know at all. Hopefully,
my fellow molecules could help me cull the list down a bit more.

That evening, I drove the car to the Bishop home. It was a
bitterly cold night and I knew Mrs Bishop would insist that her
husband give me a ride home after dinner. And I certainly did
not want to be alone in a car with Dr Bishop, where he could
question me again about security's interest in my actions.

I received another warm welcome from Ann's mother who once again lived up to her sterling reputation as a cook. Dinner was fabulous. I don't think I've ever eaten a tastier meatloaf. Everything went as usual until the end of the meal.

Dr Bishop rose to his feet and said, 'Mother, Ann, if you will excuse us, I would like to have a private word with Miss Clark in the living room. I would really not like to be disturbed.'

A lump lodged in my throat. I swallowed hard but it wouldn't go away. Did Ann mention what she did for me today? Was he going to ask me to never return to his home? Had he heard news that I'd soon be sent packing?

I trailed after him with all the enthusiasm of a condemned man heading for the noose. I remained standing, not knowing what to do until Dr Bishop said, 'Have a seat, Libby.'

I slumped into the nearest chair and summoned up the courage to meet his eyes. 'Yes sir, is there something on your mind?'

'There is, Libby. I imagine you are aware that you are under unusual scrutiny at this time.'

'Yes, sir. I certainly am. I think it's unwarranted but—'

'I am not here to chastise you for anything you have done or you've been accused of doing. I consider myself a good judge of character and I don't find yours lacking.'

'Thank you for your confidence in me, sir.'

'You've earned that, Miss Clark. And although I've been questioned about you more than once, I do not want to put you in a position where you'll feel the need to defend yourself.'

'I could—' I began.

'Quite frankly, the less I know the better. You do understand that, don't you?'

'Yes sir,' I said, as my guts clenched tight waiting for him to drop the 'but' and all that followed it.

'But, I wanted to talk with you about two things. First, although I initially decided to keep this to myself, I think you should know that I have been asked to report back on every visit you make to my home.'

'Have you agreed to do that?' I asked, working hard to keep my feelings of alarm out of my voice and facial expression.

'Yes. But I am telling you because you have never done anything here that is questionable in any way. You've always behaved like a lady and a professional. I've assured them that I have never heard you mention a word about our work in the presence of my wife or daughter. And I'll repeat that in my reports about your visits. I simply felt you had a right to know about this.'

'Thank you, sir. It is kind of you to inform me.'

'How could I do less for a fellow scientist?' he said with a smile that seemed a bit condescending. Still I smiled back.

'The other matter is my daughter. As I said, I don't know what you are involved in, but I do want to make it clear that I do not want you to drag my daughter into your problem in any way.'

Oh dear. Did Ann tell him about the list? 'I would not intentionally do anything to hurt Ann.'

'I have no reason to believe you have done so,' he said to my great relief. 'Nonetheless, I wanted to make my feelings clear. I do not want my daughter compromised in any manner. She is not as educated as you. She is far more naive than you. As her father, I want your assurances that you will not involve her in any manner.'

My conscience screamed for a confession that I'd already involved Ann but my common sense prevailed. 'I promise, sir, that in no time in the future will I ever get Ann involved in anything that is the least bit questionable.' It wasn't a lie but it wasn't the complete truth either; I added deceit onto the list of forgiveness items for my nightly prayers.

After the conversation, I escaped to the kitchen where Ann pressed to know what her father wanted. Fortunately, Mrs Bishop gave me an easy out. 'I imagine it was about work, Ann. You know scientists can't share information about their work with the rest of us. That's what it was, wasn't it, Libby?'

I was chagrined over how easy it was to say, 'Yes.'

TWENTY-NINE

Walking out to the car for the drive home, I suppressed the urge to jump in the air and click my heels. It had been far easier than I thought it would be to turn the conversation away from Ann's line of questioning and onto the

Bishops' trip at Christmastime. Ann washed, I dried and Mrs Bishop put away the dishes while memories of the family's recent holiday trip rolled off the older woman's tongue.

That woman certainly was a talker. It was difficult to feign interest as Mrs Bishop talked about people I didn't know: Aunt Flossie and her bunions, Uncle Freddy's death, a cousin's latest letter from the front and the two – or was that three? – new babies that were added to the clan in recent months. Fortunately, I was able to pay enough attention to ask the right question at the right time.

'Mrs Bishop, I can't help but wonder how you stretched your gasoline ration to travel around to all those households. Weren't you worried you wouldn't have enough fuel to make it back home?'

'Land's sakes no! It wasn't a problem at all. The families planned it all out like a military campaign before we arrived. We went straight from here to my mother-in-law's house on Christmas Eve. They delivered us to the next stop – and so on, down the line. Like a relay race. It was really lots of fun. We didn't get back to Mr Bishop's parent's home – and our car – until the afternoon after Christmas. And *that* certainly put a big pout on my little Annie's face.'

Ann rolled her eyes. 'Please, Mom,' she said and turned to me. 'I accidently left my tube of lipstick in the back seat of our car. I wanted to swing by and get it – we were awfully close when we went to Aunt Minnie's. I couldn't understand why it was out of the question.'

Mrs Bishop crinkled up her nose and pinched Ann's cheeks. 'Isn't she just the cutest thing? I tell her at her age she doesn't need any face paint – she's as pretty as she can be without it.'

Ann lightly swatted at her mother's arm. 'Mother!' she moaned, before grabbing my hands and dragging me out of the kitchen.

After tonight, I could officially scratch Dr Bishop off of my suspect list. His name wasn't Bill, and knowing he was out of town and unable to sneak back on Christmas night because he didn't have access to his automobile made it scientific certainty. Who else on the list would have been away at Christmas under similar circumstances, unable to make a surreptitious trip back to Oak Ridge? It was satisfying to know, that without trying tonight, I'd actually made the list shorter. Somehow, I was going to find answers for Irene's family. As I drove home, I thought I might smile through my dreams.

That sense of well-being dissipated the moment I pulled up to the house. A large shape blocked the steps leading up to my home. It moved. It was alive. It was a man. Should I restart the car and zoom away? But where would I go? Who could I turn to for help?

Cautiously, I stepped out of the car, standing for a moment by the open door. Then I shut it and walked toward the steps. I shuddered as a voice called out, 'Libby!'

It was a familiar voice but whose? 'Who's there?' I asked.

'It's Teddy from Alpha – your fellow Walking Molecule, at your service.'

What in heaven's name was he doing here? 'Hi, Teddy. What are you doing out here in the cold?'

'I'm hoping you'll let me inside before my jaw freezes shut. I learned some information tonight that I thought you'd want to know.'

'I didn't lock the door, Teddy. You could have gone right inside. In fact, I wish you had, you could have gotten the place toasty before I returned.'

'Libby, don't ever leave your door unlocked again.'

'Nobody locks up here, Teddy. We're not in a big city,' I said pushing open the door and stepping inside.

'Yes, but there is a killer on the loose and he could be looking for you. Promise me until he's found, you will lock your door.'

'Teddy . . .'

'Please! If you don't promise, I'll have to camp out on your steps every night.'

'All right. I promise. Now let's get that fire going,' I said and reached for the poker beside the stove. Before I could secure it, Teddy had it firmly in his grasp.

'I'll take care of that,' he said. 'Think maybe you could make us something warm to drink like some coffee or whatever you've got around that you pretend is coffee?'

'I still have some of the good stuff left from Christmas. I'll fix us both a cup.'

Was there something suspicious about Teddy's presence here tonight? Or could I accept what he said at face value. I was on edge and startled when he spoke, nearly dropping the coffee cups

I'd pulled from the cupboard. He stood in the entryway to the kitchen with the coal scuttle dangling from the fingers of one hand. 'I used up all your coal in your stove. I thought I'd refill it for you so you'd have some for the morning.'

'Oh, there's no need, Teddy.'

'Really, I don't mind. And my mother will never forgive me if I didn't act like a gentleman once in a while,' he said with a grin.

'Well then, be my guest. Grab the flashlight by the door. The coal bin is that little thing at the foot of the stairs that looks like a dog house.'

He walked back inside just as I was carrying a tray with a coffee pot, a small plate of cookies and two cups and saucers into the living room. 'Sorry, but I don't have any sugar. I used every last crystal to make these.'

'I like it without, anyway. And cookies? What a treat. Thank you.'

We sat down in chairs on opposite sides of the stove. 'Well, Teddy, you sat out in the cold waiting for me. I have a hard time imagining what tidbit of information could possibly be so important that you'd risk frostbite.'

Teddy sipped and sighed. 'I'll be honest, Libby. Now that I'm sitting here talking about it, I doubt that it's all that important.'

And just what did that mean? I forced a polite smile to remain on my face. What was he up to? 'Really? Why not?'

'You see, what I learned just made me nervous about where you were tonight and I don't think I could have slept if I hadn't made sure you got home safely.'

'How did you know where I was tonight?' I asked, my suspicions about his motivation strengthening.

'Oh, golly, I didn't mean to alarm you. I didn't follow you or anything, I swear. It was Ann Bishop. I'm not carrying a torch for her or anything like that. It's just that I've been hoping if I paid her some attention, she'd invite me to dinner at her house sometime. She doesn't live in the dorm – she lives with her parents and it sounds like her mother's a pretty good cook.'

Ah, that's a man for you. I couldn't help but grin. 'She most definitely is.'

Teddy sighed. 'I've been to her house once when I picked Ann up to go to a movie. I tried to charm her mother without coming right out and begging for a home cooked meal. So far, no luck, but I keep trying. I often asked Ann what her mother's making for dinner. When I asked her today, she told me that you were coming to the house.'

'You were worried about the Bishops?'

'No, I didn't think about them. I guess I should have but I didn't. I wasn't even worried until I went down to Joe's and bumped into an engineer named Mike DeVries.'

'Ugh, DeVries! I had the distinct misfortune of meeting him once and that was enough for a lifetime.'

'Not exactly my favorite person either. He used to live down the hall from me in the dorm. When he got one of the cemesto houses, his wife moved down to join him. But that Mike is a real drugstore cowboy. Always making passes at every dumb Dora he can find. Didn't seem to matter that he was married when his wife was out of town but I thought that would change when she moved here. But judging by his conversation tonight, I don't think it's made any difference to him at all.'

'When I met him before Thanksgiving up at the Calutron, he said he knew Irene.'

'Well, that answers that. When he said that he had a regular dame up until Christmas and finally found a new one to take her place, I asked, Was your last regular girlfriend named Irene? He squinted, glared at me and said, What business is it of yours? Then he threw a buck on the bar and walked out.'

'Yes, but just because he knew Irene doesn't mean that he was her regular boyfriend. I can't imagine what she'd see in a man like him. Why would what DeVries said make you worry about where I was tonight?'

'I went back to the dorm and it hit me. I rushed over here to look for you. I thought about walking the roads you'd take if you walked home but then realized that if you got a ride home, I wouldn't recognize the car. And until you pulled up tonight, I didn't realize you had a car.'

'Teddy, you're still not making sense. What hit you?'

'I remembered where Mike DeVries and his wife lived. They moved into a cemesto just across the street from the Bishops' house. And I started thinking, what if "Bill" was a phony name? Maybe Irene didn't know her boyfriend's real name.'

'And maybe it was Mike?'

'Well, yes. But now that you've said it, I feel like I really stretched my chain of logic all out of shape.'

'I can't argue with that assessment,' I said with a laugh, amused by his runaway concern. 'But, you never know. Do you think we need to take a closer look at DeVries?'

'Well, I'm kind of embarrassed to admit it . . .'

'Admit what, Teddy?'

'I stole his cigarette lighter.'

'What?'

'I'll give it back. It's part of my plan. You see, tomorrow at lunch, I plan to run up to his house to return it and it'll give me a chance to talk to his wife when he should be at work. Never know how much you can learn with innocent questions.'

I laughed out loud. 'That is an outrageous plan.'

Teddy shrugged. 'Desperate men – desperate times.'

'Teddy, I think you are a bit too paranoid.' Suddenly, my suspicions all felt normal in comparison.

'It seems a natural state to me, considering all the secrecy in this place.'

'And it is a sneaky plan – brilliant in its own way. But I really think it's a waste of your time.'

'Maybe. But I know I'll feel better if I follow it up. Well, tomorrow should be a busy day and we'll be meeting again after work. I better get going and let you get your beauty sleep – not that you need it.'

'Don't go all lounge lizard on me.' I was flattered but still . . .

'Wouldn't dream of it. But you take good care of yourself. Be cautious even when it makes you feel stupid. I couldn't bear it if something happened to you.'

'It sure would destroy the reputation of the Walking Molecules. Experiment declared abysmal failure after death of one of the scientists,' I joked.

Teddy laughed and then looked into my eyes. 'It's more than that, Libby. Much more.' Before I had a chance to respond, he was gone.

As I prepared for bed, I wondered if I understood the meaning of his parting words. Was he interested in me? He certainly was interesting. Was he really as progressive in his attitudes about women as he seemed? I drifted of to sleep thinking about his smile.

THIRTY

The next evening, our fledgling detective group gathered again at Joe's. When pitchers of beer and mugs arrived and the barmaid departed, I said, 'I believe I have neglected to inform you of three bits of information that may have bearing on the issue at hand – variables in our equation as it were. I would like to rectify that right now. The first two had slipped my mind. First is the anonymous gift I received shortly after Irene's death. It was left in a sack on my porch steps – a pair of mittens with a note that read: "I've got my eyes on you". Now, while I realize that could have been interpreted as an admirer, it, nonetheless, felt threatening to me because of its timing. It frightened me enough that I tossed them into the fire. And who would think of hand-knitted mittens for a gift? My logic tells me it would be an older married man, a father, someone with a wife and kids.

'Secondly, Ruth told me that Irene had always been open with her about who she was dating until this mysterious Bill came along. Never told her his last name. Ruth never saw her in public with him. When she confronted Irene and directly asked her if her Bill was a married man, Irene changed the subject. Ruth was certain he was a married man.'

'So Irene was a home wrecker,' Tom said.

'Please, Tom, let me finish. The third piece of information, I deliberately concealed. Irene was dead. I saw no reason to spread the story around. But I realize now that it is a vital piece of information. Probably the one fact that leads more directly to a married man than any other: when Irene Nance was murdered, she was pregnant.'

'What a floozie!' Tom exclaimed. 'I can't understand why we are wasting all this time and energy on a tramp. She got what she deserved.'

'You disgust me, Tom. Thoroughly. Your attitude towards women is deplorable,' I said.

Tom jerked to his feet, his eyes angry, his fists clenched. 'No woman talks to me like that.'

Teddy jumped up, mimicking Tom's stance. Gregg tried to defuse the situation with a chuckle. 'Looks like this one just did, Tom. There is a first time for everything.'

Tom took a step in Gregg's direction. 'Why, you—'

I jumped to my feet. 'And I'll say it again: you disgust me. Whatever did your mother do to you to make you so hostile to women?'

Tom raised one fist in the air and shook it. 'I'm warning you, girl. You leave my mother out of this.'

I defiantly thrust out my chin. 'Or what? Are you going to hit me, big man? Go ahead. I dare you.'

'Don't think I won't!'

Gregg shouted, 'Shut up, Tom, and sit down. Teddy, unclench your fists and get back in your seat. Libby, you sit down, too. You're not helping matters here.'

The three of us all glared at Gregg. Slowly I lowered into my seat careful to do so at the same time as Tom, to prevent him from getting the upper hand.

'First of all, Tom, Libby is right,' Gregg said.

Tom clenched his jaw so hard it throbbed. Several of the group murmured their agreement – but not Gary and Rudy, they stared at the floor. They probably agreed with Tom's philosophy even if they didn't agree with his methods of expressing it.

'You've forgotten why we are here,' Gregg continued. 'We are here because we wanted to do vital war work. We wanted to play a part in our victory. We wanted to ensure freedom and protect the American way of life – and that's for all Americans, not just half the population. For women, too.'

Teddy added, 'Where have you been the last couple of years, Tom? You've seen the change. Women in factories. Women doing what we always called men's work – and they're doing it well. The only reason they hadn't been doing it before is because we wouldn't let them. Out of misguided chivalry and an unhealthy dose of fear, we've wanted to keep them in their place – under our thumb. And we did it not because we are smarter or more capable but simply because we're bigger and stronger.'

Tom looked from face to face around the room, shrugged his shoulders and raised his hands. 'I give,' he said. 'I concede to the opinion of the majority. I'd hate for this group to break up over some woman.'

'Tom!' Teddy and Gregg exclaimed in unison.

'OK, sorry,' Tom said. 'So what's the plan? How are we going to find the guy who bumped off Irene?'

'The theory I propose is that a married man took Irene's life,' I said. 'He would have the most to lose. It puts both his personal and professional life at risk. A single man would have far less need to resort to a drastic, fatal solution to the problem of a pregnant girlfriend.'

'Just as long as we don't totally eliminate the single men and only rank their priority a bit lower, I'm fine with that approach,' Tom said. Murmured agreement circled the table.

'OK, I have a list of all the scientists here. I think we should look at all of them – not just the men named Bill. Irene's boyfriend could have lied about his name to her. Or he could have an official code name and Bill is his real name. We just don't know. I've gone through the list and put a check mark beside all the names that I know aren't married – and that includes everyone at the table. I'd like to pass it around and have all of you check off anyone I missed.'

Tom reached across the table and snatched the list out of my hands. I did not like that man and could not understand why the others invited him into the group in the first place. He seemed to be fueled by anger and his attitude was so negative. But he was a part of it. And I was the new one here. I had to find a way to smooth things out between us for the good of the group and the investigation. I doubted, though, that Tom would make that easy.

'Wait a minute,' Tom said. 'I thought we were checking off the single men but you've checked Dr Bishop. I know for a fact that he's married.'

'You're right, Tom. I neglected to mention that – it slipped my mind. The Bishops were out of town and on the night of Christmas Day, Dr Bishop did not have access to his automobile so he couldn't have slipped back here on the sly. If anyone else knows a married man who's on the list who could not have been here when Irene was murdered, please check him off, too.'

'No. That's not adequate,' Tom objected. 'We need to

distinguish between the two. Say we make a check for "not married" and an x for "not here".'

'That's fine, Tom. If that's important to you, go right ahead.'

'Are you saying it's not important?'

'No, Tom. I am not saying that.' What an exasperating man. 'I'm not arguing with you. Please change my check by Dr Bishop's name to an x. Please.'

'While we're talking about suspects, I checked out an engineer named Mike DeVries today,' Teddy said.

'I thought we were operating on the premise that Irene's boyfriend was a scientist – not an engineer,' Tom objected.

'Well, gee, Tom. Irene was a country girl. Maybe she doesn't know the difference between the two.'

Tom opened his mouth to argue the point but Gregg interrupted. 'What about him, Ted?'

Teddy related his conversation with DeVries, getting nods of understanding for his suspicion about the man. 'Today, I talked with his wife. Mrs DeVries told me that late Christmas afternoon, their little boy broke his arm. She said that she and her husband were in the hospital with their son all night – didn't return home until just after dawn.'

'That takes him off of the list of possibilities,' I said.

The pages continued around the table as everyone not working on the list talked about the news they'd heard from the front in Europe and the Pacific and the latest coming out of Washington, DC. Teddy interrupted their conversation. 'Not all the names on here are real,' he said.

'I suspected that was possible, but I wasn't certain.'

'This guy,' Teddy said pointing to the paper. 'This Dr Smith, Dr Fredrick Smith. That's not his real name.'

'Are you sure?'

'Definitely. He works in Alpha but before that he was working with Fermi up at the University of Chicago. When I was a student there, I attended the seminar he conducted.'

'Dr Smith?' Gregg interjected. 'Wasn't that the one who was glaring at you the other day, Libby? I thought his name was phony then.'

'Well, it was a Dr Smith but that's such a common name,' I said.

'What does he look like, Teddy?' Gregg asked.

'Dark, almost black hair. Big, bushy eyebrows. And deep-set eyes. His facial hair is so dark and thick, by lunchtime every day, he looks like he could use a shave.'

'That's the same one, Libby,' Gregg said. 'I was wondering if he might be staring at you because he was Irene's boyfriend and he knew about your connection to her.'

'Teddy, what's his real name?'

'Wilhelm Schlater.'

'What more do we need?' Tom said. 'Wilhelm sure could be Bill. And it sounds German, too.'

'What does that have to do with anything?' I asked.

'I guess you've been too busy in the lab, Libby, but we declared war on Germany a little while back.'

I wanted to slap his face, pop him in the nose, something. I stifled down my aggressive impulse and through clenched teeth said, 'I know we are at war with Germany but that has nothing to do with people who trace their heritage back to Germany.'

'OK, Teddy, is he German?'

Teddy looked at me, his face contorted with regret, 'Yes. He has a very thick accent.'

'There you go,' Tom said. 'That's my postulate: Wilhelm Schlater is our man. We can test it and if we're wrong move on to other possibilities. But at this point, there is a high enough probability to warrant further investigation.'

'And you think the probability is high simply because he's a German?' I snapped.

'That's one reason.'

'Although there are other facts that make him suspicious, his country of origin is not a valid one, Tom,' I argued.

'And just why not?' Tom shouted.

'Hold it down, Tom,' Gregg urged. 'You're going to get us thrown out of here.'

In a quieter voice, Tom said, 'I think we have our first suspect.'

'But we don't even know if he's married or not,' I objected.

'Fine, that'll be the first thing we'll investigate,' Tom said. 'All in favor of pursuing the investigation of our suspect Wilhelm Schlater, raise your right hand.'

I was dismayed to see every hand but mine in the air. When I looked at Teddy, he pulled his down.

'You sure about that, Teddy?' Tom asked.

Teddy nodded.

'OK, it's eight to two. Majority wins. You two in opposition still with the group?' Tom asked.

'We don't toss people out because they cast a vote different from the majority, Tom,' Gregg objected.

'I just want to know if they're with us or against us, Gregg. It's all about democracy. That's what we're fighting this war for, aren't we? If we're going fight for it, we have to live with it. Libby? Teddy? You gonna go along with the will of the people?'

I looked around the table. I didn't like the bias that went into the decision making but I didn't have a better idea for a starting point. Smith/Schlater was a definite possibility. I nodded. Once I did, Teddy followed my lead.

'OK,' Tom said. 'This is your investigation, Libby. What are we going to do to find out if he's married or not?'

'Could you ask Ann Bishop to find out?' Gregg asked.

The last thing I wanted to do was entangle Ann in this mess again. 'I don't think she'd have access to that information. They'd have that up in personnel. I don't know anyone up there.'

'Ann would, wouldn't she, considering her position? She could find out for us,' Gregg said.

Teddy said, 'I don't think we should get her involved. We all go to her for the latest gossip around here. She could let something slip.'

'OK, then, Teddy, how are we going to find out?' Tom demanded.

'I'll follow him home from work. Find out where he lives. He works in the lab next to mine. I see him coming and going most days. I probably have the best opportunity.'

After murmurs of agreement, they broke up for the night, the men heading back to the clamor of their dorms, me to my quiet home. Teddy insisted on escorting me to the front door, but I squashed his attempts at conversation. Right now, I needed to think, not talk.

THIRTY-ONE

The racetrack was in continuous operation around the clock now and the workload in the laboratories increased dramatically. Trainloads of the ore to be separated were offloaded into the Calutron building and the new loosely wrapped electromagnets no longer had issues with shorting. As I ran samples of the Uranium 235 through the spectrograph, I was delighted by the improved purity of the product. With the change in the lubricating oil, the anomalies I'd found before Christmas were absent. It was professionally – and personally – rewarding to see proof that my theories were right.

The investigation into Irene's murder, however, seemed to have stalled, making me frustrated and out of sorts. Every evening, Teddy was waiting when I finally emerged from the lab after days that averaged twelve hours. Each time, he reported his lack of success; his shoulders seemed to slump even more. Either he hadn't seen Wilhelm Schlater leave the premises or when he left, he was picked up by a soldier in a jeep.

On Friday, however, I noticed a change in Teddy's demeanor the moment I opened the door. He was pacing the boardwalk. Excited or agitated? I couldn't tell. 'Hey, Teddy, what is it?' I asked.

Teddy looked in all directions before whispering, 'I know where he lives.'

'Is he married?'

'Yeah.'

'You saw his wife?'

'Well, no. But he lives on Outer Drive in a type C cemesto. They have three bedrooms so he has to be married with at least two kids.'

'Maybe. But if he's important enough to have a code name, he might be important enough to get a larger house than his family size would dictate. We can't make assumptions. We can theorize, but we need to verify.'

'So how do we do that?'

'We can look in their windows.'

'Oh, no, Libby. How could I ever explain to my mother if I got arrested for being a peeping Tom and sent home in disgrace?'

'Fine. I'll be less suspicious than a man anyway. You can be the look-out. I'll go up to the house and see what I can see.'

'You really think that's a good idea, Libby?'

'No. But right now, it's my only idea. Let's go.'

When we reached the home, Teddy stood guard on the board-walk on the opposite side of the street, as I snuck up to the house, perched on a rise with a steep patchy lawn in front and back. On one end, the windows were too high for me to look inside of them. I crouched down as low as I could go and crept to the back of the house. Looking in the window on the kitchen door, I saw the signs of meal preparation but no one was in sight. I moved to the side of the house where the windows were closer to the ground.

I lifted up slowly, just high enough to see over the sill. The family was sitting down to dinner. Two young children, a boy that looked to be about eight years old and a girl who appeared to be about two years younger sat at a table with someone who must be their mother and Wilhelm Schlater. The tranquil, domestic scene, made me doubt that he could possibly have anything to do with the death of Irene. But looks can be deceiving.

I lingered too long taking in the scene as I suddenly heard the wife scream. Schlater jumped up from the table, glaring at me before I could duck and run. I stumbled, rushing down the hill and finally reached Teddy, grabbed his hand and kept moving. I heard the front door open and the sound of a shouting voice.

'What happened?' Teddy said.

'Not now. Just run,' I urged.

I wouldn't let Teddy stop until we reached Towncenter, where we collapsed on a bench to catch our breaths. I cast nervous glances in the direction we'd just traveled. After five minutes, I felt fairly certain we had not been followed.

'That was too close,' Teddy said.

'Yes. But we found out what we needed to know.'

'Did he see you?'

'Definitely,' I admitted.

'Did he recognize you?'

'I don't know. I looked back when I heard the front door opening. He had to have seen you, too. Do you think he would recognize you?'

'I don't know. I doubt it. I was just one student in a crowded auditorium.'

'But, we've been seen together a lot. If he recognized me, he could probably find out who you are. We'd better not be seen in each other's company for a few days,' I said.

Teddy sighed deeply. 'You're probably right. But I'll worry about you.'

'Don't. I'll keep my eyes open. If I have a problem, I'll get word to you, one way or another. Otherwise, avoid me.'

I walked away, turning back once to see that Teddy hadn't moved from the bench. Because of the distance, I could no longer discern his expression but his shoulders slumped, making him look like a lost little boy. Was Teddy that rattled by the near confrontation? Or was the idea of not spending time with me making him distraught? Not seeing him made me feel sad, too.

All day Thursday, I kept waiting for some sort of commotion over our escapade the night before. Every time anyone walked into the lab, my nerves jangled in response. I expected to look up and see Wilhelm Schlater glaring at me from the doorway again. When nothing happened all day, I was more relaxed on Friday but still maintained a state of vigilance. I didn't pay a lot of attention when Charlie walked into the lab with a pot-bellied man in a suit. A few minutes later, that man was at my elbow and Charlie was nowhere in sight.

'Mr Morton told me you impressed G.G. That is quite an accomplishment.'

I flipped over the papers in front of me. I didn't know who he was and wasn't about to assume he was authorized to view my work. My stomach fluttered and a jolt of adrenaline coursed through my veins. With his bushy mustache, button nose and bespectacled eyes, he looked harmless enough; but, then a good spy wouldn't appear sinister, would he? 'I'm sorry, sir,' I said, 'but shouldn't you be with Mr Morton?'

'Relax, Miss Clark. I'm Dr Ottinger and I am authorized to

view your facility here. Mr Morton had a phone call and told me I was free to look around.' He chuckled. 'You think I'm trying to commit an act of espionage? I'm just not the sneaky type. I came over to talk to you because you reminded me of my first love in college.'

His pleasant demeanor did not reassure me. To the contrary, it ratcheted up my anxiety and left me speechless. Was he a spy? Or was this a test?

He placed his chubby fingers on my forearm and gave it a pat. 'It's a much more dangerous world out there than it was when I was your age. Be careful at all times, Miss Clark, and trust no one.' He turned and walked toward Charlie's office just as Charlie emerged.

'I've got to get back to work, Charlie,' Ottinger said.

'I'll walk you out,' Charlie said, nodding at me when he noticed I was staring at them.

Then they were gone. I blew out a forceful exhalation that was louder than I thought it would be – loud enough to capture Gregg's attention. He tilted his head to one side, giving me a quizzical look. I shook my head and shrugged my shoulders. Inherently, there was nothing wrong with anything Ottinger had said. Still, somehow, it made me feel uneasy and disoriented. What hidden purpose lay behind his warning?

By the time Saturday came and went without any other untoward or unsettling occurrence, I relaxed in relief. Looked like we wouldn't have to pay a price for our clumsy spying.

Monday morning arrived with sunny skies and warmer temperatures than we'd had for weeks. The improved weather seemed like a good omen. I was filled with optimism, excited about the prospect of the work week ahead and eager to push forward with the investigation in my spare time.

When the boom lowered, it seemed so inappropriate, so out of place on such a promising day. I first realized that something was amiss when a uniformed man appeared at the door of the lab. The soldier whispered to Charlie Morton, who walked over to me and said, 'We're both needed over at the administrative building, Miss Clark. This soldier will drive us there.'

He never called me Miss Clark to my face. Something serious was afoot. I glanced at Gregg Abbott, then followed Charlie out of the building. At the outside door, I removed my shoes and slipped into my galoshes – the return of warmer temperatures had heralded the arrival of the treacherous mud.

The soldier drove to the castle on the hill and led us up to the top floor and to the office of Lieutenant Colonel Thomas T. Crenshaw. In the foyer, the secretary told Charlie to go right in and asked me to take a seat. At first, I clung to the vague hope that this summons had something to do with our work. Maybe G.G. had questions and wanted answers from Charlie and me. Maybe there were changes that needed to be made and we were being consulted. I couldn't hold on to those fantasies for long. The fact that I was left waiting alone made it clear. I suspected that everyone in the room was now being briefed about the problem with Libby Clark. I was in trouble – big trouble – and it had to involve Wednesday night's events or some other aspect of the investigation into Irene's death.

I ran through the periodic table in a futile attempt to remain calm, but I was so rattled, I kept losing my place. I started over from the beginning, again and again. I sucked in a harsh breath, making a small gasping sound when the door to the inner office finally opened. Teddy walked out the door with a soldier by his side. He gave me a quick sidelong glance and mouthed 'sorry' as he was led out into the hallway. I didn't have much time to worry about the significance of his presence in the room. Moments later, the door opened again.

'Miss Clark,' another soldier ordered.

I rose, smoothed my skirt and walked through the doorway. I looked first at the big glass windows of the office, taking in the sight of Oak Ridge spread out below. It looked far more massive from here than it did on the ground.

A uniformed man with an oak leaf on each shoulder – presumably the lieutenant colonel – sat behind the desk with a rigid military posture, even the brown and gray bristles on his head stood at attention. Brown eyes stared straight ahead and his hands folded together on his desk. 'Miss Clark, please have a seat,' he said nodding in the direction of the plain oak chair that looked out of place amid the other leather, tufted chairs and the burled walnut desk.

I summoned my dignity and did my best to make a gracious descent despite the shaking in my legs. 'Yes, sir.'

'I'm Lieutenant Colonel Crenshaw and we would like to ask you a few questions.'

I looked around the room at an array of suits and uniforms – except for Charlie who was still in his lab coat, looking pale and drawn. He would not meet my eyes. Dr Bishop was there, too – he looked at me, nodded and greeted me with a tight smile. I didn't know the names of any of the others and they didn't bother to introduce themselves. 'It has come to our attention, Miss Clark, that you and your colleague, a chemist named Teddy Mullins, have conspired in a rogue investigation of a scientist, who for security reasons has been given a code name by the government. Uncovering his real identity is a serious violation of security.'

He only mentioned Teddy. Does that mean Teddy didn't name names? That they don't know anything about the others? I could only hope that was true and answer accordingly. 'Teddy recognized him from his days at the University of Chicago. We knew his identity.'

'Then, why were you spying on him, Miss Clark?'

'We wondered if he was married,' I said, hoping a piece of the truth would disarm them.

'Who are you working for, Miss Clark?'

'No one, sir. I am not a spy.'

'Who are you reporting to?'

'No one, sir.'

'Then why do you have any interest in Dr Smith?'

'My only interest in him is finding out whether or not he had anything to do with the murder of Irene Nance.'

'Why do you think that has anything to do with you?'

'Because our local police force will not investigate because they are certain the crime happened outside of the fence in Knox County. And the sheriff's department said they will not investigate because they are certain the murder happened in Oak Ridge and the body was only dumped in their jurisdiction to confuse law enforcement.'

'What our police force or sheriff's department does or doesn't do is irrelevant, Miss Clark. You were told to stop your investigation.'

'But, sir, I made a commitment. I promised the family of Irene Nance that I would give them answers regarding her death.

Since no one in authority is interested in finding those answers, I had no choice in the matter. I had to pursue it.'

'You were given specific orders.'

'I know what I was told to do, sir. People were throwing around patriotic platitudes like candy at a Christmas parade. But not one person offered up one fact about the case that turned it into a genuine security issue. And quite frankly, I owe it to her family to find out why that is. Why that poor girl's murder does not matter. Why her life had no value. Can you tell me, lieutenant colonel, can you?'

'I can tell you one thing, young lady, you clearly crossed the line when you began investigating a high-ranking scientist. That is a definite security issue. That does threaten the war effort. You also seem to have no regard for the necessity to maintain high morale in this facility even though that matter was explained to you at great length.'

'Does this mean you are covering up for Wilhelm Schlater? Are you willing to give him a pass on murder because of the value of his work? Or is it because he's connected to someone rich or powerful?'

Crenshaw slammed a fist down on his desk with force, causing a pen to skid across the surface and land on the floor. 'Enough! This will stop right now. I am ordering you to cease and desist in this investigation from this moment forward.'

I was raised by a mother who taught me that you catch more flies with honey than you do with vinegar. Had none of these men ever heard that from their parents? If so, were they intentionally trying to provoke me? 'Sir, I must respectfully remind you that I am not in the military. Since I am not, you cannot court martial me and I am not required to obey your orders, even if this is war time.'

The smile that slid across Crenshaw's face churned up nausea in my stomach. 'Of course you aren't military, Miss Clark. You would have never survived in that environment. Mr Morton?'

I looked at Charlie. He appeared sadder than I'd ever seen him before. 'Miss Clark,' he said, 'I must insist that you stop your investigation and to never speak of it again to anyone – here or elsewhere.'

'That was your supervisor, Miss Clark,' Crenshaw said. 'Now let's see what his supervisor has to say. Dr Bishop?'

'Morton, I will hold you personally responsible if the actions of your employee have a deleterious effect on morale, productivity or security.'

They both complied with the lieutenant colonel's wishes but not in the same way. Charlie was unequivocal – his words were clearly etched in black and white. Dr Bishop, on the other hand, made a statement that left him room to maneuver depending on his personal analysis of any situation he faced. Was Bishop's wording intentional? Or was I reading too much into it?

'Now, Miss Clark, is the situation clear to you? I hope that settles this matter,' the lieutenant colonel said, his face looking smug and confident. 'Even outside of the fence, you will not investigate or speak of this matter ever again.'

I heard a roaring sound that made it impossible for me to think. Outside the fence? Was I about to be sent home in disgrace? Quite possibly. I had no choice – to safeguard my job, I'd play the only card I had. I didn't know how to follow through if they called my bluff, but I'd worry about that when and if that happened. I stood, forcing my wobbling knees to hold me upright. I placed a hand on the back of the chair to steady me in place. 'I am sure G.G. will be disappointed to learn of this. I imagine he'll feel rather ashamed of sharing a uniform with a pack of men who are protecting a killer and obstructing justice for a poor country girl who never did anyone any harm. When I hear back from him, I'll try to let you know what he said before he arrives here.'

I pirouetted on my toes, released the chair, held my breath and walked to the door, not stumbling or faltering by sheer force of will. A soldier said, 'Shall I go with her and make sure she clears out?'

'I am countermanding that order, soldier. You are dismissed.'

Had I just gotten a reprieve from the shame of termination? What a relief. Bringing up G.G. had secured my position – at least for now. I wouldn't stop, though, until I had answers for the Nance family. I would not rest until someone was held to account for her death. But I had no idea of how to contact G.G. and someday, I might have to pay a price for my arrogant misuse of his name.

THIRTY-TWO

Returning to the lab, I did my best to put the meeting out of my mind and concentrate on the work in front of me. A backlog of reports and samples needing analysis had piled up in my absence. I jumped when Ann whispered in my ear, 'I need to talk to you.' Then she spoke in a louder voice. 'It's a personal problem, please.'

I followed her into the ladies' restroom where Ann said, 'Tom in the Alpha lab – you know who he is right?'

I nodded.

'You're not seeing him, are you? He's all wet.'

'No, I'm not seeing him. What about him?'

'First he asked me to let you know that Teddy Mullins was summoned to the administrative building. When I told him that you and Charlie Morton had been taken there, a little while after Teddy, he asked me to watch for your return. He said that if you came back and Teddy didn't, I should ask you if Teddy was still wherever you were. Does that make any sense?'

'Oh my. This is all my fault.'

'What's wrong, Libby?'

'Tell Tom that Teddy left before I did. I don't know where he is. Then tell Tom that you can't deliver any further messages.'

'It's not a problem, Libby. Really. I don't mind.'

'Yes but your father minds. He made me promise that I wouldn't get you involved in my problem.'

'What problem, Libby?'

'I can't tell you. Your father would be furious with me. If he even knew I was asking you to deliver one final message, he would never forgive me.'

'Oh, horse feathers. My father thinks he controls me but he doesn't. He has no idea of half the things I do.'

'This time, I think you need to listen to him, Ann. You really do not want to get caught up in this.'

'If you have a problem, Libby, I want to help.'

Placing a hand on Ann's arm, I looked into her eyes. 'The

best way you can help me right now is to do nothing that might anger your father. I think he's on my side at the moment – but I don't think anyone else on the management level is. Please, Ann.'

'OK. But if you change your mind, let me know. I consider you a friend, Libby – a good friend – I'll help you in any way I can.'

'We need to get back to work. Can you grab a piece of tissue and dab at your eyes a bit, like you were pouring out your heart to me?'

Ann grinned. 'Just watch me,' she said as she opened the lavatory door, sniffling as she stepped into the hallway.

Returning to my work station, I shuffled through the paperwork until I found the piece of paper I needed. Holding it up in the air, I spoke in a loud voice, 'Gregg. Gregg Abbott.' He looked up and I continued, 'I have a few questions about the report you submitted this morning. Could you please step over here for a minute?'

Gregg walked over and said, 'What's the problem?'

'This figure here,' I said poking at the paper. Lowering my voice to a whisper, I continued, 'Keep your eyes on the report. Nod and point as if we are discussing it. I was called before Lieutenant Colonel Crenshaw. So was Teddy. He was in there before me and left before I went into the inner office. Fortunately, Crenshaw was under the impression it was just the two of us involved in investigating Wilhelm Schlater and Irene's death.'

'I'll get the word out to the group. Maybe someone else knows what happened to Teddy.'

'I'll have to work late tonight.'

'I think we all will. I'll set the meeting for nine.'

'See you then,' I whispered. In a louder voice I added, 'Thank you, Mr Abbott.'

I barely got out of the lab in time for the Walking Molecules meeting. As I pushed open the side door to enter Joe's, Ottinger was on his way out of the bar. 'Don't forget what I told you, Miss Clark. Trust no one,' he said.

The comment was troubling. I looked over the faces arrayed around our table. Did Ottinger know something about one of these men that I didn't know? Was the whole group a set-up to lead me astray? Or was Ottinger just trying to unsettle me? If so, why? What possible purpose could he have?

The moment I slipped into a chair, Tom said, 'What happened to Teddy?'

'I don't really know.'

'Why are you here and he's not? Did you pin everything on him?'

'No, Tom. I didn't,' I said clenching my teeth. Why did Tom always assume the worst of me? 'I thought Teddy was off the hook until I returned to the lab and got the message from you that he hadn't gotten back yet.'

'So what about the rest of us? Are we next?'

'I don't think so. I didn't mention any of you and I don't think Teddy did. They seemed to think it was just the two of us involved.'

'Well, you got us into this mess, what are you going to do for Teddy?'

'Libby!' a voice cried out from across the room. We all turned toward the sound and saw Teddy walking towards us. 'Hey, Libby, am I glad to see you. I thought you'd been shipped out.'

'We thought you were, Teddy,' I said. 'Great to see you. Where have you been?'

'I spent most of the day wondering how I'd explain to my parents about my unexpected return home,' Teddy said, 'and then everything changed.'

'What happened?' I asked.

'After you saw me leaving Crenshaw's office, Libby, I was escorted back to my dorm and told to pack my things. I was ordered to stay in my room and make no attempt to communicate with anyone. I finished packing and sat there for a while before opening my door to go to the lavatory. That's when I realized there was a soldier posted outside my door. He didn't want to let me leave at first but when I explained the situation, he escorted me there. On the way, I passed someone in the hallway I knew who greeted me. When I responded, the soldier gave me a shove in the back and said, 'No talking, Benedict Arnold.' I turned around and said, 'I'm no traitor.' He just gave my chest a shove and said, 'No talking.' When I finished, I went back to my room and waited some more.

'Finally, another private arrived along with a sergeant and they escorted me out to a jeep and drove to the gate. I handed over my badge to the guard. He went into the guard house, came out and waved the sergeant inside. They were in there a few minutes. When the sergeant emerged, he told the private behind the wheel to turn around and take me back to the dorm.

'Course, I had a lot of questions but nobody gave me any answers. I unpacked my bags, realized there was no longer a soldier at my door and left my room to look around the dormitory for someone from the group. When I couldn't find anyone, I came here. Nobody seemed to be following me. So, I guess I still work here. What did you do, Libby, to make them change their minds?'

'Don't celebrate too hard, Teddy. I bluffed them. If anyone calls my bluff, we'll be back in hot water again.'

Joe, the quietest one of the group surprised us all by speaking up, 'Maybe we'd better drop this investigation. Maybe we ought to walk away while we can.'

'And let that German get away with murder?' Tom asked.

Joe cringed at the harsh tone of Tom's voice, making me wonder if he'd ever say a word again. 'We don't know that he's the one who killed Irene, Tom,' I said.

'But everything we learn points in that direction. And the brass are protecting him. What other possibility could there be? And besides, as I said, he's a German – they're a bloodthirsty lot.'

'Tom, please, give the man some credit. He left Germany, didn't he?'

'A German is still a German. Always a German. We should round them all up and lock them away.'

Thinking of Aunt Dorothy's housekeeper, Mrs Schmidt, I was alarmed by Tom's attitude but didn't know how to respond.

Gregg did, though. 'Shut up, Tom. There are a lot of Germans over here helping us beat the Nazis at their own game. And back in Germany, there are plenty good Germans living under the heel of the brown shirts.'

'Oh, bring out the violins,' Tom said, as he mimed playing the instrument.

'I'm exhausted,' I said. 'Too tired for stupid arguments. I'm going home to get some sleep. Tomorrow promises to be another grueling day.'

Despite what I said to the group, I was in no hurry to get back home. My little house would feel extra lonely and lifeless after the day's upsetting events. Maybe I should get a cat. With all the farms in the area, someone was certain to have a litter of kittens this spring. At least then I'd have someone to greet me at the end of the day.

THIRTY-THREE

Tuesday morning, I ran tests of the spectrograph. Charlie seemed to be trying to steer clear of me as much as I wanted to avoid him. I didn't notice that Ann had entered the lab until I saw a piece of paper drop on the counter and caught a glimpse of Ann's back on the way out of the room.

The note read: 'Ladies' Room. Now. Urgent.'

I checked the progress of the ongoing tests and then went down to the restroom. Pushing open the door, I said, 'Ann, you've got to stop this. If your dad thinks we're conspiring together, he's going to forbid you from seeing me.'

'Not this time,' Ann said with a grin. 'This message is from my dad.'

'Really?'

'Oh, yes! Let me tell you what happened last night. Dad came home and he was in a state. He mixed a drink and swallowed it down even before he said hello. Then he asked my mother what she planned for dinner the next night. When she said meatless spaghetti, he said you're going to have to do better than that. Well, Mom didn't like that, not one little bit. She started in on how hard she struggled to be able to serve a decent dinner every night. I almost thought she was going to start throwing things.'

'Your mother?' Libby asked.

'I have never seen her angrier. But Dad calmed her down when he said that she did a terrific job and he had no complaints, it was just that he had to have someone over for dinner the next night and he needed something special so his invitation couldn't be turned down.

'Mom told him she couldn't perform miracles and asked why it had to be that night and who was so all-fired important. And he said, "Because of what happened today, I need to speak with

Libby and I can't do so at the lab." So Mom asked what happened today and Dad, of course, told her he could not talk about it. Then Mom said, "Are you going to send Libby back to Philadelphia?" And Dad looked horrified and said, "No, I'm trying to protect her from those who want to do that." Then Mom wanted to know who wanted to do that and Dad again said he couldn't talk about it. Mom threw up her hands and served dinner.

'After we ate, she left me with the kitchen and dishes and she took off for the farm where she buys eggs and came back with a chicken. We're having fried chicken tonight and you're invited.'

'Although the thought makes my mouth water and I really want to hear what your dad has to say, I don't know if I can get away in time for dinner.'

'You have to,' Ann said. 'You work for Charlie, Charlie works for my dad. It should be a piece of cake.'

'Not if your dad doesn't want Charlie to know about this invitation . . .'

'Just tell me you'll come, Libby. It must be important. I haven't seen Dad act this way in a long time. These days, he suggests things to Mom, but he never says it has to be one way or another. At least, he hasn't been doing that in front of me.'

'OK. Let your mother know I'll be there. I'll come even if I have to return to the lab afterwards.'

'Swell! I'll see you tonight,' Ann said, darting out of the ladies' room.

All day long, I couldn't help but speculate about what Dr Bishop had to say – it made it difficult to get my work done. Dinner time came around more quickly than I thought possible, but looking back on the completed tasks, I was pleased with what I had accomplished, despite my mental distractions.

At Ann's house, Mrs Bishop's welcome was even more effusive than the last visit. Dr Bishop stood quietly to the side while his wife gave me a hug. When we parted, he said, 'Libby, I've asked Mrs Bishop to hold dinner for a bit while we talk. I know I'll find it easier to enjoy my meal if we have our discussion out of the way and I imagine you will, too.'

I followed Dr Bishop into the living room as Mrs Bishop hustled her daughter into the kitchen. Sitting on the edge of a chair, I braced myself to hear the worst.

'I was very troubled by yesterday's meeting. Like you, I am

appalled that the authorities are not interested in justice for a young country girl and for her mother who entrusted us with her care. I knew Irene . . .'

'You knew her? Why have you been keeping that a secret?' I studied Dr Bishop's face uncertain with what was hidden there – or even if anything was. He paused long enough that it appeared as if he were making a decision – was he choosing truth over a lie or just the opposite?

He shook his head before answering. 'I trust you will keep this to yourself, Libby. But Mrs Bishop is a very jealous woman. If I mentioned that I knew the girl, she would assume the worst.'

'The worst? She would think you killed her?'

'No, not that, but she'd think, well, you know.'

'Oh.' I wanted to ask if Mrs Bishop had good reason for being that suspicious, but that was a bit too far to push against a man who was, indirectly, my supervisor.

'Really, Libby that's all beside the point. I just wanted you to know that I went along with what occurred in order to be able to learn everything I could about the situation – not because I approve of any of it. I imagine it's probably difficult for you to trust anyone right now, but I hope you will accept my sincerity.'

'Yes, sir,' I said, but I didn't feel as positive as I tried to make it sound.

'There are things you need to know that were hidden from you. First, the plan was to dismiss you that day, over my objections and, I must add, Charlie Morton strongly argued for a less draconian solution to the problem. But Charlie thought that the presence of administration higher-ups would intimidate you and get you to comply. I insisted that you were not the type of person that crumbled when confronted by bullies. I was right, wasn't I?'

'I'd like to think so, sir.'

'When you threatened to contact G.G., a number of people in the room thought you were bluffing and wanted to call your bluff.'

It was a close call, then. 'How? Were they going to call G.G.?'

'That was suggested after you left. But those of us, including Lieutenant Colonel Crenshaw, who witnessed your meeting with General Groves, cautioned it would be a mistake. And quite frankly, in all things military, Crenshaw was calling the shots. So you get to keep your job, for now.'

'What about Teddy Mullins?'

'It took a little longer to convince everyone that dismissing Teddy Mullins would be a mistake. I said that I believed it would make you even more intent on securing justice for Irene Nance. Was I right?'

'Probably. Hard to be certain how I'd react until it happened,' I said, hedging my bets unless and until I felt more comfortable with Dr Bishop.

'It was one of the Roane-Anderson administrators who made the argument that won the day. He said that Teddy was obviously stuck on you and because of that, easily manipulated by you and shouldn't be punished for being young and in love.'

'Dr Bishop, we're just friends . . .'

'Maybe so, Libby. Seeing Mullins talk about you did give credence to the argument that there was more to it, at least on his part. Anyway, Mullins' dismissal was rescinded but I would strongly encourage you to steer clear of him, for his own good.'

'But, sir . . .'

He raised his hand, palm up. 'Hear me out, Libby. For his own sake, you need to cut him off completely. If your interaction continues, Crenshaw might reconsider and decide that dismissing him would serve as a warning to you.'

I nodded even though I had no intention of doing as he said. However, I would take care that Teddy and I would not be seen together. All the while, I needed to keep in mind that what Dr Bishop was saying might be honest and open. Or it might be a disarming move. He could be taking this stance with me with Crenshaw's blessing or because he was trying to steer my investigation for some reason that wasn't apparent.

'But I know you will need assistance to get to the bottom of all of this. I'm willing to step in and serve in that capacity. I am in a position to aid you far more than Teddy Mullins ever could.'

'After that meeting, you want to help me?'

'It's because of that meeting I want to help you. I don't like the military putting on pressure to hide the facts. I know it will require you to place a lot of trust in me. I know that will be difficult after what you've experienced. But I really do think I can make a positive contribution to your effort.'

Ottinger's words danced through my head. 'Trust no one.' But I couldn't be that absolute in my thinking. Risk was essential to progress. 'Do you know anything that could help the investigation now?'

'Yes,' Bishop said with a nod. 'I know that Dr Smith, whom we both know is Wilhelm Schlater, could not have attacked Irene Nance on Christmas night. One of his children brought the mumps home the last weekend of school before the holidays and Schlater came down with them mid-week. He was in bed and miserable for a few days. He did not leave the house until after lunchtime the day after Christmas,' Dr Bishop said. His face turned red as he added, 'I do not doubt that he was homebound because, well, I don't want to go into any details but rest assured that an adult male with mumps would not be moving around anywhere.'

I blushed in response, not quite sure what he meant, but understanding it involved men's private parts. 'Sir, are you certain he had mumps? Or is it possible that is just the story they concocted to protect him?'

'That's what they told me, Libby, and I have no reason to doubt it.'

'Really, sir? After this morning, you are still willing to accept what they say at face value?'

Bishop sighed. 'You make a good point. But, what—'

'What about Mrs Bishop? Does she know Mrs Smith? Could she find out if it was true?'

'I can't drag my wife into this situation,' Bishop objected so forcefully that I didn't try to convince him otherwise. It was quite touching that he didn't want to involve his wife in anything remotely sordid.

'Anyway,' he continued, 'I have another possibility for you: Dr William Ottinger. You know him?'

'I met him briefly when he visited Charlie last week in the lab. And I bumped into him the other night at Joe's. I don't, however, recall seeing his name on the list.' The second those words came out of my mouth, I realized my mistake.

'What list? Where did you get a list?'

Panic clutched my chest. I couldn't tell him that Ann drew up the list. I shrugged as nonchalantly as I could and forced a blasé tone into my voice. 'Oh, nothing much. Just a roster of Y-12 scientists floating around the lab. There are a lot of chemists who think they'll be out of work when the war's over and they want contacts to help their career when it's time to leave.'

'You need to be careful of that sort of thing, Libby. It can easily be misconstrued. If you see it again, you'd better destroy it before someone gets into serious trouble.'

I blinked hard to keep the expression on my face as placid as possible as I pictured the list sitting in a dresser drawer under my stack of nightgowns. 'If I see it floating around the lab, I'll make sure it goes no further.'

'Good,' he said. 'Now back to Dr Ottinger. I know a few things about him. He doesn't work at Y-12. He's at K-25.'

'I'd heard that facility was progressing rather quickly but I don't know anything about the work they're doing there. Do you?'

'No,' Bishop said, shaking his head. 'I don't know what is being done at K-25. And I don't know what Ottinger is doing since he's come here. But I do know that he has worked on isotope separation in the past.'

'Are they duplicating our efforts or are they using a different methodology?'

'Don't know with any certainty, at all. I can only postulate and my assumption is that they're not using the same mechanical process that we are.'

'Do you know anything else about Ottinger?' I asked.

'Just what I've heard from my wife. Mildred mentioned that the Ottingers were having marital difficulties. Nell Ottinger confided that she had threatened to leave him on a number of occasions because of his long history of philandering. Mildred said that Nell never followed through because she had four small children, had no money of her own and since they're Catholic, divorce would not be an option.'

'That rotund little man is a Casanova? I certainly can't see the appeal.'

'You'd be surprised how easy it is to impress the country girls around here if you can put doctor in front of your name. Most of them never left their native counties before the war.'

'But, surely, the military would have no interest in covering up the tracks of his adulterous behavior.'

'It depends,' Bishop said. 'I think that the possibility he is doing vital work at K-25 is very high, making him someone the governmental and military authorities would want to protect. The fact that his past history of indiscretion didn't stop them from hiring him reinforces that fact, I think.'

'He made me very uneasy, Dr Bishop. He's told me twice now that I should trust no one. I don't know why he's warning me like that . . .'

'Maybe, it's a simple case of intimidation. Maybe he's afraid of you. Maybe he thinks you'll find something he's hiding. And maybe that something has to do with Irene,' Dr Bishop speculated.

'You may be right, sir. But that sounds like a big leap of faith, rather than a solid deduction. Can you find out anything more about him?'

'I will try. I'll have to be discrete but I'll pass along anything I learn. There is something I need to know from you, Libby. Did you recruit anyone besides Teddy to help you? It seemed to me that you would but the others at that meeting thought otherwise.'

As much as I wanted to trust him not to betray me, I certainly had no faith at all in his protective feelings toward any of the others. 'You have no idea of how difficult it was for me to make one friend among my fellow scientists. There are a lot of them who don't think women belong in any field of scientific endeavor.'

'Ah, well, patience on that front. It will change with time.'

Eager to change the subject before he could ask any additional questions along that same line, I asked, 'Did you know that they moved Irene's body from the high school bleachers to a spot outside of the fence?'

'I knew from the first part of the meeting, before you and Teddy came in, that you were claiming that. It wasn't until the end of the meeting, though, that they actually admitted doing it.'

'I guess I should be grateful that they are not lying to themselves.'

'I imagine that's some small comfort but I was – and still am – appalled. They said they had dual grounds for that decision: national security and community morale. I said that I didn't think either made any sense.'

'I suspect they didn't take that well.'

Bishop grimaced. 'Not at all. I had to endure a lecture about the security risks of allowing state authorities to come inside the fence to investigate what was a violation of the laws of Tennessee and about the likely loss of some workers and the loss of productivity by all the others if they no longer believed that the community was safe and crime-free.'

'Do you think those arguments have any real merit?'

'I think it's all baseless, but I'd stopped arguing my point, just the same. In fact, I pretended to be in accord with their viewpoint. I knew I couldn't change the attitudes in that room but hoped if they were convinced I was on their side, I could be more effective in assisting you.'

'It could hurt your career if they knew that, Dr Bishop. Why are you willing to take the risk?'

'I understand your skepticism,' Bishop said with a nod. 'In fact, I'd expect nothing less from someone with a scientific mind. But a young woman is dead. She was the same age as my daughter and she was murdered. She was a human with feelings and family and dreams . . .' Choking on the last sentence, he paused to clear his throat and swallow before continuing, 'And she was an American. If we have no interest in pursuing justice for her, then this whole war is a sham. I don't know if they know who killed her and think he's worthy of their protection or if they simply fear finding out the identity of the man who committed the crime because they are afraid of the answer.'

'You got a better glimpse into their thought processes than I did,' I said. 'What do you think is the most likely scenario?'

'I think it's probably the latter. I believe that they are honorable men who feel they can wrestle with the theoretical without taking action, but couldn't live with themselves if they knew who did it and did nothing about it.'

'Seems as if they all believe the ends justify the means.'

'I can't argue with that – and I can't subscribe to it, either. And looking at it from that perspective, I realize you are right about Mrs Bishop. I will ask her to try to verify the story about Dr Smith and the mumps – I'll present it to her like a lark to chase down gossip. And I'll see if I can get you anymore information about Ottinger. Let me know if you identify any other possible suspects.'

'If we can eliminate both Ottinger and Schlater, we can move on to others. Do you know anything else about Schlater?'

'Yesterday I learned that Dr Smith – please refer to him by that name rather than his real one – is hostile toward you. Mullins told us about him glaring at you in the lab and I asked why he'd do that. A couple of the men at the meeting laughed and one of them said, "She showed him up. He should have known the oil they were using would put impurities into the system but he missed it. He'll never forgive her for that." Then Crenshaw said that once Smith caught you spying on him, he started spreading the story that you were only able to figure out the problem with the oil because you'd stolen reports from his desk.'

'I did not!' That really angered me – that a fellow scientist would suggest I'd do such a thing was an outrage.

'I never for a moment thought that you did – and no one else did either. The consensus is that Smith was trying to save face when he pushed to have you charged with treason. But don't worry: they're all laughing at him about that.'

Despite his assurances, it was unsettling to know that an accusation of work-related sabotage had been leveled at me. That kind of poison lingers in the back of people's minds long after the suggestion has been dismissed, just waiting for a moment of doubt to cause its resurrection.

'I think it's probably wise if we don't interact in the lab any more than we've done before – which hasn't been much at all,' Dr Bishop said. 'I'll pass along information through Ann.'

'But I thought you didn't want her involved.'

'I didn't when I didn't know the nature of your problem. Now I do. I do not, however, want either her or my wife to have any more knowledge about the details than they need at any given time. I want to keep them in the dark, for the most part, until this issue is resolved.'

'No problem, sir.'

'Fine,' he said with a shake of his head. He rose from his chair, offered his arm, and said, 'Miss Clark, may I have the honor of escorting you to dinner? Fried chicken awaits and Mrs Bishop makes the best I've ever tasted.'

THIRTY-FOUR

Although the Calutron operation was now running smoothly, it still seemed to be a terribly inefficient process. I believed that there must be a better way to achieve the separation, something faster and more productive. At this rate how could we ever get the job done? The gaseous diffusion process developed by the Brits before we got into the war had shown real promise. Was that research still ongoing? Maybe this was what Ottinger was involved in at K-25? I certainly couldn't ask anyone about it. Scientific inquiry had been blindfolded, gagged and bound; the natural exchange of scientific ideas throttled in its sleep.

It all circled back to the same old conundrum. The fissible material we produced was needed to build and use a bomb the likes of which the world has never seen, but if it were built, would we use it? The immediate death toll would be high but justifiable to end the war. But what additional damage would be done? Was it morally questionable to participate in this project or was it morally wrong to abstain from using my talents and knowledge to bring the war to an end in the belief, hope or desire that, in the end it would actually save lives?

Regrettably, those answers would not be apparent until the war was over and the damage done. But if the Germans developed this awesome new weapon first, there were no doubts in my mind that they would use it. Before the Allies had even heard of their success, the new bomb would fall on Britain or the United States – maybe both at the same time. If that happened, all questions of morality would be moot and I could never forgive myself for not doing more.

I worked hard for the next two days, keeping focused on my work while I waited for more information from Dr Bishop. On Friday morning, it finally came.

Ann walked up to me in the lab and in a normal tone of voice she said, 'The answer to the first question is confirmed. The answer to the second question is "nothing more pointing in either direction at this time".' Then she whispered, 'Libby, does that make any sense to you?'

'Oh, yes,' I said, knowing now that Wilhelm Schlater really was sick with mumps on Christmas Day and incapable of murdering Ruth's sister and that Dr Ottinger remained a possibility as a suspect.

'You've got to tell me, Libby. What are the questions? What are you and Dad up to?'

'You'll have to ask your dad.'

'Oh, I did. All he said was that if I cared about you, I need to do exactly as he told me. Then he made me repeat the message twice to make sure I had it down. What's going on, Libby?'

'Ann, I promised your dad . . .'

'What good is friendship if some silly promise to some old guy can get in the way of it?' Ann said and flounced out of the lab and down the hall.

Her words hurt. I wanted to answer Ann's questions but knew that would be selfish. It would ease my mind but it would put Ann at risk. I crossed my fingers and sent up a little prayer that the damage to our friendship would only be short-term.

It was after eight that night when I was finally able to leave work behind. Arriving at home, I found a letter from Ruth.

> Dear Libby,
>
> I was glad to hear things are going well for you and you are making friends. I miss you and hope someday we'll see each other again – maybe after the war, just like everything else. Ha Ha Ha!
>
> Things are a bit rough here at home. Besides everything else, Mama worries every day about Hank. She's so afraid he won't come home alive after the war. She says that she couldn't bear to become a Gold Star mother and have to put on a brave face every day.
>
> I would like to ask you to do me a favor. Could you go see Sally at the guest house? She used to work with Irene on the second shift. She sent Mama the nicest letter but Mama has not been able to answer it. Every time she sits down to try, she starts crying and the ink starts running all over the place. Anyhow, could you tell her that her letter meant a whole lot to Mama and she'll write back to her just as soon as she can?
>
> Thank you, Libby. You are the best friend ever.
>
> Your pal,
> Ruthie

It was all so sad. I went into the kitchen to fry up a piece of spam and warm up a can of beans. Poor Ruthie. Poor Mrs Nance. When I flipped the spam over to fry the other side, it hit me. Ruth must have written and rewritten that letter to make sure she hadn't said anything to catch the attention of the censors. She must have concealed a message.

I slid the spam and a spoonful of beans on a plate, grabbed the letter and sat down at the table to read it again while I ate.

The only thing that stood out the second time though was that Ruth wanted me to speak to Sally. And it could be important. Second shift was from two in the afternoon until ten at night. If I hurried, I could catch Sally before she left for the day – if she'd worked that day. If not, it would all be a waste of time.

I gulped down the rest of my meal and raced over to the guest house. When I walked up to the reception desk, there were two women behind the counter and I had no idea which one – or if either one – was Sally. The shorter of the two had her blonde hair swept up in an elaborate style as if she hoped the piled-up locks would make her appear taller. The other woman wore a more simple hairstyle sporting short bangs and hair on the sides that flipped up at her shoulders. Both of them were engaged in conversations with people who appeared to be guests.

The first woman free was the short blonde. Approaching her, I said, 'Hello, I'm looking for Sally.'

The tall brunette turned towards me, holding an index finger up in the air. The blonde said, 'Are you sure I can't help you?'

'Yes. I have a message from a friend for Sally.'

As the people walked away, the brunette walked over and said, 'How can I help you?'

'I got a letter from Ruth Nance this week . . .'

'Oh dear, how is she doing?'

'I think she's doing all right, considering. She wanted me to let you know that her mother really appreciated your letter and wanted to write one to you. But then every time she started, she'd cry all over the paper and couldn't go on.'

'Oh, poor thing. I certainly didn't expect a letter back. I know how it is. My mom is a Gold Star mother.'

'Oh, so sorry to hear that. I lost a cousin in Pearl Harbor.'

'You know then. Well, anyway, it doesn't matter how you lose a child, it's awful. I don't think I could bear it. I know we're supposed to want to get married and have babies but that always comes with the risk of losing them. I don't know if I'm strong enough. My mom tells me I'll feel different when the war is over. I doubt it. Between now and then, I imagine a lot more of our boys will die. Listen, I've got to get back to work.'

'Say, are you working Sunday? If not, I'd love to have you over for Sunday dinner. It might only be spam or canned salmon, but I'll try to find something else at the market.'

'You have your own place?'

'Yes, I do. It's a flattop.'

'Spiffy. I haven't seen the inside of one of those. I'd love to come over Sunday – even if it is spam.'

I walked home, tired but cheerful. I had expected that any friend of Irene's would be a bit shallow but Sally seemed quite nice and actually capable of thinking for herself. My first dinner guest besides Ruth – how exciting. I'd have to get to the market before it opened to have any chance to get any fresh meat at all – that would make me late to work, but it was a Saturday, Charlie wouldn't come down on me too hard.

The next morning, I arrived at Towncenter forty-five minutes before the doors of the market opened and already there were at least two dozen people ahead of me in line. I was afraid that all the meat would be gone before I got to the counter but I stood in place hoping my patience would be rewarded.

I heard someone shout my name. Looking around, I saw Mrs Bishop near the front. 'Young lady, you get up here with me right now. Where did you get off to? Don't dawdle, Libby.'

I edged my way to the front, expecting someone to make an angry remark but most of them just smiled and shook their heads. They must have assumed that I was Mrs Bishop's daughter and she was scolding me for being disobedient. What a brilliant strategy. Was it the first time she'd used this particular subterfuge? She was obviously good at it. I'd been underestimating Ann's mother.

When I joined her, I said, 'Yes, ma'am. I'm sorry. I just got distracted.'

'Don't let it happen again, Libby. It's difficult enough shopping without having to keep up with you.' She slid a hand into mine and gave it a squeeze.

I was able to buy two lamb chops – small but so welcome. I grabbed a couple of potatoes and a can of peas and went through the check-out and waited for Mrs Bishop to finish her shopping. We walked out of the store together and once we turned a corner, Mrs Bishop said, 'I was surprised to see you here. I thought you'd be at work.'

'I should be but I really needed to get to the market before all the meat was gone. Thank you very much for helping me.'

'Sometime you can return the favor if you get a chance.'

'Yes, ma'am. Thanks again. I need to get this food home and get to work. See you soon.'

'Just one more thing, Libby.'

'Yes, ma'am?'

'You and my husband are dealing with some sort of problem . . .?'

'Oh, Mrs Bishop I'm sorry, but I can't—'

'I know you can't tell me anything about that, dear. I was just curious about where you meet to discuss the problem – besides the office and our home.'

'No place else, Mrs Bishop.' What kind of question was that?

'Are you sure? Not even once or twice? Did you talk at your little flattop or anyplace else?'

What was going on here? 'Absolutely not, Mrs Bishop. Why do you ask?'

'Oh, someone told me that you were at Joe's the other night with a bunch of scientists and I thought my husband might be one of them.'

'I was at Joe's but your husband wasn't there.'

An indecipherable look passed over her face. She sighed, her expression softened and she smiled. 'Ah, I was just worried about the two of you. Well, I'd better let you get on to work.' She turned and walked away.

I puzzled over the odd line of questioning as I hurried home, caught the bus and raced to Y-12. No matter which way I looked at Mrs Bishop's question, it still did not make much sense. With all my rushing, I was a bit out of breath by the time I got inside and suddenly, there he was, Wilhelm Schlater, walking straight at me. I tucked my head down and walked past him, hurrying to my work space as if it were a refuge from the war, seeking anonymity and shelter.

His footsteps faltered as they passed me. Then I felt a firm hand grasping my shoulder and spinning me around.

'Vat are you doing here?'

I was too terrified to speak – all that came out of my mouth was an inarticulate gurgle.

'Get out of here!' he shouted.

'Excuse me, sir,' Charlie said. 'I would appreciate it if you would keep your hands off of my staff.'

'I vas assured she would be gone. Immediately. You know this to be true. You vere there. You heard them say so. I vill report this. But I vant her out of this lab now.' Schlater grabbed my upper arm and pulled.

Charlie in turn grabbed Schlater's arm and said, 'You unhand that young lady or I will call security.'

'Oh, ya, go right ahead. You know she should not be here. You know it.'

'You're wrong, Dr Smith. The decision was changed.'

'I don't belief you.'

'Dr Smith, I suggest you discuss this matter with Lieutenant Colonel Crenshaw.'

'Ach, I vill. You'd better belief I vill,' Schlater said, shoving my arm away with force, causing it to swing wide and hit Charlie. 'Und I vill be back here with soldiers to take her away.' He spun around and walked off, his footsteps echoing down the hall as he marched away.

'Are you OK, Libby?'

'No damage done.'

'I would have thought someone would have spoken to him about the change of plans. In fact, I was told not to let you know that there had been an order to send you home – but now you do.'

'Thank you for coming to my rescue, Charlie, but if Schlater hadn't confronted me, would you ever have told me?'

'I couldn't, Libby. You know how it is. I am happy about the outcome, but I could not influence it. I did try.'

'Sure, well, let me get to work.' Some people will follow rules and orders, under any circumstances. No matter how unfair, how unjust, the rules were paramount. Now, in this time of war, that attitude seemed to spread to nearly everyone. It seems, I could trust someone like Charlie in a black and white situation, such as this one, but if there was a grey area, it was clear I'd be on my own.

THIRTY-FIVE

On Sunday morning, I went through my house, straightening up clutter and dusting off surfaces in preparation for my guest. When Sally arrived, she was more than impressed with the space.

'Well, isn't this the cat's meow. Almost like living in a doll house, Libby. And it's all yours. I can't tell you how green I am. I only had one roommate when I got here, but two weeks ago, I got a second one. I hope the three of us have enough patience to last through the war – the only thing that saves us from driving each other completely wacky is that we all work different shifts. But this,' she said spreading her arms wide, 'this is heaven.'

'Thank you, Sally. I'm very fortunate but sometimes I forget my good luck on a cold and windy night. It's draftier than the chicken coop at my dad's farm. Make yourself at home, I need to get back into the kitchen and finish fixing our dinner.'

'Can I set the table?'

'As you can see the table's tiny. We'll have to serve up the food on the plates and carry them out here, but you could lay out the utensils.'

After doing that, Sally stayed in the kitchen with me, chatting about the mud, dances and the poor quality of the cafeteria food. Sitting down to eat, we both cut a piece of lamb chop and popped it in our mouths, relishing the flavor as we chewed. After swallowing, Sally said, 'I forgot how good a lamb chop could be. I can't remember when I last had one. How did you ever get them?'

'Lots of luck and a friend at the front of the line at the market,' I said with a laugh. 'Glad you're enjoying it.'

Sally started to cut off another piece then set down her knife and fork. 'Libby, I figured you asked me over because you wanted to talk to me about Irene. You don't have to make any more small talk. Just go right ahead, ask me anything.'

'Thanks, Sally. I wasn't sure how to start. But eat – don't let your dinner get cold. We'll have plenty of time to talk when we finish.'

Sally said, 'Say no more, this is the best meal I've had since I moved into the dorm.' She ate another bit of chop, a mouthful of mashed potatoes and a forkful of peas. 'I really liked Irene. There was a lot more to her than most people gave her credit. Sure, she liked to have a good time but she had a goal. She wanted to find a man she could love, who could take care of her, who could take her away from the sticks, give her a nice life in the city.'

'You talked a lot?' I asked.

'Sometimes we worked like spinning tops with questions and

problems from the guests. Other times, we'd go an hour or more without seeing anyone but each other. And Irene? A lot of people thought she was just looking for fun all the time. But when the war was over, she didn't want to go back to the farm and settle down with one of the local boys. That's why she dated a lot of different men. It wasn't because she was wild – well, she was a bit wild – but what I'm saying is, she'd date a man two or three times but as soon as she realized he wasn't the one, she just moved on to someone else – a bunch of someones actually. I was green as could be at times. Hardly enough men to go around and they all seemed to want to go out with Irene.'

For a few more minutes, Sally concentrated on the food on her plate. Then she said, 'I wish I could be more like her.'

'In what way?'

'When we first started working together, it seemed like she was making eyes at every man who walked through the door. Then I realized that she was simply at ease with all of them, didn't matter if it was a young private or one of the old guys working a desk job up at the castle. She just liked men – and women, too. And everybody felt that from her.'

'The women, too?'

'Listen, you could tell which of the married couples staying in the guest house were happy and which ones had problems just by watching how the wives acted around Irene. If they had a good marriage, they smiled and laughed with Irene every time they saw her. But if things were bad between a woman and her husband, she'd be just as bristly as a porcupine. Wives like that were suspicious of Irene. And sure enough, the husbands of those women were the ones who were a bit too bold, asking every woman that worked there to take a walk or go out somewhere.'

'Were there any men who paid special attention to Irene?'

Sally laughed. 'Yes, all of them. But seriously, if a man was staying at the guest house with his wife, she was friendly with them but it ended there.'

'What about a German guy named Dr Smith? He lived in the guest house for a while back before his family came down and moved into a cemesto house. Do you remember him?'

'Thick accent, mean eyes?'

'That's the one,' I agreed.

'Wish I could forget him,' Sally said. 'What an unpleasant man. No matter what problem he had, like if he ran short of towels or soap, it was as if someone did it to him deliberately. No one could stand that nasty man – not even Irene and she was everybody's friend. I was glad to see the last of him.'

'How about a Dr William or Bill Ottinger?'

Sally furrowed her brow. 'Hmmm? Oh, was he married to that little woman who looked like she got her face out of a sour pickle jar every morning?'

I laughed at her imagery and answered, 'I don't know.'

'I bet it is. He was a real drugstore cowboy. Had a couple of lines he used on every woman who worked there. First, he'd say she reminded him of an old flame and then he'd warn her not to trust anyone – I suppose he thought saying that would make us distrust everyone but him. He asked us all who worked there to step out with him and he could be really fresh. He made me blush almost every time he spoke to me. Got so fresh with Irene once she slapped him right in the kisser.'

'Really?'

'Don't remember what he said but I felt like cheering when it happened. He stormed off as if he didn't think he deserved that kind of treatment, but I bet it wasn't the first slap that man had gotten.'

'When did that happen?'

'I don't remember exactly but it was after Thanksgiving and close to Christmas – maybe halfway between the two.'

People had been killed for lesser reasons than a slap and a bit of humiliation. Was that the motive for Irene's murder? 'Did he stay angry with her?'

'For a couple of days he didn't speak to her but then he was back to sweet-talking every time he walked by. Men like that never learn.'

'Would she have gone out with him? Maybe just for an apology?'

'Not that I know but I suspect it was possible. Every day she left work, there was somebody waiting to walk her back to the dorm. I suppose he could have been there one night. Irene never seemed to hold a grudge against anybody.'

'So, Irene didn't seem to pay anyone any special attention?'

'Oh, I didn't say that. There was someone special. Don't know who he was but just before Thanksgiving she told me she was in love.'

'You have no idea who it was?' I asked.

Sally shook her head. 'She never said – acted all mysterious about it. But she said he was the one. She said after the war they'd be moving out of here. Probably to California, she said.'

'You never noticed her treating anyone special?'

'No, like I said, Irene was friendly with everyone.'

'Anyone treat her special?'

Sally laughed. 'They all did – even that little Italian fella who said his name was Eugene Farmer.'

I exhaled a big sigh.

'You're asking all these questions for her family, aren't you?'

'Yes,' I admitted. 'They want to know what happened to Irene. But it would be real nice if you wouldn't tell anyone I was asking.'

Sally mimed zipping her lips shut, locking them and throwing away the key. 'Like the billboard says, what I see here, stays here.'

'Thanks, Sally. If you could just think about it and let me know if anyone comes to your mind.'

We picked up our plates and carried them into the kitchen. Despite my protests, Sally insisted on helping me clean up. I washed, Sally dried and soon all was clean and put away. As she set down the towel, Sally said, 'There was this one fella, a little older but not too old. I saw him slip her a note a couple of times. She tucked them away real quick and never talked about them even when I teased her.'

'Who was that?'

'I don't know. He wasn't a guest at the house. He just showed up a lot. He brought people there who had just arrived on the train. He picked them up sometimes in the morning and whisked them off somewhere or another. Always the men who were here for a short time. I figured they were important visitors. He treated them like they were. But he never introduced himself – not to me, anyway. Irene did look at him a little differently. Now that I think about it, she was a little quieter around him, not quite as brassy and forward as she could be. I didn't think anything about it then, but now that I'm talking about it . . . well, it makes me wonder.'

It made me wonder, too. Ottinger was still a possibility. But who was the mystery man? And did Irene's behavior toward him mean anything at all? The questions and speculation kept me tossing and turning in bed for hours.

THIRTY-SIX

On Monday, all morning long, I tried to find a few minutes to chat with Charlie. I hoped he would tell me who typically met the visiting scientists at the train station. However, work kept me extremely busy as the morning went by in a blur of frenzied testing. I didn't even notice as one chemist after another left for lunch. Charlie startled me when he approached from behind and said, 'Libby, you've got to get something to eat.'

'I haven't reached a stopping point, Charlie. When I do, I will.'

'How about if I run to the canteen and grab a couple of sandwiches? You can bite and chew while you work, can't you?'

'Sure, Charlie.' I never noticed him leave and was not at all aware of the passage of time, making his return with food feel like magic.

'C'mon, Libby. You've got at least fifteen minutes before you need to intervene in the process. Sit in my office and eat lunch with me.'

'I don't know, Charlie. I don't like to walk away in the middle of—'

'Libby, honestly, at this stage, you don't need to hover over it. You know that.'

He was right, I couldn't argue. I followed him back to his office, realizing how hungry I was the moment I took the first bite. The question I wanted to ask popped back into my mind. 'Charlie, when I first got to Knoxville, you met me at the train station and drove me inside the fence. Did you do that with everyone here?'

'Oh mercy no.'

'Who brought them to the labs?'

'They had to get here on their own in those army cattle cars they call buses. You've gone to Knoxville in one, haven't you?'

'No. My old roommate was always asking me to go into town with her on Monday night but I never managed to get around to it.'

'They're really primitive, Libby. Plywood seats and usually not enough of them. You want it to stop and you pull a chain that's supposed to ring a bell in the cab of the truck but it usually doesn't work. Some of the guys here said everyone would pound on the sides but often still couldn't be heard. Sometimes, the riders have gotten so frustrated that they start deconstructing the thing from the inside, pulling out slats around the locked door just to get out.'

'We don't make visitors come here that way, do we? I mean, important scientists, General Groves, people like that?'

'Oh no. The general and other high ranking officers get met by a military driver. The scientists have a car pick them up. I've done that a couple of times, filling in for Dr Bishop when he couldn't get away.'

'Dr Bishop?' I struggled to hide the feeling of alarm his comment induced.

'Yes. He's usually the one to escort them to the guest house and to the lab but occasionally he's not available.'

'Well, I'd better get back to my lab bench.' I walked away very disturbed. Not Dr Bishop. He couldn't have been having an affair with Irene, could he? No, I needed to put that thought out of my mind. Impossible.

That afternoon, I didn't dare allow my mind to wander away from the work at hand until around four o'clock, when I was interrupted by Ann. I looked up to see her standing stock-still, staring at me. I blushed, embarrassed that she might have read my thoughts about her father.

'Dad said you have to come to dinner tonight,' Ann whispered. 'Mom's not too happy because she was just planning on leftovers. Told Dad the only other thing she had was a couple of cans of spam and it was too late in the day to go find anything else. I've been listening to Dad insisting in one ear and Mom complaining on the phone in my other ear. All I know is that you'd better be there even if Mom is serving cardboard.'

'If I can get this done in time, Ann.'

'You'd better. Be there at six. You and Dad are driving me crazy, Libby!' Ann spun around and flounced out of the room.

At 5:45, I wanted to start another test but relented and headed out the door and up the hill to the Bishop residence. When I arrived a few minutes after the hour, Mrs Bishop seemed a bit put out. No warm welcome that day. Was she irritated that I was late? Or simply annoyed that I was there? Conversation at the dinner table was stilted and focused completely on practical matters, like 'please pass the salt' and 'thank you'. I hadn't felt so relieved to push away from a table since I was a child.

I wanted to help Ann and Mrs Bishop clean up but Dr Bishop insisted that we go into the other room to talk.

'I think Bill Ottinger is your man,' he began.

I looked into his eyes but the moment I did, his darted away from mine. My suspicions from earlier that day returned, etching on my nerves like acid on glass. 'What made you reach that conclusion, sir?'

'I've asked around and it seems he left Columbia University after a bit of a scandal. It involved affairs with several of his students. One I heard was carrying his child. He left town as quickly as he could, deserting that poor girl. And, now, tucked away here, no one can come after him.'

'That does raise some suspicions,' I conceded.

'You said Irene was pregnant when she died, didn't you?'

'Yes. Yes she was.'

'You see, this time he couldn't run away. He knows too much. He's involved in something top secret at K-25 and he's pivotal to the work. Not only would they hunt him down if he ran off and either bring him back here or charge him with treason, but if he stayed put, they'd protect him at all costs even if he had killed Irene.'

I came close to telling him about Ottinger's unpleasant interaction with Irene at the guest house, but an intuitive impulse urged caution so I listened without making any objection. What he said was certainly plausible but what if it was all a lie – a fabrication to divert attention from himself? I felt like I was treading water in a murky swamp of uncertainty. In a lab, there are tests for that; in real life, it was hard to know what to do. To Dr Bishop, I simply nodded and said, 'You make good points. So what do we do now?'

'I've already spoken to Lieutenant Colonel Crenshaw. And to the chief administrator at Roane-Anderson. They have promised me they will look into it.'

'But I thought you said they would protect him at any cost?'

'Yes and they will. I asked them what they would do when they found out I was right. Crenshaw said, "We can't lose him but we will keep him closely contained."'

'What does that mean?'

'It means nothing will happen to him now – maybe he'll be charged after we win the war. But right now, they'll have military personnel following him everywhere. He won't be able to engage in adulterous activity. If he can't do that, he can't kill anyone else.'

'That's not exactly what I would call justice,' I objected.

'It's the most you can expect right now, Libby. We are at war and Ottinger is indispensible – winning the war is more important than some little girl from the country. I know that sounds unfair, but that is the way it is.'

'And what if the military decides you're right? And what if both of you are wrong? Does that mean someone, somewhere, is free to take another girl's life?'

'Just hope I'm right, Libby. Get your coat, I'll give you a lift home.'

That invitation made me nervous. Something felt wrong. Concerns about Ottinger's possible involvement made sense but Dr Bishop's certainty seemed out of proportion with the evidence. 'No, no thank you. I'd like to walk tonight.'

He objected but I brushed away his concerns. Once again, the thought of being alone with him made me very uncomfortable. I thanked Mrs Bishop for supper and she snapped back, 'Sarcasm is not becoming in a young lady, Miss Clark.'

I started to object – admittedly the spam and baked beans were a bit boring, but the homed-canned applesauce Mrs Bishop had pulled out of her pantry made the meal a treat. However, seeing the look in the other woman's eyes I simply said, 'Goodnight, ma'am.'

Walking home I tried to figure out the meaning of what had happened that night. Ann had hardly spoken to me. Mrs Bishop, the most welcoming hostess I'd ever known, was now hostile and unfriendly. And Dr Bishop? He was the most puzzling of all. He was jumping – leaping – to conclusions. He was a scientist. Scientists don't do that. We always want definitive proof. By the time, I reached home, things made even less sense to me . . .

THIRTY-SEVEN

I felt dreadful the next morning. Sleep had been elusive, fitful, haunted by frightening dreams that I could not remember except for the stark image of Irene's body, strangled under the bleachers. Every time I awoke, I reminded myself that, for now, the Ottinger problem was out of my hands, the investigation into his possible involvement out of my control.

In the cold light of morning, though, I wondered if I'd get any answers no matter how well the authorities investigated. Would I ever be told about the conclusions they reached, the actions they'd taken? Probably not. That meant I'd have to find out more information about Ottinger and his whereabouts on Christmas night. That was dangerous territory. Making inquiries about a scientist of his caliber could be interpreted as digging for secrets about his work.

Maybe the Walking Molecules could figure something out at their regular meeting tonight. If not, I'd have all day Sunday to sort through the problems and decide who was the most likely to have had an affair with Irene, to have killed Irene. Was it Ottinger? Dr Bishop? Or someone else entirely?

As a scientist, I'd been trained to compartmentalize. I needed to use those skills now; my attention must be on the work at hand. I was engrossed until Gregg walked past my station, poked my side and said, 'Looks like you're needed,' as he nodded towards the door.

There was Ann, hands on her hips, feet spread, a scowl on her face. Oh good heavens, what now? I did a quick check on the progress of the spectrograph; I had a few minutes to spare. I brushed past Ann and headed straight for the restroom. I leaned on the wall with my arms folded across my chest and waited for Ann. As soon as she opened the door, I said, 'What now, Ann?'

'What are you doing?'

'I was running some tests when you interrupted me.'

'Don't be a smart aleck. You know what I mean. What are you and Dad up to? What is going on?'

'Ann, you know I can't answer those questions.'

'Don't pull that security line on me. Don't tell me it has to do with your work. It's something personal. I know it.'

'Yes, in a way, it is. But your dad made me promise not to tell you.'

'I thought we were friends, Libby. Whatever you're doing is tearing my family apart.'

'What are you talking about, Ann?'

'Last night, after they thought I was asleep, my parents were arguing. I didn't understand what they were saying. I even wondered if you and my dad were having an affair, but I just couldn't believe that could be true.'

'It's not true, Ann.'

'Well, then, what is it? Why were they arguing about you?'

'Obviously, your mother didn't want me to come to dinner last night.'

'But why not, Libby? Why not? She's been encouraging me to spend time with you and now she doesn't want you around? What gives?'

'Exactly what were your parents arguing about – what about me caused their disagreement?'

'Mom said that you knew. She said that she was sure you knew. Knew what, Libby? What was she talking about?'

'How did your father answer her?'

'He said that he didn't think so. He said that you were focused on Dr Ottinger now. Who's Dr Ottinger? And what are you doing with him?'

'What did your mother say when he said that?'

'She said, "You're wrong, Marc. I saw it in her eyes. You need to leave, now, before they start questioning you." Who are "they", Libby and what would they question him about?'

'Ann, just tell me the whole conversation first and I'll see if I can figure it all out.'

'Then my dad said, "You know I did nothing to hurt that girl. You know I wasn't there. You know it wasn't me." And Mom said, "It doesn't matter what I know. If the truth comes out, it will be a scandal. But if you run off and hide somewhere until after the war, everyone will forget. Ann and I can live with my parents for the duration. You have to think of us first." Dad left the house then. He slammed the door when he did. Dad never slams doors. I lay awake for hours waiting for him to come back, worrying that he had left for good. Then a little after three, I heard the door open and close and finally I could get to sleep. Libby, you have to tell me what's going on. I'm scared. I'm confused.'

I gently placed my hands on Ann's upper arms and looked straight into her eyes. 'I am sorry for what you are going through, Ann. Right now, though, I don't have any real answers. I'm confused, too. But I'm going to figure this out. One way or another, I will find answers. When I do, I will let you know. Just now, I feel like I've been turned upside down and shaken, and set back down with the ground shifting beneath my feet. I imagine you feel that way, too. But, please, trust me, for just a little bit longer.'

'I don't know how long I can stand this, Libby. I feel worse than when I was a little girl and the milkman ran over my puppy with his truck. I never thought I'd ever feel any worse than that, but I do.'

I wrapped my arms around her and gave her a hug. 'I'm sorry, Ann. I'll do everything I can to make the world right again for all of us. Right now, though, I need to get back to work and try to do what I can to end this war. You understand that, don't you?'

Ann's long face looked bleak. 'Yeah, the war,' she mumbled, 'the war always comes first.'

As her slumped shoulders and weary shuffling feet left the restroom, I hustled back to my tests, regretting everything.

When chaos erupted in the Calutron area, I looked over at Charlie on the other side of the room. Without a word, we both raced out of the lab to find the source of the problem. The moment we reached the machinery, the situation was obvious.

A man was pinned to the racetrack, held there by a sheet of metal plate. He'd obviously gotten too close to the Calutron with the piece of metal in his hand. We'd all been warned about the proximity of anything that responded to magnetic pull. It was clearly a careless mistake.

Charlie shouted, 'Why the hell did he bring that in here?'

'It doesn't matter now,' engineer Mike DeVries shouted back. 'Shut down the magnet!'

In moments, the cry of, 'shut down the magnet,' were coming from nearly everyone gathered in the vicinity.

'I'm not going to do it,' the foreman yelled. 'Listen, people, there are three hundred people an hour being killed in this war. If I shut down a magnet, it could take us as long as a week to get it back up and stabilized and producing again. A week lost, more than two thousand dead. I will not do it.'

Charlie shouted over the noise, 'We can't just leave him there.'

'It's our job to stop the war.' Pointing at the pinned man, he said, 'It's his job to stop the war. Right now, we all have to act as if we were the only people in the world with that responsibility. Any damage done to this man is already done. Shutting down the magnet won't change that.'

The cries to shut down faded away. Clusters of people gathered in conversation. I felt so helpless. I tried to conjure up a solution but nothing was coming to mind. Was the man crying or moaning? It was impossible to hear above the clatter of the relentless race-track spinning away.

DeVries ran up to the foreman, leaned into his ear. The foreman nodded and yelled, 'Two by fours. We need some two by fours.'

A couple of men came running up with lumber. They shoved the boards under one side of the plate and put all their weight on it to leverage it away from the magnet. Their veins bulged, sweat appeared on their foreheads. Finally, their efforts paid off. The sheet of metal pulled away, and clanked to the floor. The man slumped to the ground. Men with a stretcher appeared out of nowhere, picked him up and hurried him away.

Like everyone else who'd witnessed the event in the Calutron room, Charlie and I both had trouble concentrating on our work. We frequently exchanged glances of concern across the room. Hours later, Charlie stood beside me and said, 'He's going to be all right.'

'Really? Are you sure?'

'Yes. He's got bruises and a few cuts. But no internal bleeding. The doctor ordered bed rest for a couple of days and then he should be back at work. And, hopefully, more careful.'

The day had been emotionally draining. I just wanted to go

home and curl up by the fire with a book. But I had a Walking Molecules meeting and a commitment to Ann and to Irene's family. I pulled on my galoshes and trudged out the door to Joe's.

THIRTY-EIGHT

When I stepped outside, Teddy was standing on the sidewalk. I'd pressured him into agreeing not to meet me alone anywhere, any time, until the situation was resolved. But there he was.

'Before you say anything, I have no excuse but now that I'm here, we might as well walk to the meeting together,' he said.

I should refuse. I should chastise him. But, in all honesty, I was really glad to see him. 'You're right. Harm's already done. Let's go.'

As we walked up the boardwalk, Ottinger hurried toward us. One hand held his hat in place, the other waved wildly in the air. As he got closer, he shouted, 'Clark! Elizabeth Clark!'

Teddy stepped between me and the onrushing man. 'What do you want?'

'I need to talk to Miss Clark.'

'About what?' Teddy said, holding his ground.

Ottinger tried to push him aside. Teddy shifted his weight and held firm. 'I think you'd better tell me what this is all about.'

Ottinger ignored him and said, 'Miss Clark, I need to talk to you.'

Curious and feeling secure with Teddy by my side, I said, 'Yes, what do you want?'

'You need to stop this.'

'Stop what, sir?'

'You need to stop persecuting me. I didn't do anything.'

'Sir, I do not know what you are talking about.'

'Irene. We're talking about Irene.'

'What about her?' Teddy asked.

'We had a little incident at the guest house and I have barely spoken to her since.'

'I understand she slapped you in the face,' I said.

'Yes and she made me cut my lip on my tooth.'

'And you were pretty angry about that, weren't you?'

'Well, wouldn't you be?'

Teddy stepped forward, putting his face right up to the man's.

'You are Ottinger, aren't you?'

'Yes, yes, yes,' he said, waving Teddy away as if the fact was insignificant. 'Miss Clark, you've got to stop lying to the authorities about me.'

'I think you'd better move along, sir,' Teddy said.

'Wait a minute, Teddy. Dr Ottinger, what makes you think I spoke to the authorities about you? Did they tell you that?'

'No. They wouldn't tell me a thing. But I asked around. I know you've been trying to find out who killed Irene. And I did not do it.'

'I didn't talk to authorities about you, Dr Ottinger,' I said.

'Well, if it wasn't you, who did talk to them?' he asked.

'I can't tell you that, Dr Ottinger.'

'Do you know, Libby?' Ted asked.

'Not now, Teddy.'

'I wasn't even here at Christmas,' Ottinger objected. 'And now they're going to talk to my wife. What is she going to think of me?'

'Well, Dr Ottinger, you might have thought of that a long time ago.'

'I admit I joked around with all the girls and took a couple of them out for a beer at Joe's. I know my wife wouldn't like that. But still, it's not as if I were doing anything else.'

'Oh, really, Dr Ottinger? What about the scandal at Columbia University?'

'What scandal?'

'You know, you and your students. And particularly the one student who was carrying your child.'

Ottinger's hands flew to his head, knocking off his hat. He grasped the thinning hair on both sides of his head. 'What are you talking about?'

'Oh, please, Dr Ottinger,' I said with a sigh.

'I swear to you. I only left the university to continue my work here. There wasn't any scandal. Students? A pregnant student? You're talking about adultery? I am a Catholic, Miss Clark! I would never . . . Who told you that? That is outrageous!'

'If it's not true, Dr Ottinger, I am sure it will be easy to find out,' I said, not really believing what I said, but hoping to call his bluff.

'So you're going to keep persecuting me? Are you going to talk to my wife, too? My colleagues at the university? Asking insinuating questions? Those questions just don't go away, Miss Clark. No one will back that story because it's not true. But the suspicion will remain there. You will destroy me, my reputation, my work, my marriage.' He lunged toward me and his nose collided with Teddy's fist. Ottinger made a hard pratfall onto the boardwalk. He looked dazed. A tiny rivulet of blood trickled out of one nostril.

'C'mon, Libby,' Teddy said, grabbing my hand.

'But, Teddy, he's hurt,' I objected.

'Yeah, he is. So hurry while we still have time to get away from here.'

We ran hand in hand down the boardwalk. The darned galoshes limited my speed. The rubbery slap on the wood made me giggle. Then, Teddy joined in, laughing louder than I was. By the time we reached Joe's, we were both laughing so hard that we could barely stand upright.

As we ran, I didn't give a thought to my hand entwined with Teddy's. Once we came to a stop and Teddy still held on firmly, I grew instantly self-conscious about the intimacy. 'Uh, Teddy . . .' I said, lifting our hands up high.

'Right,' Teddy said loosening his grip and slowly releasing my fingers. 'Don't want to give anyone the wrong idea.'

Breathless we arrived at the table commandeered by the group. For a moment, no one said a word. Tom spoke first. 'So you're both breathless and your faces are red. Do you care to explain what you've been up to?'

We ran through a tag-team explanation of our encounter with Ottinger. 'Do you believe him?' Gregg asked.

'I don't know,' I said. 'Do any of us know anyone at Columbia?'

'I have a cousin there but she's an English major. I doubt she'd know anything about anyone in the science departments,' Gregg said.

'A scandal like that should have covered the campus,' I suggested. 'Could you check with her?'

'I imagine I could get her phone number from my mother but

how could I call her and ask about a scientist here when they're listening in to all our phone calls?'

'Get the number and call her from a pay phone in Knoxville,' Teddy suggested.

'I'd have to wait until Sunday to do that. I'll try to get her tonight and keep my questions vague,' Gregg said.

'Before you go to all that trouble,' Tom said, 'we should know who made the allegations. That person might have an ulterior motive for spreading the rumor. Who told you about it, Libby?'

I paused, trying to find a good reason to not answer the question. When that failed, I said, 'Dr Bishop.'

'Bishop? You can't be serious?' Gregg said.

From there a discussion about Bishop divided the group. Those who knew him, thought he was a credible source. The other chemists were far more skeptical.

'I think,' Tom said, 'that to determine his objectivity on a more logical basis, we need to ascertain his motivation. As I see it, there are two possibilities. Either Bishop is telling the truth or at least talking about something he believes is true, or he has concocted this story for some hidden purpose. If the latter is true, it points suspicion away from Ottinger and straight to Bishop.'

'Hold on,' Gregg said. 'There is no way Bishop could kill anyone.'

'How can you be so sure about that, Gregg?' Tom asked. 'You have an affair. The girl gets pregnant. You don't want anyone to find out. Sounds like a strong motive to me. How well do you know this man, Libby?'

'I've had dinner at his home a few times. He's stood up for me and he's given me other information.'

'Come on, Libby. If he was having an affair with Irene and he killed her, wouldn't he want you to think he was on your side?'

Did Tom make a logical point? I wasn't sure but I nodded anyway.

'Don't we want to find out about Ottinger before jumping to that kind of conclusion?' Gregg said.

'I don't see the two questions as mutually exclusive,' Tom said. 'Set your emotions aside, Libby. Think logically. Is it a plausible scenario?'

All eyes turned to me. I thought about my answer before saying it. 'I have given this possibility some thought before tonight. At first, I could not imagine Dr Bishop having an affair with anyone. The more I considered it, though, I realized it was possible. However, no matter how I turn it over in my mind, I find great difficulty in thinking he could have killed Irene.'

That remark spawned another argument where one group of scientists was pitted against the others. When the speculative debate about Bishop started running in circles, Teddy interrupted the group. 'We're not going to agree on probability here. I think we just need to plan our next steps. To be thorough, we must investigate both Ottinger and Bishop. Gregg, you agreed to check out the Ottinger scandal with your cousin, right?'

Gregg nodded.

'So what do we need to know about Bishop?' Tom asked.

'We need to know if he had any opportunity to return to Oak Ridge on Christmas night. I had dismissed him as a possible suspect right away because he didn't have access to his car. Now I wonder if there was another way for him to get back here that night,' I said.

'How can we find that out?' Teddy asked.

'I'll have to talk to Ann. Her father made me promise that I wouldn't tell her anything but I don't think I can keep my word on that any longer. Ann will know if there was any way for him to get back here.'

'What if she tells her father? And he is the one responsible for Irene's death? Won't that put you at great risk?' Teddy asked.

'The whole world is at risk right now, Teddy. I can't let that get in my way. I'll talk to Ann and deal with the consequences if needed.'

THIRTY-NINE

After the meeting, I insisted that I didn't need an escort home. The most persistent offer came from Teddy. I would have liked having him walk me back but, despite our earlier indiscretion, I needed to keep him at arm's length until the problem was solved one way or another.

At home, I put on the kettle to make a cup of tea, fantasizing about having a cup of green tea or oolong but I hadn't seen either of them since the war started. The only thing I could get nowadays was black tea grown in India. While it steeped, I debated whether or not to dig into my dwindling supply of sugar to sweeten the cup but decided that adding a few drops of milk would suffice.

I sat down in front of the coal stove with my cup and *The Song of Bernadette* that Mrs Bishop had loaned to me the previous week – my, how things had changed in a week. Way back then, Mrs Bishop treated me like a second daughter. Last night, she had treated me like the mud on her shoes.

I was lost in the book when I heard a knock, banging me back into the real world. I glanced at the clock – almost 10:30. My arms tingled, my mouth dried. I was afraid to answer the door but too anxious to ignore it.

I rose, crossed the room, pressed against the door and asked, 'Who's there?'

'It's Sally. From the guest house. I'm sorry it's so late. I just got off work.'

I opened the door and shut it as quickly as I could; the wind outside was absolutely frigid. Even with the door closed, I could feel it seeping around and past the sill, making me shiver. I hurried back to the stove to warm back up.

'Again, I'm sorry,' Sally said. 'But I did think this was important.'

'Would you like a cup of tea? I still have hot water on the stove.'

'Oh, thank you, yes.'

'Come on in the kitchen with me and tell me what's so important while I fix your cup.'

'I know who that man is – the one who passed notes to Irene.'

'Really, who?'

'Someone named Dr Bishop.'

'Are you sure?' Oh, please tell me you're not.

'Yes. I hope I don't get in trouble. We've been told over and over not to question the guests about anything. He's not exactly a guest and I'm hoping he won't say anything. But I know I broke a rule.'

'What did you do?'

'I asked him his name,' Sally said.

'You just came out and asked him?'

'Not exactly. He came to escort a visitor to one of the labs.

He asked me to let the man know he was here. I pulled out a piece of paper, wrote down the date and time and said, "May I tell him who's calling?" He just stared at me at first. I was really nervous. So I said, "New policy, sir. We have to keep a record of everyone who comes to see one of our guests." He raised his eyebrows at me and said, "Dr Bishop." And I wrote it down.'

Was it Dr Bishop or was it someone else using his name? 'Let's go back in by the fire. This house is so drafty.' Back in the living room, I asked, 'What did he look like?'

'Dark hair with a wave in it. A little gray at the temples. Brown eyes. A dimple in his chin. Distinguished looking. Taller than average. But not too tall.'

That description fit Dr Bishop well – too well. 'What did he sound like? His voice, I mean. Did he have an accent?'

'Not much of one. Sounded a little bit like Tennessee. Like he was born here but had spent some time away. You know what I mean? Shoot, a year ago, I wouldn't know what that meant. But with all the people coming and going through the guest house, I'm becoming an expert on accents,' she said with a laugh.

'So his voice was a bit like mine?'

'A bit. But you definitely don't sound Tennessee underneath your Yankee polish but there's obviously a southern influence in your voice.'

Oh, dear, that did sound like Dr Bishop – another arrow pointed in his direction. Could I be wrong about him? Could he be capable of killing Irene? I realized that Sally was waiting for a response to something but I had no idea what she'd asked me. 'I'm sorry, Sally. My mind wandered.'

'I was just wondering if you knew this Dr Bishop. But you look tired, I'd better get going and let you get some sleep. If I can help you with anything else, let me know. And thanks for the tea.'

I almost urged her to stay. I needed my sleep but at that moment, I did not want to be left alone with my dark thoughts. I didn't want to believe Dr Bishop was involved with Irene but I couldn't deny the reality of what Sally said. An affair. I can accept that. But did he kill her, too? I didn't want to believe that yet – and I wouldn't – unless Gregg learned that the story about Ottinger was a lie. That would change everything.

In the meantime, I needed to get confirmation of Dr Bishop's alibi from Ann. I hoped she knew something that made it totally impossible for him to have returned to Oak Ridge that night.

When I walked into the lab Thursday morning, I went past Gregg's work station. As I approached, he shook his head. 'Couldn't get her,' he said. 'I'll try again tonight. You won't believe whose phone I used.'

'Whose?'

Gregg nodded his head to his left. 'Charlie's.'

'Really?'

'Yeah. I went to his house after the meeting that night. I told him that I was concerned about some information I received that could indicate a security problem but I didn't want to say anything to any of the authorities until I could confirm the accuracy of the information.'

'That was bold, Gregg.'

'Actually, he commended me for not taking any risks with someone's reputation until I knew what I heard was fact. Anyway, he said I could come back tonight and try again.'

'I know Dr Bishop was involved with Irene. One of her co-workers identified him as the man who was slipping notes to her. That doesn't mean he killed her, but that does make his credibility about Ottinger a major concern.'

'Don't worry. I'll follow up tonight,' Gregg said.

While I worked, I tried to think of a good reason to go to Ann's desk. Failing to come up with any good ideas, I kept an eye on the hallway, hoping to see her pass by on the way to the rest room. It took a couple of hours, but, finally, there she was. I followed her.

When I opened the door, Ann spun around and said, 'What do you want?'

'I need to talk to you, Ann. I need to tell you what I've been doing and how you can help.'

Ann folded her arms across her chest. 'OK. What's going on?'

'I've been looking into Irene Nance's death. Some people – important people – haven't been happy about that.'

'That girl they found outside the fence?'

'Yes. But Ann, please don't tell your dad I talked to you.'

'Of course not, Libby. I'm surprised you even said that. But why do you care about what happened to that girl?'

I searched Ann's face. Her expression had softened and her folded arms didn't cling as tightly to her body as they had a few seconds ago. 'Her sister was my roommate when I lived in the dormitory.'

'Oh, so you're doing it for her? What about the police or the sheriff – aren't they investigating it?'

'Ann, I found her body . . . well, my old roommate and I did. When we saw it, it wasn't outside the fence. It was at the high school.'

Ann's eyes widened. 'Did you move the body outside the fence?'

'Good heavens, no.'

'Then who did?'

'The army,' I said.

'Whatever for?'

'They claim it was both for the sake of security and for the morale of the community.'

'That doesn't sound right, but we are at war. You said I could help. How?'

'I need to know if there is any chance your dad could have come back here to Oak Ridge Christmas night.'

'You think my dad . . .? How could you?' Ann said, her arms flying out from her body and pinwheeling in the air.

'I can't believe your dad would kill her but I do believe he was having an affair with her.'

'You are a liar! You are trying to destroy my parents' marriage. Why is that, Libby? You want my dad for yourself?'

'Of course not, Ann, I—'

'You just get away from me, Miss Elizabeth Clark. You stay away from me. You stay away from my dad. You stay away from my home. You hear me?' Ann shoved the restroom door hard and stalked down the hall.

Oh dear, that was a mistake to try and explain the situation to Ann; I should have realized that being told her father had had an affair would be too much of a shock for her to handle. What could I do about it? Not much. Not now. I filed it away for later consideration and focused anew on the work at hand.

At the end of another long day, I bundled up before stepping outside. My hand was on the door when I heard my name.

I tensed when I saw Ann hurrying towards me. 'Wait up, Libby.'

I fought the urge to run outside and all the way home.

'Boy, you sure work late. I've been waiting forever for you to finish up for the day.'

'Well, I'm done now. What do you have to say?' I braced for the worst.

'I need to talk to you. Come on, let's go. I'll walk you home.' We walked quietly for a couple of minutes. Instead of looking at Ann, I focused on the boards beneath my feet. Finally, she said, 'I'm sorry, Libby. I shouldn't have jumped on you like I did earlier. I've been thinking about what you said and it made my parents' fight make more sense. How do you know about my dad having an affair?'

I hated telling her about it. 'He used to slip notes to Irene. Someone who worked for her said she was in love and they thought he was the one.'

'But see, you don't definitely know, do you?' Ann asked.

'Not one hundred per cent. But it doesn't look good.'

'But just because he might have been having an affair, doesn't mean he hurt that girl. In fact, I know he couldn't have.'

'How do you know that?' I asked.

'Because Dad couldn't have gone anywhere on Christmas night – my aunt's car disappeared.'

'How do you know he didn't take it?'

'My cousin and I were up late playing Monopoly – the game went on forever. Anyway, about ten o'clock, my dad asked my Aunt Mabel where her car keys were. They both looked around without finding them and Dad went outside. When he came back in, he said that the car was gone. My aunt said that nobody should expect him to go to a meeting on Christmas night anyway.'

'Where was the car?' I asked.

'I don't know.'

'Who couldn't have taken it? Do you have an uncle? A cousin? Could it have been your mom?'

'My Uncle Henry and my mom had both gone to bed. I was playing with one cousin and my other cousin had shipped out with the Navy. But anyway, around midnight my Aunt Mabel and my dad went to bed. It was after two in the morning before I landed on Boardwalk where my cousin had a hotel and I lost the game. The car wasn't there then. It was there the next morning but nobody wanted to talk about it. My cousin and I both asked about it but all we got was: "It's here now, that's all that matters." But it wasn't there when my dad went to bed so I know he couldn't have gone to Oak Ridge. He wanted to go, but he couldn't.'

'Irene came home early on Christmas night. She wasn't supposed to come back until two days later. But she planned on meeting someone that night.'

Ann sighed. 'Probably was my dad. But he didn't make it. She had to have met up with someone else.'

'Thank you, Ann, for telling me about this. Do you want to come in? I don't have anything but eggs and spam but I'd be glad to share it with you.'

'Nah. I need to get home. Mom's already going to be mad because I'm late for supper. She's been so touchy the last couple of days. I don't want to give her another reason to get all steamed up. You won't tell her about my dad, will you? She'll probably find out if she doesn't know already. But if you tell her, she might tell me I can't see you again.'

I fixed supper thinking about Dr Bishop. I was pleased that there was now a very strong possibility that he could not have killed Irene. But where did that leave everything? Why did Irene say Dr Bishop was named Bill? Is that what he told her? Or did she just make it up to protect his identity?

And who did kill her if it wasn't Bishop? Did Irene pick up with someone else when Bishop stood her up? Or did someone just happen to run across her and take advantage of finding her all alone, waiting for her lover? But if they always met at Towncenter, how did she get to the high school? Did they change their meeting place? Or did she know the person she encountered at the usual place? Could it have been Dr Ottinger?

FORTY

When I stepped out of the house Friday morning, someone was huddled beside the coal bin. I walked down a couple of steps, and he turned around. 'Gregg, what are you doing here?'

'I thought walking you to work would be a good time to talk. I reached my cousin last night,' he said.

'And?'

'I asked her if there'd been some sort of scandal involving a professor last year. She said she didn't know of any but said if I told her a bit more, she'd ask around. So, I told her what Bishop told you but I didn't mention Dr Ottinger's name.

'And she said, "Oh, that wasn't my school – that was Teresa's. That's all she wanted to talk about last summer at the family reunion." Teresa is my second cousin. She goes to the University of California. I hadn't heard about it because I couldn't go to the reunion since I already went up to Rochester at the time. So, I got Teresa's phone number and talked to her later that night.'

'And what did she say?'

'I asked her the same question and she confirmed the scandal, said it was horrible. One girl left in disgrace – total disgrace. I asked her if that girl was pregnant. And she said, "What do you think I am telling you?" I almost came over after I got off of the phone with her but it was pretty late by then. The time difference out in California made it hard to get hold of her at a civilized hour.'

Wasn't Dr Bishop at the University of California? I wondered but didn't dare say those words out loud.

'I really didn't want to use names over the telephone line. But I had to know, so I asked her, "Dr Ottinger, right?" And she said, "Ottinger? I never heard of him." And I asked who it was. She said she couldn't remember the name off the top of her head. All she could remember, she said was that his name had something to do with church. So I said, "Parrish?"'

'Who's Parrish?' I asked.

'I don't know. I just made it up – trying to prod her into remembering. But she said that wasn't it. So I said, "Chapel?" And again she said "no" but insisted she'd know it if she heard it. So I said it. I asked her, "Bishop? Dr Bishop?" And she said, "Yes, that's it. Dr Bishop – Marc Bishop if I remember correctly. They said that no female chemistry student was safe around him. There were a lot of other girls besides the one who got pregnant".'

I stopped walking and stood still, my mind racing as it sought a way to discredit or minimize what I'd just heard. Gregg went a few steps and then came back to my side. 'I didn't want to believe it either, Libby. But there it is. He had several affairs with students. One of them got pregnant. He got into a lot of trouble for that. If he got another girl pregnant maybe this time he'd handle it differently.'

'He'd kill her?'

'That's what I'm afraid of, Libby. It sure follows the laws of probability. And the simplest solution is usually the right one. It's logical that whoever had an affair with Irene is the one who killed her.'

'But he couldn't have, Gregg,' I said and started walking again.

'Why not?'

I told him about the vehicle situation on Christmas night and said, 'See. He had no way to get here when Irene was murdered.'

'Think about it, Libby. If he were planning a murder, don't you think he's smart enough to cover his tracks? What if he hid the car earlier and put on that little act. And when Ann thought he was going to bed, he slipped out the back door or a window and went to the car, drove down here, bumped off Irene and drove back?'

'I can't believe that's true, Gregg. Marc Bishop isn't that unusual a name, is it? And there'd be signs, wouldn't there? I mean, he seems so nice and . . .'

'I'm having a hard time with it, too, Libby. I think we need to get the group together and try to hash this all out. Someone, like Tom, who doesn't know Bishop, might be able to show us where our logic is faulty. Or maybe we'll convince him that Bishop isn't the kind of man who'd commit murder. I'll spread the word and see when we can get together. I don't think I can pull it off tonight. How about Saturday night at Joe's?'

'It's too loud there on weekend nights to think and impossible to have a conversation. What if everyone comes to my place – Sunday afternoon?'

'Are you sure that's wise? It might look suspicious.'

'Nothing is wise right now, Gregg. But it would look less suspicious during the daytime than it would be if all of you snuck into my place after dark. And we've got to sort this out. If we reach any strong conclusion, I'll go see the lieutenant colonel on Monday. If not, we can plan what to do next. In the meantime, I'll try to get a minute with Ann and find out if they were in California.'

'OK, I'll see if I can gather all our molecules together.'

I giggled at the sound of his words. 'I'm sorry. It just sounded so silly.'

'No apologies needed. I told you it was a goofy, alcohol-induced name.'

Once again, I worked with an eye on the hallway, watching for Ann. When I spotted her going down the hall, I waited a couple of minutes, hoping to make the encounter appear serendipitous. I walked in as she emerged from a stall. 'Hi, Ann. How are you?'

'Typing like mad. It seems as if everybody wants a letter sent out today – typical Friday.'

'I wanted to ask you about something.'

Ann turned a sad face towards me. 'About my dad?'

'Oh, no. Nothing like that. It was just wondering about your accent. I was talking to a girl about all the different accents around here and she was trying to figure them all out. It made me think about you. I know your family all lives in Tennessee but you don't have a real definite Tennessee accent.'

'That's because I moved away from the state years ago and just moved back this year.'

'Where did you go? Up north?' I prodded.

'No, we went out west. California. Berkeley, California.'

'What were you doing out there?'

'It was because of my dad,' she said with a smile. 'He was a professor at the University of California. I thought you knew that.'

'If I did, I'd forgotten.' I slipped into a stall, hoping Ann would go away.

She shouted, 'Talk to you later,' and went out the door.

I didn't want her to say that. I wanted Irene's killer to be anyone but Dr Bishop. If he was charged with murder, I knew my friendship with Ann would be over. Even if Ann didn't cut it off, she and her mother would move away from Oak Ridge. I'd never see her again. At least not until after the war. The last phrase curdled. I was so tired of waiting for 'after the war'.

*   *   *

At the end of the day, Gregg reported on his progress, 'The old lab telegraph is working well. Caught up with most of the guys. Me or one of the other guys will talk to the remaining three at the dorms tonight. We'll all be at your place on Sunday afternoon at two.'

Each little step in the right direction gave me a good feeling. As usual, everything was moving too slow for my taste – but I had to admit that I always felt that way in my life and in my work for as long as I could remember. I always wanted to charge ahead much faster than the situation would allow.

When I reached my block, I saw a light shining in my house. Had I forgotten to turn them off that morning? I didn't think so. Someone must be inside. I stopped on the boardwalk, unsure of whether to go into the house or run for help. I grappled with my emotions by running a quick logic check: I'd told several people to feel free to come in out of the cold if I was not there when they arrived; and wouldn't anyone with a reason to harm me want to catch me unawares? The light was on. It was not a surprise attack.

I couldn't see any flaws in my line of logic but still, I was apprehensive about the reliability of my conclusion. I mounted the stairs with heavy feet and opened the door. Mrs Bishop was sitting under the lamp by the coal stove. Knowing who was there did little to alleviate my anxiety. Our last encounter had not been pleasant. Maybe Ann told her about my suspicions. Maybe that was why she was here.

Mrs Bishop stood and said, 'Good evening, Libby. I hope you don't mind me coming inside. I was getting cold out there on your stairway.'

'I'm glad you did,' I lied, standing between Mrs Bishop and the door.

'First of all, dear, I wanted to apologize for being in such a foul mood the other night. It wasn't you. I was rather irritated with Dr Bishop.'

I wasn't sure if I believed that, but the couple had had an argument after I'd left. Maybe it was true. I relaxed a bit and smiled. 'Think nothing of it, Mrs Bishop.'

'That's not the only reason I'm here. I'm worried about Ann. She's hasn't been herself. I don't know what to do and was hoping you could help me.'

'I'll certainly try, Mrs Bishop. How about I make some tea for us first?'

'That would be delightful, dear.'

I went into the kitchen with Mrs Bishop trailing behind me. As she stood behind me, it seemed as if she was constantly moving out of my range of vision. Her movements made me feel uneasy but I pushed that feeling aside, chastising myself for being a nervous Nellie and imagining danger where none existed.

I was pouring water from the kettle into the teapot when something flew past my face and jerked me back. My throat tightened. The kettle clattered to the floor. Hot water sloshed from the spout scalding the skin on my legs. But worse, I suddenly couldn't breathe. I tried to cry out but only squeaked the puniest of sounds. What was happening? At first, I had no idea but when I did, panic washed over me.

Mrs Bishop had cinched something around my neck and she was tightening it more with every passing second. I clawed at my throat, trying to relieve the pressure and kicked my feet back at Mrs Bishop, but she shifted around, keeping me off-balance and unable to land a solid blow. Why was she doing this?

In the drawer, there was a knife, but I couldn't reach it. My head was swimming. I had to act immediately or it would be too late. Desperate, I lunged forward, falling on the counter. Mrs Bishop tightened her grip.

I fumbled open the drawer and felt inside until I found the handle of my biggest knife. I whipped it out and stabbed backwards.

Mrs Bishop shouted out and fell to the floor. A scarf fluttered down on the linoleum beside her. Mrs Bishop wasn't moving. Blood pooled on the floor. The knife protruded from her side.

My head was spinning but I could breathe. I took a deep breath, reveling in it but when I took a step, I nearly lost my balance. I used the counter and the walls to keep upright as I staggered to the front door. Outside on the landing, I inhaled deeply again, trying to regain my equilibrium. I felt very unsteady but my fear summoned sufficient adrenaline to move my feet down the stairs and up the boardwalk. I moved as quickly as I could on my uncooperative, shaking legs. I didn't stop until I collapsed against the counter at the police department.

FORTY-ONE

wanted to slip to the floor and rest, just rest. But I had no
time to spare. Mrs Bishop might still be alive, but she needed
immediate medical attention. I heard the desk sergeant say
something but his words were not loud enough for me to understand over the sound of my own ragged breath. I pressed both
hands into the wooden counter, pushing upward as I gulped for
air.

'Ma'am, is someone chasing you?' the desk sergeant asked.

'I don't know,' I said, panting between each word.

'Then why were you running?'

'I . . .' I inhaled sharply and spoke as I exhaled, 'I may have
killed someone.'

'You killed someone?'

'I don't know. I left her on the floor.' I sucked in another hard
breath. 'She was bleeding. I stabbed her. She might still be alive.
You need to help her.'

The sergeant pulled out a form and asked, 'What is your
name?'

'Clark. Elizabeth Clark. But please, you need to get someone
to my house to help her.'

'Elizabeth Clark?'

'Yes. But hurry. I don't want her to die.'

The sergeant came out from behind the counter, and placed a
hand around my upper arm. 'I understand, Miss Clark. Why don't
you come in here and sit down? I know your work is very
stressful.'

'This has nothing to do with my work,' I said struggling against
the tug on my arm.

'Officer Ambrose, could you give me a hand out here?'

'Let me go,' I insisted. 'Listen to me. A woman might be dying.'

I didn't stop struggling but, with the help of a uniformed
officer, the sergeant trundled me down the hall and into a room
where they forced me into a plain wooden chair. 'You stay right
here, Miss Clark,' the sergeant said. 'I'll get you help right away.'

'I'm not the one in need of help,' I objected, trying to rise from the chair but being firmly pressed down into it.

'Miss, you just sit here. Officer Ambrose will be right outside the door. You're safe now.'

I slumped into the chair feeling defeated. 'I'll stay here but you need to get someone to my house. You need to get help for that woman.'

The sergeant and officer walked out of the room without saying another word. And there I sat helpless and confused. What did they think was going on? How long were they going to hold me? Would they send someone to the house? They had to. Mrs Bishop might bleed to death if they didn't. But why did I care? She tried to kill me. Obviously, she saw me as a threat to her husband, her family. Could I completely blame her for wanting to protect them? No. Not completely. When Dr Bishop killed Irene, he set this all in motion.

I jumped up and pounded on the door. 'Officer! Officer! You need to get help for Mrs Bishop. She might bleed to death. Please help her.'

'Miss Clark, you need to calm down,' he shouted through the door. 'If you don't, I'm going to have to handcuff you to the chair. Please don't make me do that.'

'But she might die . . .'

'Miss Clark, please.'

I slouched away from the door and returned to my seat. They must have been told some strange story about me. They were treating me as if I were mentally unstable. I looked for a way out of the room. But there were no windows. No other exits. The only way out was through that door and the officer was bigger and stronger than me. I slumped in the chair and waited.

Time passed with the speed of an opossum lumbering across a country road. If someone was going to go to my house, they would have been there and back by now. If they'd done that, they would know I was telling the truth.

I walked over and knocked politely on the door. 'Officer Ambrose, sir.'

'Yes, miss.'

'I need to go to the lady's room.'

'Miss, I am sorry. I was told to keep you in this room.'

I slid as much southern sugar into my voice as I could muster,

'But sir, please. I really need to go to the ladies.' I sniffled for effect. 'I really can't wait any longer.'

For a moment all was quiet. I loudly choked back a sob. The lock clicked and the door opened.

'Thank you, thank you, sir,' I said coming through the door, wiping away imaginary tears.

'It's down this hall. Walk ahead of me and don't try to run off.'

I slipped into the restroom. In the stall, I planned my next moves. Flushing the toilet, I walked over to the sink. I turned on the water and let it run for a moment. I bunched up a towel and dampened it, and turned off the water. Opening the door to the hallway, I smiled, hung my head and said, 'Thank you, sir.' Then I threw the towel in his face and took off running.

He was standing between me and the lobby with the front door, so I took off in the opposite direction. There had to be a rear exit and I would find it. Every moment, I faced another decision. Turn right. Turn left. Go straight. I no longer had any idea of my relative position in the building.

Suddenly, I faced a dead end with an open door to another room. Would I find a way out in there? Looking through the entry, I saw windows. Windows can be broken. I rushed into the room, thinking it was empty but then heard a voice saying, 'She's quite hysterical.'

'I am not hysterical. She tried to kill me. Look. Look at my neck,' I said raising my chin and pulling down on the collar of my blouse.

The man on the phone spoke again into the receiver. 'And it looks like she injured herself to give credibility to her story.'

'I did not do this,' I shouted as Officer Ambrose pulled my arms behind my back. 'I stabbed her. Go to my house. Take care of her.' Cold metal encircled my wrists. A loud click echoed in my ears.

The man at the desk disconnected his call. 'Miss Clark, I am very sorry for having to restrain you but it's for your own good.'

'Go to my house!'

'We did, Miss Clark. There is no one there.'

'Did you look in the kitchen?' I shrieked as Ambrose led me out of the room.

'Yes, Miss Clark. I am very sorry. We have a doctor on the way to help you.'

'I'm not the one that needs help,' I shouted.

Ambrose manhandled me down another hallway to a barred cell. He unlocked the door and shoved me inside. I stumbled and didn't regain my balance until I ran into the opposite wall.

'The doctor will be here soon, Miss Clark. Try to pull yourself together,' the officer urged.

'If she dies, her blood will be on your hands, too.'

He looked at me, shaking his head sorrowfully. 'I'm sorry. When you get better, you'll understand. Sit on the bench and be quiet. If you settle down, maybe we can take those handcuffs off.' He walked away, his head swinging back and forth with every step.

A few minutes later, Ambrose and the sergeant led a man with a doctor's bag up the hall. He was short with gray hair, balding on top and drooping across his forehead. Gray stubble marched along his jawline. 'It's very sad,' he said to the policemen. 'But often the line between genius and insanity runs very thin.'

'I am not a genius,' I objected.

'There, there,' the doctor said. The three men waited until two white uniformed hospital orderlies carrying a stretcher arrived outside the bars.

'What are you going to do to me?' I asked, jumping to my feet.

The cell door opened and all five men converged on me. 'You're going to have to take the cuffs off so I can give her an injection.'

'No. No. I don't want an injection. Stay away from me,' I said as they backed me into a corner. I hissed at them, feeling primitive, animal, savage – I was ready to do anything to get away but with my hands fastened behind my back, I was helpless.

Ambrose flipped me around as if I was weightless and pressed my face into the rough wall as he unfastened the cuffs. The second my wrists were free, he spun me back around. I lashed out with my arms now, swinging punches but the orderlies easily overpowered me, pushing shoulders back, pinning in place like a dead butterfly.

The doctor reached for my arm. I tried to pull it away but the sergeant grabbed it firmly by the elbow and forced it out toward the doctor. The doctor squeezed my fingers under his arm and wrapped and tied a rubber tube above the sergeant's encircling hands. He palpitated my vein. I willed it to flatten, to no avail. When the needle pierced my skin, I screamed.

In seconds, a warm sensation coursed through my limbs making me feel light and weightless. Hands slipped under my arms and ankles. Before I knew what happened, I was lying flat on my back. I looked at the lights in the ceiling passing over my head. And then, I was gone.

FORTY-TWO

I was foggy-headed when I awoke. And frightened. I didn't know where I was. I blinked as I looked around the room. Was I still in Oak Ridge?

'She's opened her eyes,' someone shouted out.

'Miss Clark,' someone else said while placing a hand on my shoulder. I flinched away from his touch. 'You're OK. Everything is all right. But we need you awake. Can you sit up if I help you?'

I nodded. 'Mrs Bishop?' The croaking voice I heard did not sound like mine. My mouth was so dry that my tongue cleaved to the roof of my mouth. My throat hurt. 'Water. Please.'

A nurse handed me a glass and I took one greedy gulp after another. When I handed the glass back, another nurse handed me a cup of coffee. 'It's a little hot, can you manage it?' I nodded. 'Drink up. We need to get you alert. We need your help.'

They needed my help? What had happened while I slept? 'Mrs Bishop – did you get to Mrs Bishop? Is she still alive?'

'We think she's alive but we're not sure. We're going to get you over to her house as soon as we can,' a voice said from the other side of the room.

Why would they want to take me to the woman who had tried to kill me? I looked toward the person who last spoke. It was the same man I'd seen talking on the telephone in that room at the end of the hall.

'Who are you?' I demanded to know.

'Lieutenant Hammond. We met earlier but you might not remember.'

'Oh, I remember all right.' I turned away from him and looked at the nurse. 'What's going on?'

Before the woman could respond, Hammond said, 'I'll explain to you on the way over to the scene.'

'What scene?' I asked.

'I'll explain in the car,' he said.

'No! I will not go anywhere with you.'

'But Miss Clark, you are needed . . .'

'I'll go where I'm needed but not with you, not in a police car and not with any officer of the law.'

'Miss Clark, you are acting crazy,' Hammond snapped.

If he was calling me crazy, he obviously didn't believe I was an insane person who needed to be humored. That was definitely an improvement. Still, I wasn't going anywhere with a policeman.

'Oh, leave her alone,' one of the nurses said. 'You treated her like she was crazy when she was telling you the truth and now you're calling her crazy when she expresses a healthy skepticism about your intentions. I'll drive her over there.'

Things had really changed while I was asleep.

'She needs to be briefed,' Hammond objected.

'I know enough. *I'll* tell on the way over,' the nurse insisted. 'C'mon, Libby.'

In her car, the nurse said, 'I don't know the whole story but I'll tell you what I know.'

'First, what time is it?' I asked.

'1:45 a.m.'

'How long was I out?'

'Just short of four hours. We gave you another injection to bring you around – not the best things to do to a body. You will probably not react well to it.'

'What do you mean?'

'In all likelihood, you will develop a splitting headache later this morning, along with a seemingly unquenchable thirst. And when that hits, the only thing that's going to make you feel better is a long, long sleep.'

'Not exactly a cheery prospect. Tell me, what is going on here?'

'After you were brought over to the hospital, there was an

argument between the military and the physicians. We thought you should be in a proper mental health facility where you could be evaluated and treated. They argued that it would compromise security by bringing unwanted attention to our mission here. They worried about the risk that in your state you might reveal important information about your work here.'

'What did you all decide?'

'We didn't have time to make a decision. The argument was still underway when one of the Bishops' neighbors called the police station and reported he heard shots fired and a woman screaming and thought it came from the Bishop house.

'An officer responded to the Bishop home but when he knocked on the front door and got no response, he eased the door open. At that moment, a shot rang out. The officer was hit – it was only a flesh wound but it was enough to make him lose his footing. He stumbled off the steps and fell on the ground, and broke an arm.'

'Oh no. The same arm that was shot?'

'Yes, but at least he has one arm that still functions. We patched him up, too, while you slept. Meanwhile, Lieutenant Hammond was concerned enough about what was happening over there, that after he sent in help and reinforcements for the injured officer, he personally made a trip to your house. He didn't find a body but he noticed a throw rug on the kitchen floor that seemed to be in a peculiar spot. He lifted it and saw smeared blood on the floor. Then, he looked in your trash can and found towels stained with reddish brown. And he came to the hospital and here we are.'

'So what's going on at the Bishop house?'

'That I don't know. But right now, the police are assuming it's a hostage situation. They just don't know who the hostages are and who is holding them.'

As we pulled up to the scene, the situation looked anything but normal. Patrol cars filled the street in front of the Bishop home. I stepped out of the nurse's car and looked around for a familiar face. I heard a voice shout, 'Over here, Miss Clark.'

I turned and saw Lieutenant Colonel Crenshaw and Charlie Morton standing side by side. I walked over to them and saw relief wash over Charlie's face. 'Thank God, you're OK, Libby.'

'What happened? What's going on inside the house? Is Ann in there?'

Crenshaw placed a hand on Libby's shoulder. 'Let me explain, Libby. Let's go sit in my car.'

I didn't particularly trust Crenshaw either but I slid into the passenger seat just the same. I did, however, keep a hand on the door handle, just in case. 'How did you get involved in this?'

'You look wary, Miss Clark. I can't say that I blame you. Lieutenant Hammond called me over to your house. Besides the evidence in your kitchen, we found a trail of blood leading down your steps. It ended just where someone would have stood to get into an automobile and drive away.

'Both the lieutenant and I thought it was possible that the story you told was true. I admit that I was still skeptical. But I couldn't neglect what I saw with my own eyes. When we arrived over here, I became a believer. I'm sorry for doubting you – we all regret it.'

'I think this is connected to Irene's death.'

'In all likelihood, that is correct. What do you theorize happened?'

'Dr Bishop was having an affair with Irene Nance,' I began.

'Correct,' Crenshaw said.

'Irene was pregnant.'

Crenshaw nodded.

'Bishop had been in that situation before. This time, he decided to eliminate the problem by killing Irene before she could kill his career.'

'That part of your theory needs to be reconsidered, Miss Clark.'

'Why?' I asked. 'Do you have evidence pointing in another direction?'

'Just before midnight on Christmas evening, a car belonging to Mrs Bishop's sister did go through the gate into our facility.'

'Well, that puts Dr Bishop here and gives him the opportunity to commit the crime.'

'Not exactly. There was only one passenger in the vehicle. It was not Dr Bishop. It was a woman – his wife, Mildred Bishop.'

'But I thought she was protecting her husband. I thought that's why she attacked me.'

'Apparently, she was just trying to save her own neck.'

'So she must be the one firing the gun inside the house?'

'Probably. But it is also possible that Dr Bishop has the weapon and thinks somehow he can protect his wife. Or maybe we heard gunfire because he killed her when he found out what she had done.'

'But she was injured. How did she get to her house?' I asked.

'We found the car parked a block up the street. There was blood on the driver's seat and a spotty trail of blood up to the house. We assumed she drove herself home.'

'So where do things stand now? What do you need from me?'

'It's a long shot. But we were hoping that you could try talking to Mrs Bishop on the bullhorn. Maybe your presence would catch her off guard. Maybe you could convince her to release her daughter. It seems worth a shot.'

'OK,' I agreed. 'I don't think it will do any good but I'll try.'

The police provided me with as much cover as possible. I lifted the instrument to my lips and shouted. 'Mrs Bishop, this is Libby Clark. I need to talk to Ann. Could you let her come out, please?'

A shot fired out from the house, shattering the headlight on a patrol car. A second shot dinged a lamp post. I sighed, turned the bullhorn over to the officer standing beside me, and walked over to where Crenshaw waited. He gave me a grim smile and said, 'Thank you for trying.'

FORTY-THREE

The military reinforcements that Crenshaw requested marched forward to firm up the barrier with more bodies and more fire power. The time ticked by. I had nothing to do but observe and listen. Officials, it seemed, were torn between the fear that any move on their part could harm those whom they believed might be hostages and the anxiety that doing nothing might be even worse. The decision making was complicated by the presence of two commanding officers: Lieutenant Hammond of the police force and Lieutenant Colonel Crenshaw who was in charge of the unit of soldiers.

The thin light that arrived just before dawn was seeping into the sky when sudden movement erupted among the soldiers and police. They all went into shooters' stances and drew beads on the front of the house. I followed the direction of the gun barrels and saw the spark that caused the flurry of action. The door was opening slowly. Through the crack, a hand emerged waving a towel. 'Hold your fire' screamed up and down the line surrounding the house.

The door opened further, then all the way. Ann Bishop stepped out on the front porch.

Instinctively, I ran towards her but was stopped before I got far. Soldiers stormed up the steps; one grabbed Ann and took her down the stairs, the others rushed inside. In a moment, another uniform walked out holding up Dr Bishop, whose pants leg appeared torn and darkened as if by blood. Medics loaded him into a waiting ambulance.

Crenshaw stepped up to me and said, 'Thank you for your persistence, Miss Clark. We owe you a debt.'

I looked away. Too little. Too late. I wish I'd done something differently. I didn't know what but there must have been a better way to resolve the situation.

A soldier stepped out on the top step of the house. 'Lieutenant Colonel Crenshaw, you're needed in here.'

'Well, Miss Clark, they must have subdued Mildred Bishop. I'll be back as soon as I can,' Crenshaw promised.

A minute later, Crenshaw emerged and walked straight back to me. 'Mildred Bishop is dead, Miss Clark.'

'Dead?'

'Yes, from the looks of it, she bled to death while we waited for her to surrender.'

'I did kill her then.' A torrent of guilt flooded me with a fresh wave of pain. I caused the death of another human being. I made the wound that caused her to die. What Mrs Bishop had done was horrible but still she was Ann's mother. I had no right to kill her.

'Don't blame yourself, Libby. She would have been captured or killed, now or later. Just like Hitler. Violence leads to a violent end. You've done no wrong. You are a heroine.'

I heard his words and believed he was sincere. 'Thou shalt not kill' thundered in my head. 'If she'd been captured sooner, she'd still be alive.'

'And with that outcome, there would be a trial. Not only would it be a security risk but it would cause prolonged anguish for her husband and daughter.'

Yes, but Ann might forgive me then. I could never expect that now. I'd violated one of God's commandments. It seemed in both my private life and my work, I was following the same path. Who was I to judge when to kill and when to not?

FORTY-FOUR

I climbed into one jeep for a ride to the guest house, Ann got into another. I don't know if Ann was aware that I was even there. She didn't even spare a glance in my direction. Dr Bishop was already on the way to the hospital to be treated for the gunshot wound he'd received when he tried to rush his wife and take away her weapon. After his injury was addressed, he, too, would return to the guest house where we would all stay while police finished their investigations. Lieutenant Colonel Crenshaw promised all of us that the military would come in and clean all the biological contaminants out of both of our homes. The military sure had fancy terminology for bloody messes.

By the time I arrived at my temporary residence, my head was throbbing, just as the nurse said it would. Each beat of my heart seemed to worsen the pain. I turned down an offer of breakfast, slipped into a pair of pajamas that the police thoughtfully retrieved from my home. As I collapsed on the bed, my last thoughts were of Irene Nance – Irene, who worked right here in the very place I was falling to sleep. Irene, who didn't deserve to die.

When I awoke, darkness had returned. I must have slept ten hours or more. My head still felt fragile as if the headache would come crashing back if I made any sudden moves. But, boy, was I hungry. I picked up the telephone receiver by the bed but couldn't get a dial tone. I checked the closet but there was no other clothing anywhere except for a terry cloth robe draped across the foot of the bed. Someone had removed my blood-stained garments while I slept. Would they try to clean out the stains? Or had they disposed of them already?

I shrugged into the robe and stepped to the door. Grabbing

the knob, I twisted but it didn't move. I pounded on the door with a fist.

The door opened a crack and a soldier said, 'Yes, ma'am, what can I do for you?'

'Why am I locked in my room?'

'For your protection, ma'am.'

'Right. Well, I don't need protection any longer. And my phone is dead. I need to go downstairs to speak to someone at the front desk.'

'No, ma'am. You can't do that.'

'Are you telling me I'm a prisoner?'

'No, ma'am. You just can't leave the room until Lieutenant Colonel Crenshaw gets here to talk to you.'

'So I am a prisoner.'

'No ma'am, you are not. In fact, I've been instructed to get you whatever you want from the kitchen. It's dinner time so you can have dinner – there's a menu on the table by the window. But since you just woke up, I'll be glad to bring you a breakfast tray if you prefer.'

'I understand. You don't like the word prisoner. Would it be easier for you to say I am under arrest?'

'No, ma'am, because that is not the truth. You are not under arrest and you are not a prisoner.'

'Then, please, let me leave the room.'

'That is not possible, ma'am. I can't let you speak to anyone but me until the lieutenant colonel gets here. So what do you want to eat?'

I was getting nowhere arguing with him. Maybe I could slip out while he was gone. 'All right, soldier. Two eggs over easy, home-fried potatoes, grits and bacon.'

'You want any toast with that?'

'Sure.'

'Juice?'

'Just coffee, please.'

He nodded and pulled the door shut.

I waited until his footsteps faded away before trying the door. Unfortunately, he had remembered to lock it. I rummaged around the room looking for something I could use to pick the lock. The closest possible thing to a tool I could find was the toothbrush in the bathroom. One escape route cut off. I peered out the windows.

I wasn't on the ground floor and saw nothing below it to break my fall if I jumped except for a few puny bushes that looked like they'd collapse if I dropped a pillow on them. That's an idea. No, actually, that's a pathetic, ridiculous excuse for an idea. I sat down to wait for breakfast.

I'd finished eating and was sipping on the last cup of coffee when a knock at the door signaled the arrival of Lieutenant Colonel Crenshaw. 'Good evening, sir. I'd offer you some coffee but I'm drinking the last cup now. Should I ask for another pot?'

'Not unless you want it, Miss Clark. If I drink anymore coffee now, I'll never get to sleep and today has been far too long already.'

'Now why don't you explain to me why I've been held here against my will?'

'Miss Clark, you said you'd be happy to stay in the guest house while we sanitized your home.'

'Yes, but I didn't expect to be locked in my room like a prisoner.'

'Prisoner is a harsh word.'

'Yes, it is. Why am I under arrest?'

'I wish you wouldn't look at it that way,' Crenshaw pleaded.

'Just tell me what you want to tell me. I'll listen carefully and hope my reward is my returned freedom. This isn't Germany, you know.'

'I see that you are still a bit overwrought. We simply did not want you to speak to anyone until we reached an understanding.'

Interesting choice of words.

'Here is our situation,' he continued. 'The killer is dead, the population is safe. Justice has been satisfied. There is no need for further action. Do you agree?'

'In principle,' I said.

'There is also no need for anyone not directly involved to know anything about this incident.'

'What about Irene's parents? Don't they deserve answers?'

'Yes, they've been told the killer of their daughter is dead. Their sense of justice has been satisfied.'

Did 'satisfied' adequately describe how Ruth was feeling right now? I hoped she was coping well with the news and made a wish that one day I would be able to see her again. Crenshaw cleared his throat, bringing my focus back to him. I asked, 'What about the Bishops' neighbors? There's no way they could have missed all the excitement. They'll need to be told something about what happened.'

'We've talked to everyone of them. They have an understanding of the events that transpired.'

'And just what do they understand, sir?'

'They understand that Mrs Bishop had a nervous breakdown, administered a serious self-inflicted injury and died in her home.'

Amazing how well he could lie without the slightest crack in his façade. 'You sure know how to spin a yarn, sir. It's a shame it doesn't resemble the truth.'

'If it's repeated enough, it will become the truth.'

'Oh, so we *are* learning valuable lessons from Nazi Germany.'

'Don't be trite or petty, Miss Clark. In this war, the fate of our nation, the future of the world is at stake. We are hoping you will do the right thing and cooperate with us in this matter,' Crenshaw said.

'And if I don't?'

'No threats, Miss Clark. Nothing will happen to you personally. But I do think you should keep the possible consequences in mind.'

'Consequences? That sounds very close to a threat.'

'It's not personal. I think you need to understand that the loss of one brilliant scientist like Dr Bishop will cost us time . . .'

'Why does Dr Bishop have to leave?'

'It is what he wants, Miss Clark. He can't bear to live in that house or to stay here knowing that what he's done precipitated his wife's action. The loss of a scientist with his expertise puts us further behind in our mission. If the workers here knew all the details, they would be anxious, fearful – they'd lose their sense of safety and community. I'm confident they'd get it back sooner or later. But that disruption in the *esprit de corps* would slow everything down, once again costing us time and keeping us from reaching our goal. And we must reach it before the Germans do. I'm afraid, right now, that they just might be in the lead.'

'I suppose I can't ask what that goal is.'

'You can ask, Miss Clark, but I can't answer. We have great respect for your intellect. We admire your persistence, your loyalty, your commitment to a cause. We need scientists like you.'

'There is one question that you might be able to answer. Who moved Irene's body from the bleachers to outside of the gate?'

'We did – the army did – Miss Clark. But we will deny that if you repeat it.'

'And would you have done anything to secure justice for Irene Nance and her family if I hadn't pushed it to the point where you had to take action?'

'Do you think we would allow a killer to roam free among our civilian population?'

'You haven't really answered my question, though, have you, sir?'

Crenshaw stared out the window, his face unreadable. When he turned back, he asked, 'Is there anything else you'd like to ask, Miss Clark?'

'What about Teddy Mullins? Has he been told what happened?'

'Only that you are safe and that Irene's killer is dead. We thought you'd want to explain the rest to him since the two of you were working together. We request that you impress upon him the need for secrecy.'

The thought of seeing Teddy again made me smile. With a man like him, maybe it would be possible to have a relationship and a career at the same time.

'Miss Clark, it's a bit troubling to see you sitting there with an enigmatic smile on your face after I asked you for your pledge of secrecy.'

'You really did think it was just the two of us, didn't you?'

'It wasn't?' Surprise disturbed his features briefly bringing a broader smile to my face.

I looked down at the floor and shook my head. 'Not hardly, sir.'

'Who else was involved?'

'With all due respect, sir, that is something I will never tell you.'

Crenshaw sighed and said, 'I can understand that. But how many of you?'

'Oh no, you won't get me to give up that bit of information away either. Let's just say that our group of volunteer detectives easily exceeded the size of the average family.'

'Fine, Miss Clark, just make sure you impress on them the need for secrecy.'

'All of us chemists understand that, sir. After all, we have a lot of experience working with Tube Alloy, as we are required to call it.' The bigger question raced back through my thoughts. Were we all contributing to the development of the world's most deadly bomb – one that could kill thousands? Did the ends justify the means? When the war was over would I – would the others – regret their role in its making?

'Tube Alloy. Yes. Quite. We can count on you then?'

'I wouldn't put it that way sir.'

'No?' Alarm flashed across his face with the speed of a bolt of lightning, disrupting his normal impenetrable expression once again.

'Let's just say that my country can count on me. That's what really matters, isn't it, sir?'

Lightning Source UK Ltd.
Milton Keynes UK
UKOW02f0643010215

245425UK00001B/2/P

9 781847 515278